HELL HATH NO FURY

Center Point
Large Print

Also by Charles G. West and available from
Center Point Large Print:

A Man Called Sunday

**This Large Print Book carries the
Seal of Approval of N.A.V.H.**

HELL HATH NO FURY

A John Hawk Western

Charles G. West

CENTER POINT LARGE PRINT
THORNDIKE, MAINE

This Center Point Large Print edition
is published in the year 2017 by arrangement with
Kensington Publishing Corp.

The text of this Large Print edition is unabridged.
In other aspects, this book may vary
from the original edition.
Printed in the United States of America
on permanent paper.
Set in 16-point Times New Roman type.

ISBN: 978-1-68324-622-0

Library of Congress Cataloging-in-Publication Data

Names: West, Charles, author.
Title: Hell hath no fury : a John Hawk western / Charles G. West.
Description: Center Point large print edition. | Thorndike, Maine :
     Center Point Large Print, 2017.
Identifiers: LCCN 2017041662 | ISBN 9781683246220
     (hardcover : alk. paper)
Subjects: LCSH: Large type books. | GSAFD: Western stories.
Classification: LCC PS3623.E84 H45 2017 | DDC 813/.6—dc23
LC record available at https://lccn.loc.gov/2017041662

FOR RONDA

CHAPTER 1

"Crowder, go find Hawk," Lieutenant Mathew Conner ordered. "Tell him I wanna see him."

"Yes, sir," Private Crowder responded, and hurried down the bluffs to the river where the men were watering their horses. "Seen Hawk?" Crowder asked as he passed through the small detachment of soldiers. One of them pointed upstream, so he hustled on toward a slight bend in the river. A couple dozen yards farther along he spotted him, a tall man wearing cavalry trousers and a buckskin shirt. On his head he wore a flat-crowned hat with a hawk's feather stuck in the hatband. Standing on a low hummock of grass that protruded out over the edge of the water, he was watching his horse, a big buckskin gelding, drink. "Hawk," Crowder called out. "Lieutenant Conner wants you."

Hawk figured as much when he saw Crowder hustling along the bank in his direction. "Is that so?" he responded. "Did he say what he wanted?"

Crowder shrugged indifferently. "Just said to go find you."

"All right, I'm comin'." He stepped back off the hummock and whistled softly. The buckskin in the shallow water immediately jerked his head up and left the water to follow the scout and the soldier back toward the other men. Hawk took hold of the reins and led the horse, aptly named Rascal, across a wide grassy patch where some of the cavalry horses were grazing. He left him there and proceeded on with Crowder to a small group of cottonwoods where he found Lieutenant Conner sitting in the shade, studying a map.

"Hawk, where in hell are those Indians going?" Conner asked as his scout approached.

"I thought Nestor told you where they're headed," Hawk replied, referring to Roy Nestor, the other scout assigned to the patrol.

"Nestor said they were heading back to their camp somewhere on the Yellowstone, but we damn sure lost them now." The tracks they had followed since morning seemed to indicate Nestor might be right. But they ended at this point when the Sioux had entered the river with the obvious intention of losing anyone following them. The horses needed rest, so Conner decided to halt the patrol there since there was some disagreement between his scouts as to what the hostiles' intentions were. With rations for fifteen days, Conner's detachment of fifteen troopers were in day twelve of a search for a hostile Sioux war party that had struck several farms along the Yellowstone River. That morning, they had come upon a small rancher who had just been hit by a raiding party. He told the lieutenant that the Indians had not attacked the house, but had stolen half a dozen cows. Conner's two scouts disagreed on whether or not it was the same party that had burned and killed along the river.

"Where is Nestor?" Hawk asked.

"I sent him on up the river to see if he can find where those Indians came out of the water," Conner said. "I was hoping he'd be back by now."

"Waste of time," Hawk stated impassively. "Like I told you this mornin', this ain't no war party we're trailin'. This bunch ain't no more than six or eight bucks and they stole that man's cows because they're runnin' short of food. They've got some hungry folks somewhere and that's where they're headin'. They ain't that war party we're looking for." He was repeating what he had told him earlier that morning, but Nestor had insisted that it was the war party that had killed a settler and his family three days before.

The lieutenant knew there were hard feelings between Nestor and Hawk, and he had complained to Major Brisbin when the two were assigned to his detail. The fact of the matter was, Conner thought John Hawk was by far the best scout in the entire regiment. But Nestor was so sure, adamant, in fact, that he was right about the small band they had been following all morning, so Conner gave him the benefit of the doubt. His decision to send Nestor out alone to verify his contention that they were on the trail of the Sioux raiders was greatly influenced by his desire to stop the murdering savages. It would definitely be a positive mark on his service record if he did. "All right, damn it," he confessed. "I know what you said, and I know we damn near wore the horses out trying to catch up with them." Hawk had agreed with Nestor, but on only one thing. The tracks were fresh. Nestor was so sure the war party was running up the Yellowstone that Conner had decided he might be right. Consequently, he pushed the horses hard, thinking they could overtake them. And by the time they were forced to rest the horses, they discovered that there were no more tracks to follow. "So now, you tell me where this party is that we've been following," he said to Hawk.

"Well, if it was up to me to get a bunch of soldiers off my tail, especially if I was drivin' cows, I'd go in the river and double back the other way before I came out. I expect those Indians likely watched us go flyin' past 'em while they were hidin' back there along the river somewhere. So if you really wanna track that bunch down, then we'd best head back downriver and find the place they came out of the water. Maybe we'll pick up their trail and that'll tell us where they're really headin'. And if I had to guess on where that might be, I'd say most likely up toward the Big Belt Mountains."

Conner said nothing for a couple of minutes as

he stared at the somber scout. When he finally spoke again, it was with a guilty smile. "That makes sense to me. The horses should be rested by now." He turned to another soldier who was standing close by. "Corporal Johnson, get 'em mounted. We're riding out of here in fifteen minutes."

"Yes, sir," Johnson replied, and ran to obey the lieutenant's orders, yelling at the troopers to saddle up and get ready to ride.

"Are you gonna wait for Nestor to get back?" Hawk asked.

"Hell, no," Conner answered. "If he's as good a scout as he claims he is, he oughta be able to track a cavalry patrol."

"I reckon," Hawk said, although his personal opinion was that Nestor couldn't find a biscuit in a sack full of them. "I'll ride on out ahead, see if I can pick up a track. I'm bettin' on this side of the river, 'cause I'm thinkin' they've got a camp up in the Big Belts somewhere." He ambled unhurriedly to saddle his horse, then rode out, still with plenty of head start before the column formed up. He just needed enough time to scout the bluffs before the cavalry mounts added more of their tracks on top of those they had already laid down when they were heading upriver.

He held the buckskin to a comfortable lope across the open patches where hoofprints would be spotted at once. Reining Rascal back to a walk in places that looked more likely to disguise an exit from the river, he managed to stay ahead of the troopers following along behind him. He had ridden what he estimated to be about two and a half miles when he came to a place he considered perfect for the Indians' purpose. He reined his horse to a stop and dismounted in order to take a closer look. A rock-strewn stream emptied into the river, cutting a narrow gully through the bluffs, which were about six feet high at this point. The bottom of the stream was just rocky enough to prevent clear impressions of hooves. The job now was to find enough sign to prove him right. This didn't take as long as he had expected, for he found half of an unshod print at the very edge of the stream where its waters spread to join the river. One cow got a little too close to the edge, he thought. There was just that one print, but it confirmed what he suspected. They were heading north and they were still driving the cattle.

Walking up the stream, he found nothing more until he came to the tracks left by the soldiers' horses, as they had ridden upriver. He had to look closely to find more unshod prints mixed in with the soldiers' where the patrol crossed the stream. But he found what he was searching for, several clear prints of Indian ponies as well as a couple of cow tracks, running perpendicular to the soldiers', again confirming what he had figured. The Indians had entered the water at the spot where the soldiers had stopped to rest the horses. They doubled back then, reversing their line of flight to the point where he now knelt. Leaving the river, they rode up the creek, crossed the trail left by the soldiers after they passed by, and headed straight north. He got to his feet and looked out in the direction indicated by the hoofprints. In the distance, he could see the southern slopes of the Big Belt Mountains. Satisfied, he squatted on his heels and awaited the column.

In a few minutes, the patrol arrived and Hawk got up to meet them. "Here's where they left the river," he said to Conner, and pointed to the tracks crossing those of the cavalry horses. "And yonder's the way they headed." He pointed toward the distant mountains. "Shouldn't be any trouble to follow that trail."

"Right," Conner said. "You go on up ahead in case Nestor's right about that party we've been following and there's an ambush waiting for us." He grinned as if apologizing for doubting him. "I don't wanna be surprised, so keep a sharp eye."

"Always do," Hawk drawled, and stepped up into the saddle. With a gentle nudge of his heels, he started Rascal out over the low, grassy hills on a line toward the distant mountains.

As he had predicted, it was an easy trail to follow. The party of Indians must have assumed the threat of soldiers was past them now, for it appeared they saw no need to take extra precautions. Even so, it was obvious that they wasted no time in their efforts to distance themselves from the soldiers. Their trail was so obvious, in fact, that he didn't worry about losing the soldiers behind him. Still, as a matter of procedure, he would hang back occasionally to let Conner catch sight of him. As the miles added up, it looked like he was not going to catch up to them before it would be necessary to rest the horses again. And in that event, it indicated the chase would have to continue the next day, because it would be close to dark by that time. Judging by the tracks and the occasional droppings left by the ponies, the Indians managed to maintain the same lead they had gained by doubling back at the river. When he came to the lower foothills of the mountains, he crossed a healthy stream that looked to be a good campsite, so he dismounted and let Rascal drink. There was plenty of sign telling him that the party he followed had stopped there before him. There was still an hour of daylight left, but the horses were bound to be tired, so they might as well stop here where there was good water. He waited for the column to catch up.

"Figured you might wanna make camp here," Hawk greeted the lieutenant when the patrol caught up to him. "It's gonna be too dark to

14

follow their tracks in a little while, especially if they cut up into these hills somewhere."

"I thought we were gonna have to shoot that damn buckskin of yours if we were gonna rest our horses," Conner complained. "I wish to hell we could have caught up with that bunch before dark, but I guess we'll have to take up the chase in the morning." He gave the order to dismount and told Corporal Johnson to make camp.

The horses were taken care of and cook fires started by the time Roy Nestor rode in, his horse lathered and panting. He looked to be heated up, himself. "Damn, Nestor," Johnson needled. "Where the hell have you been? We thought maybe you rode on up to Butte."

Nestor didn't bother to respond, instead he went straight to confront Lieutenant Conner. "I had to ride like hell to catch up with you. I thought you was gonna wait till I got back before you decided to ride off in some other damn direction."

Conner didn't care for the scout's tone of voice, but he didn't respond in kind. Instead, he calmly asked, "Did you find the trail you were looking for?"

Nestor sputtered for a moment before admitting, "Well, no, I didn't run up on it yet, but I was about to, only I thought I'd best report back to you to let you know." He looked around him as if searching for someone. "Then, come to find out, you'd rode off on a wild-goose chase."

"I wouldn't call it that," Conner said, still calm. "We found the place where the Indians doubled back and headed up this way."

"I expect Hawk told you they went this way," Nestor charged.

"As a matter of fact, he did find the tracks we're following," Conner said. "Now, I suggest you take care of that horse you damn near rode to death and settle yourself down for the night. You're getting to the point where I don't like your tone. A little bit more and I think I can do without your services. Do I make myself clear?"

Too angry to speak for a moment, Nestor sneered at the young lieutenant until the corporal and a couple of the men close by moved up around him. Aware then that he might be going too far, he did an about-face and walked away still fuming. While he would have liked to have told the lieutenant to go to hell, the main target for his anger was seated by a small fire, calmly enjoying a cup of coffee. *Smug son of a bitch,* Nestor thought. *One of these days I'm liable to stomp your ass in the ground.*

The object of his scorn was indifferent to Nestor's dislike. He was aware of the belligerent scout's childlike jealousy of his natural ability to read sign and track game or men. But he could never understand why there should be a competition between them. From the time when Hawk was a young boy, he had lived with a

16

village of Crow Indians where the skills of the forest were taught naturally to the young. As a young man, he befriended a Blackfoot warrior and lived with his people for a while. As a result, he moved freely between the two tribes, even though they were enemies. As with the Indians, Hawk got along with most of the other white men he worked with—that is, with the exception of Roy Nestor. Nestor was a vile man of hot temper and questionable character. So Hawk preferred to have as little to do with him as possible. His thoughts of Nestor were interrupted then when Corporal Johnson came to join him by his fire.

"You didn't build a very big fire," Johnson teased. "Looks like you ain't expectin' company."

"If I'd known I was gonna have the honor of your presence, I'da built a bonfire," Hawk replied, drawing a chuckle from the corporal.

"I figured you scouts would take supper together for sure," Johnson went on.

"Did you just come over here to aggravate me while I'm tryin' to enjoy a cup of coffee?" Hawk japed.

Turning serious then, Johnson said, "I thought ol' Nestor was fixin' to jump on the lieutenant for a minute there. I ain't sure all the wheels are turnin' in the right direction inside that man's head." When Hawk failed to comment, Johnson asked, "How come he's got a bone in his craw about you? I never saw him act like he does

17

around you with any of the other scouts."

"I don't have any idea," Hawk said. "So how 'bout not spoilin' my coffee talkin' about him."

"All right." Changing the subject, Johnson asked, "You think there's any chance Nestor's right about this party we're trailin'?"

"No, I don't," Hawk stated. "This bunch don't ride like a war party. You look at the tracks. They're leadin' four horses that ain't carryin' much of anything and they're still leading those cows they stole. They're tryin' to take that meat to a camp somewhere so they can butcher it and feed their folks. They're gonna have to stop and butcher the damn cows before very long. They didn't take time to do it back there, just took the whole cow, hooves, head, and all." He didn't tell him why he didn't argue with Nestor when he insisted they were following a war party intent upon running straight up the river. He would have been happy to see the Indians get away with their stolen beef while Nestor led the soldiers on a wild chase. But when Conner asked him straight away if he agreed with Nestor, Hawk had to tell him the truth. Now, if they did find these hungry Indians, he supposed Conner would have to arrest some of them for cattle rustling. He could hardly let them go unpunished, so he'd have to take them back to Fort Ellis to stand trial. Hawk regretted the part he was forced to play in it because, if the government hadn't sanctioned the killing of all the buffalo, the Indians wouldn't want the damn cattle. He couldn't bring himself to mislead the lieutenant, however, so he would do what the army hired him to do and lead Conner to the guilty party. *I need to get away from this business for a while,* he suddenly told himself. He had lived too long with the Indians to not see their side of things. There was a good bit of work to be done on his cabin on the Boulder River. Now would be a good time to do it. *I'll get this patrol done, then that's what I'll do,* he decided.

Pickets were set for the night and the patrol bedded down, intent upon getting an early start the next morning. The night passed peacefully enough and they were underway again before sunup with just enough light to see the tracks they followed. The scouts were sent out up ahead of the column as it approached the mountains, still capped with snow from the winter just past.

The trail led them around the east side of the mountains for a distance of about two miles before turning to follow a ravine up to a shelf thick with pines. The narrow trail that led through the pines was not wide enough for two men to ride abreast. The scouts were forced to meet at the head of the trail to decide what to do. "I think we're gettin' close," Hawk offered his opinion.

"Yeah?" Nestor responded. "What makes you think that?"

"I smell smoke," Hawk answered. "And if you listen real good, you can hear a waterfall through those trees up ahead, about halfway up the mountain."

"Yeah, I've been smellin' that smoke for quite a while now, and I can hear that waterfall," Nestor claimed. "I didn't figure you heard it." In truth he hadn't smelled smoke and he couldn't hear a waterfall, but he would never admit that to a man he so despised. Thinking now that they might be approaching the Sioux camp, they could find themselves caught in an ambush. That trail looked so narrow that, if it opened into a clearing, there could very well be a Sioux welcoming committee waiting with rifles. Never one to stick his neck out if he could help it, Nestor said, "One of us will have to go back to tell the lieutenant what the setup is. I reckon I'll do that, since you're the one that found this trail."

"Yeah," Hawk said. "One of us had better go back to bring the patrol up to this ledge. I'll follow this trail a little farther and see where it comes out."

"Yeah," Nestor said. "Good idea, you see where this trail leads." *And maybe if I'm lucky, you can get your ass shot off,* he thought. He backed his horse away to give it room to turn around and rode back down the ravine.

Hawk watched him ride away until he was out of sight. *That's right, you lyin' son of a bitch,* he thought, *you go on back and get the soldiers.* Nestor hadn't smelled any smoke and he didn't hear any sound of a waterfall—and neither did he. He was confident that there was a Sioux camp where this narrow path through the pines came out on a grassy expanse by a small pond created by the rapid flow of the stream from above it. He knew this because he had camped there, himself, while hunting in these mountains. It was well known by the Blackfoot, and apparently by the Lakota Sioux as well. And he knew the party he followed was going there as soon as they turned up into the ravine. Now, with Nestor out of his way, he could follow this trail and see who was camping by the pond.

With the gentle slap of pine boughs against his arms and shoulders, Hawk nudged Rascal forward, following the narrow passage so thick with pine trees that the sun was blocked out. The only sound coming to his ears was the gentle plodding of Rascal's hooves on the thick carpet of pine needles. He proceeded for about fifty yards before seeing the sunlight filtering through the opening ahead. He dismounted then and walked to the opening, leading his horse behind him. From that point on, it was wise to be cautious. He remembered this place well and knew there was still plenty of cover in the meadow beyond in the form of two rock formations that jutted out from the face of the mountain. When he reached the opening, he looped the buckskin's reins around a pine bough, drew his rifle, and checked the load. Then he ran across the open expanse of grass to the first of the rocky outcroppings. From this point, he was able to see the camp, but he needed to get closer. He could see a fire with some people around it, but they all looked to be women and children.

Another expanse of grass, this one about thirty yards wide, would have to be crossed before reaching the second rocky outcropping. He paused to scan the area before him. It appeared to be a peaceful camp. No one seemed to be alert to the possibility of attack. He took a deep breath and sprinted across the grass to the rocks beyond. After a couple of minutes waiting, it appeared that no one around the fire had noticed him. From this position he had a better view of the camp. He could see their ponies grazing on the far side of the pond and children running among them, playing. *Where were the men?* Then he spotted a couple of old men who appeared to be staking meat out to be smoked. He was not sure, but he felt as if he had seen one of them before. Straining to see more, he noticed a boy of perhaps twelve or thirteen standing by the fire. This was hardly a war party, and as he peered at the boy and the women, he was struck with a stunning realization. These were not Lakota Sioux. They were Blackfeet! He looked again at the old man and realized that he had seen him in Walking Owl's village when he had hunted with his friend Bloody Hand. He had lived with the Blackfeet. Seeing this pitiful gathering of old men, women, and children, his first inclination was to shout out to them, tell them to get on their ponies and run. But he knew it was inevitable they would be caught, and he would be instrumental in bringing the soldiers down upon them.

His mind was racing, for he had to do something quickly. He didn't have much time. Conner and his men were waiting at the base of the mountain for word from his scouts. How long would it take Nestor to get back down to get them? Knowing it would be one hell of a long shot to pull off, he decided to do the only thing he could think of at the moment to keep his Blackfoot friends from being hauled back to Fort Ellis. He was well aware that he was risking his employment with the army. "To hell with it," he muttered, and stepped out from behind the rocks. "Hey-yo," he called out, and strode boldly toward the small gathering around the fire. "I am a friend."

Their reaction was swift, but nonthreatening, for there was not one firearm in the party of old men, women, and children. Armed only with bows and knives, several old men and the few boys old enough to use them, stood ready to defend their camp. "Hawk!" one of the old men called out, recognizing the scout as a friend of

Walking Owl's. He came forward to meet Hawk, telling the others as he walked that there was nothing to fear from the white man. To Hawk, he said, "Welcome. My name is Big Otter. You came to our village on the Musselshell with Bloody Hand. We have fresh meat. Come and eat with us."

Hawk remembered then why the old man had looked familiar to him. It was two years ago when he and Bloody Hand visited Big Otter's village. Now he couldn't help wondering what had happened to the rest of the village, if this handful of desperate people was all that remained. There was no time to catch up at the moment, however. Somewhere on the other side of that thick belt of pine trees, Lieutenant Conner with a scout and fifteen soldiers were even now making their way up the mountain. "Big Otter," he greeted him hurriedly. "Thank you, but there is no time to talk." He paused just a moment to make sure of his Blackfoot words. "Close behind me, the soldiers come. They come to punish those who stole the cattle."

Big Otter, as well as those close enough to hear, reacted immediately with gasps of alarm. Hawk could see that they were completely surprised, probably thinking that they had lost the soldiers at the river. At once frightened, the women began to run to gather their children, preparing to escape into the pines. "Wait," Hawk

24

said. "How much of the meat has been prepared?"

"Most of it," Big Otter answered, and turned to get a nod of confirmation from another old Blackfoot man, who had joined them by then. "It is wrapped in the hides and ready to pack on the horses."

"Where are the heads and hooves of the cows?"

"In a big hole on the other side of the pond, near the horses," Big Otter replied. Again his friend nodded excitedly.

"All right," Hawk said, talking to both of them now. "Here's what we've got to do and it has to be quick." Having to hesitate now and again to make sure he was using the right words, and not slipping into the Crow tongue, he told them what they must do to keep from being arrested. Eager to do his bidding, for they had no protection against a cavalry patrol, the whole camp followed his orders without question. They had accomplished about as much as they could before Nestor had gotten back to report to Conner that he spotted Hawk's horse tied to a tree near the end of the path.

"Where the hell is Hawk?" Lieutenant Conner asked when Nestor reported. "You sure that was his horse you saw and not some Sioux pony?"

"It's his horse, all right," Nestor replied, "that buckskin he loves so damn much."

"But no sign of Hawk?"

"No, sir. Course, his horse was tied near-bout

at the end of this damn pine tunnel we've been movin' through. And I couldn't see what was on the other side of that horse, but it was in the open. That Sioux war party coulda been waitin' for me to step out of them pines, but I ain't that dumb."

Conner thought about that for a moment before continuing. He could well understand why Hawk had no use for the man. "You do know why we employ scouts, don't you?"

"Sure, I do," Nestor replied, oblivious to the sarcasm in Conner's tone. "You need us to find the Injuns for you, not to get ourselves killed."

"All right, let's get moving," Conner said, his patience with the obnoxious scout exhausted. He turned in the saddle and signaled the column forward. When they neared the end of the forest trail, they saw the opening out onto the grassy meadow, but there was no sign of Hawk's horse. Conner halted the column, thinking it best to take no chance on the possibility his men might be riding single file into a wall of rifle fire.

"I'll go take a look, sir," Corporal Johnson said when Nestor showed no inclination to, and Conner motioned him on. Johnson was back within minutes. "Hawk's standin' about fifty yards away near a pond. Looks like he's talkin' to some Injuns standin' around a fire. Don't look like he's in any trouble. They're just talkin'."

Conner looked at Nestor. There was no effort to hide the disgust in his face. "You could have told

26

me that, if you'd gone all the way to the opening when you were here before."

"Like I said," Nestor replied, "I ain't gettin' paid to get shot."

Conner gave the order to proceed, along with a precautionary order to load their carbines, and the column rode out into the mountain meadow. Hawk turned and waved them over. "Looks like we got our trails mixed up somewhere back on the Yellowstone, Lieutenant. These folks ain't Sioux, they're Blackfoot. This is Big Otter. He says they ran across some tracks of a party about the same size as theirs. I reckon we tied onto the wrong band."

Conner didn't say anything for a long moment while his eyes swept across the gathering of women and children staring back at him with eyes wide and uncertain. He returned his gaze to Hawk, who was watching him and waiting. "What's in the packs loaded on those horses?"

"Meat," Hawk answered. "Deer meat. Big Otter said they lucked up on a big herd a couple days ago—made a big killin'." He pointed to the one boy in his teens, who made it a point to stand close to Big Otter, fiddling idly with a deer hoof. "That's Broken Wing," Hawk continued. "He got his share of the deer." Hawk could sense Conner's skepticism and feared he had not prepared the Indians enough.

"All with bow and arrow," Conner remarked.

"Yes, sir," Hawk replied. "These boys can shoot."

Back to the meat loaded on the horses, Conner remarked, "It looks like they wrapped all that meat in the deer hides. I don't believe I've ever seen Indians wrap meat with the fur inside like that. Is there a reason to have the fur touching the meat?"

Damn, Conner, Hawk thought. *How many more questions are you going to ask? What the hell do you care how they handle the meat?* To the lieutenant, he answered, "They just do that sometimes when it might be a while before they get it back home—keeps it cooler." Noticing the wry smirk across Conner's face, it struck him then. *The son of a bitch is playing with me. He knows what's going on, and he just wants to make me sweat.* He suddenly realized that Conner was going to go along with his attempt to save his Blackfoot friends. He knew about Hawk's friendship with the Blackfoot Indians. As soon as he released a sigh of relief, he was startled by the lieutenant's next comment.

"It's been a while since I've tasted venison. Maybe your friends might want to share some of their fresh kill. We could leave them some of our salt pork in exchange—give us both a change." Hawk tensed. He could dare not look at Big Otter, afraid he would see the panic in his eyes, for the old Indian understood a little English. Before

Hawk could answer, however, Conner said, "On second thought, I don't think we'll take the time for it. We've already spent too much of the army's time chasing the wrong Indians. Johnson, turn 'em around and let's get the hell out of here." As he wheeled his horse, he favored Hawk with an amused smile. "You coming, Hawk?"

"I'll be along," Hawk replied. He decided at that moment that Mathew Conner was a man with the right moral compass and was a friend of John Hawk's. He whistled for Rascal and while he waited for the buckskin to trot over from the pond, he said farewell to Big Otter. The old Blackfoot was well aware of the chance Hawk had taken and thanked him for his compassion. "You can thank that lieutenant, too," Hawk said to him. "He could have taken all that meat from you and probably hauled you and two or three others to prison." He would have warned him not to steal cattle, but knew that when the food got scarce, they would take it wherever it was and whoever it belonged to. "Where are the young men?" Hawk asked, and was told they had moved north to avoid being sent to the reservation. "Why did you people not go with them?"

"We are too old to make a new place across the medicine line in Canada," Big Otter said. "There were some women and small children left behind also and we didn't want them to live on the reservation. So we live as we have always lived,

29

but my eyes are old and can no longer aim my bow as I did when I was a young man."

Hawk felt compassion for the old man's plight, but there was nothing he could do to help. "I must go," he said, and stepped up into the saddle. "Just be careful when you steal the white man's cattle."

CHAPTER 2

"How many cows did that fellow say the Indians stole of his?" Lieutenant Conner asked Hawk when they stopped to rest the horses.

"He said six," Hawk replied. "But I figure it was more like three or four." He didn't tell the lieutenant the reason he thought that was because the Blackfoot camp had only four horses loaded heavily. He was still not ready to admit the hoax he attempted to pull on Conner. There was the chance that he had misread Conner's comments, so why risk it? Conner's next comment settled that question.

"Even if there were only three cows stolen," Conner went on, "I didn't see that much meat packed on those horses. Where do you suppose the rest of that venison was?" The broad grin on his face was evidence of the enjoyment he was getting from japing the rangy scout.

"In a gully beyond the pond, settin' on top of a pile of horns and hooves," Hawk answered. "They were runnin' outta time and deerskins," he said, emphasizing *deerskins*.

Conner threw his head back and enjoyed a good laugh. Afterward, he assured Hawk that he wouldn't let on to anyone that he had a compassionate spot in his heart. Easing up on his teasing then, he turned to more serious talk. "We wasted a helluva lot of time running this little group of Blackfoot down. My mission was to track that Sioux raiding party that burned a farmhouse to the ground and ran his stock off. I thought sure we were on their trail when we got the word about the cows. Unless Meade had better luck than we have, those Sioux are still gonna be killing and robbing settlers up and down the Yellowstone. We've only got rations for three more days. I wish to hell we could run across those Sioux before I have to take this patrol back to Fort Ellis. Have you got any notions where they might show up?"

Hawk shook his head slowly. "I ain't got any idea. I don't think they know where they're gonna show up. From the way they've been bouncin' back and forth across the Yellowstone, it looks to me like they're just keepin' on the move, hittin' everything they stumble on. Go north, go south, whatever notion strikes 'em."

Conner nodded thoughtfully. Hawk was right, of course. This band of warriors was just out to raise as much hell as they could, take as many horses as they could steal, and kill any white man they stumbled across. Conner didn't know what to do except to return to Fort Ellis and see if there were any further reports on the whereabouts of the hostiles. Possibly Lieutenant Meade, who led another patrol, might have had better luck. "Well," he decided, "we'll head back to Ellis in the morning. With the rations we've got left, we can take an extra day and ride south to Three Forks, then swing back east from there."

"Headin' back to Bozeman, are we?" Roy Nestor asked, having heard Conner's last remark as he walked up to join them. "Too bad about them Blackfoot. I knew we'd run off in the wrong direction when you found their tracks. I coulda told you it warn't the same trail we started out on. I'da picked up them Sioux again if I hadn't had to come back to see what happened to you. I reckon we could go back and pick it up again, but it's been too long now."

"I reckon we shoulda checked with you before startin' out after that party of Blackfoot." Hawk couldn't help a snide reply.

"Might have, at that," Nestor was quick to agree. "Didn't do us a helluva lotta good trackin' down a party of old men and women, did it?"

Interrupting the sniping between his two scouts, Conner gave them his orders for the trip back to the fort. "We'll pull out of here in the morning and head south toward Three Forks. I'll send you two out a little ahead, one on each flank of the column." His purpose now was to return his patrol safely to the fort and maybe pick up any sign of hostile activity in the grazing lands just north of Three Forks.

• • •

The patrol awoke to a steel gray sky and a light snow shower the next morning. Unexpected this late in the spring, but not unheard of, it nevertheless caught the sleeping soldiers by surprise, as evidenced by the griping and cursing about their wet bedrolls and cold boots. Accustomed to the chorus of complaints from the soldiers, Hawk had long since decided that bitching never seemed to improve conditions. He saddled his horse and took a long look at the sky before approaching Lieutenant Conner for any last orders before he set out.

"You and Nestor hold up a little while," Conner said upon greeting him. "It's kinda a nasty morning, so I'm gonna let the men make some coffee before we start—give 'em a half hour or so to warm up a little. But we won't cook up any breakfast until we have to rest the horses."

"Suits me," Hawk said. "I'm always ready for a cup of coffee." He looked up at the sky again. "This ain't gonna last long, though."

"Is that so?" Conner asked. "How do you know that?" He was always skeptical of anyone predicting how long bad weather would last simply by looking up at an overcast sky.

His question caused Hawk to pause, puzzled. He'd never thought about it before. "Hell, I don't know," he said. "You just know by lookin' at it."

Enjoying the discussion now, Conner continued to push him. "You say it won't last long. How long is that—an hour, a day, how long?"

Aware that Conner was japing him, Hawk nevertheless took the bait. "Looks to me like it'll clear up and warm up by the time we stop to rest the horses," he predicted.

Nestor walked over to join them then, as he usually did anytime he saw Hawk and Conner talking, convinced as he was that Hawk was out to gain the lieutenant's favor. Conner decided to continue the game he had started. "What do you think about this turn in the weather?" he asked Nestor.

"What do I think about the weather?" Nestor repeated, confused by the question. "I think it ain't worth a damn. Why?"

"How long will this snow last?" Conner pressed.

"Well, how the hell would I know that?" Nestor replied. "Till it's over, I reckon." Unable to believe that the two of them had been talking about the weather, he couldn't resist a snide comment. "Why don't you ask Mr. Hawk, here? He's the one who spends so much time with the damn Injuns. Maybe he's got some big medicine from them Blackfeet." Conner just laughed and gave Nestor the same information he had given Hawk about delaying the march for about half an hour.

∙ ∙ ∙

With the scouts out to either side and riding about a half mile in advance of the column of troopers, Conner's patrol rode south, close to the creek that served as a boundary between the ranges of two cattle ranches. Both outfits had been subject to some cattle rustling in the past couple of years. And with the current activity of the raiding Sioux, they would both seem to be potential targets for the war parties. The patrol was about five miles north of the Gallatin River when Hawk spotted the circle of buzzards over a stand of cottonwoods near a small creek. He turned Rascal toward it, thinking some rancher might have lost a cow.

As a precaution, he pulled the buckskin up to a stop on a low rise some fifty yards short of the trees and paused there for a minute to scan the trees in each direction before riding down to investigate. It was only then that he spotted a thin ribbon of smoke beyond the trees. A campfire, maybe—it was no more than a wisp of smoke. There appeared to be no activity in the trees, no sign of horses, cows, or men, so he rode on down to the creek. Guiding on the buzzards above the trees, he walked Rascal slowly through the cottonwoods until hauling back suddenly on the reins when he came upon the source of the feast. He immediately drew the Winchester from his saddle sling and hurriedly looked all around him to make sure he was alone. Reassured, he gave Rascal his heels and charged forward at a gallop, scattering the squawking birds in all directions. He pulled the buckskin to a sliding stop a few feet from the remains of a corpse and jumped out of the saddle. From what was left of the body, Hawk figured he was a cowhand, judging by his clothes, which were in tatters. They had been ripped away by the vicious claws of the hungry scavengers in their frenzy to get to the flesh, of which there was very little left. In fact, there was not enough left of the poor victim to speculate over, and little need to speculate at that. There were many hoofprints, all left by unshod horses, and long marks in the creek bank, leading from the water, told him the unfortunate man's story. He had been dragged in the creek and pulled out of the water at this point. Hawk hoped the poor devil was already dead by then.

He hesitated for a moment before firing his rifle to signal the patrol, as he lunged first this way, then that way, trying to keep the anxious buzzards from returning to the feast. If he fired a couple of shots, would he also be signaling the savages who did this? Taking another look at the corpse, he decided the party that did this thing was long gone. To reinforce that opinion, he looked at the tracks around the body and the creek and decided they were hours old. When he looked back at the body, he saw the buzzards gathering around it again, so he fired a couple of shots into the bunch, sending them scurrying again. He realized then that there was not enough of the victim left to fight the buzzards for, so he gave up on his efforts to save what remained. The shots should bring the patrol to find him, so he decided to look for the source of the smoke he had seen, wondering if there were more bodies to be found.

Leaving the noisy birds to finish their banquet, he stepped up into the saddle and started toward the smoke, now barely visible through the branches of the cottonwoods. He rode no more than fifty yards before coming to a small clearing and the smoldering remains of what must have been a line shack. It was a relief in a way, because he had feared he might find a wagon and the remains of a woman and children. "That ain't to say I'm not sorry you had such poor luck, partner," he muttered. "I'm just glad it wasn't worse." He didn't spend much time scouting around the cabin. There was nothing left to speculate on, so he rode back to the buzzards to await the patrol's arrival.

Lieutenant Conner was about to call his detail to a halt when he came to a creek. He had planned to make it to the river before stopping to rest the horses, but they were showing signs of fatigue. The sky had cleared above them and the morning had even warmed a bit. As soon as that registered on his mind, he couldn't help grinning. *It's time to rest the horses and the weather has cleared,* he thought, *just like Hawk said it would.* He chuckled to himself then, causing Corporal Johnson to give him a questioning look. *Just a lucky guess,* he told himself. *Or maybe he does have big medicine.* Moments later, he heard the rifle shots. They sounded as if they had come from farther up the creek he was just then approaching.

"How long ago?" Conner asked when he rode up the creek to find Hawk waiting for him.

"Can't say for sure," Hawk said as he watched the soldiers trying to scare the buzzards away from what was now no more than a skeleton. "Mighta been last night. I can't find any tracks that look fresh. I figure this fellow was usin' that line shack up the creek a ways."

"Right," Conner said. "Let's go take a look at that shack." He turned to the corporal standing close by. "Johnson, have a couple of the men dig a hole and bury that poor devil." Back to Hawk, he asked, "You're sure whoever did this isn't still around?"

"Long gone," Hawk answered.

The lieutenant and his two scouts rode up the creek to the charred remains of the line shack. Upon seeing the lightly smoldering timbers,

Nestor stated the obvious. "This place burnt down a long time ago. Those bastards are long gone."

"Any guess as to which way they went from here?" Conner asked, addressing Hawk.

"I'd have to look around before we'd know for sure," Nestor answered before Hawk could reply.

"They headed out that way," Hawk said, pointing south. "Toward the river and Three Forks." He had already scouted the creek bank while he waited for Conner to bring the patrol to meet him and found a plain trail left by the hostiles.

"Maybe they did and maybe they didn't," Nestor spoke up at once. "I'll take a look, myself." He wasn't happy with the way Conner seemed to be asking Hawk all the questions.

"Always a good idea," Hawk commented. "I mighta missed something."

Conner ignored Nestor's comment, still focusing his questions on Hawk's findings. "You don't suppose they're planning on hitting Three Forks, do you? Hell, that's not much more than five or six miles from here. As far behind them as you say we are, they could already be there."

"We could hear some shootin' if they were attackin' the town," Nestor said.

"I expect so," Hawk agreed. "But as far behind

as we are, they most likely would have already been there and gone. I don't think this bunch would hit Three Forks, anyway."

"Why not?" Nestor asked at once. "How do you know whether or not they'd hit Three Forks? Hell, that's what war parties do. They go out and kill white folks."

Hawk refused to rise to Nestor's bait, although it was getting more and more difficult to ignore his every challenge. "When you take a look at the tracks, you'll see why, Nestor. I figure this party ain't much more than half a dozen warriors. And I don't think they'd wanna take a chance on raidin' a town the size of Three Forks. There's too good a chance half of 'em, maybe more, would get killed."

"Maybe," Nestor allowed. "To be sure, I'd best go scout those tracks, myself."

"Good idea," Hawk said. Back to Conner then, he said, "There's a more likely target, I'm thinkin'. There's a rancher between here and Three Forks that's a much more likely target than the town. That's the folks I'm worried about, and the only hope we've got is that these raiders might be layin' around waitin' for night before they hit 'em."

"Damn, you're right," Conner said. "That makes a lot more sense. Do you know where the ranch house is?"

"Not exactly," Hawk answered. "At least not

from where we're standin' right now. Do you, Nestor?" Nestor had to say he didn't, so Hawk continued. "I rode by that place about a year ago. It's close by the river, but from where we're standin' right now, I couldn't point right at it. So I think as soon as the horses are rested, we need to follow the trail the Indians left us and hope we can get there in time."

"What if the damn Injuns ain't goin' after that ranch?" Nestor saw fit to ask. "What if they're fixin' to raid somewhere else?"

Conner answered him. "We don't know where else they might raid. And Hawk's right, they aren't likely to take a risk attacking the town. So this ranch is the only place that makes sense. We have an obligation to tell the people at the ranch that this man was killed, anyway, so that's where we'll go." After resting the horses, although for not as long as they normally would have, the soldiers moved out, following the tracks left by the Sioux.

As usual, Hawk and Nestor were out ahead of the column, this time riding together since the tracks were plain to see. After riding a distance of approximately two miles, they came to a low ridge covered with pine trees. The trail they followed led up the ridge to the top where the tracks told them the Indians had paused there to look around them. The reason they had remained there for a while was obvious to see. "There's the ranch house," Nestor said as they looked across about a half mile of open prairie to a log ranch house and barn with a corral attached. Beside the barn, opposite the house, stood what could be assumed to be a small bunkhouse. Completing the ranch headquarters was a smokehouse and an outhouse. All were standing in good shape and there were horses in the corral. "Looks like everythin's all right to me," Nestor commented. "Them Injuns must be headed somewhere else."

Hawk was not so sure. The Sioux might have headed off in another direction from this spot on the ridge. Their tracks down the other side should tell them that, but he was of the opinion that it was more likely they had decided to hide out and wait for darkness to strike. If that was the case, he felt the lieutenant was in luck, for the cavalry had arrived in time. "I'll bring the lieutenant up," he said to Nestor, and turned Rascal back the way they had come.

"I'll wait," Nestor said, "and take a look down this hill to see where they headed from here."

In a short while, Hawk returned with Conner. "You're right," the lieutenant said. "They're holed up somewhere waiting for darkness." Like Hawk, he was speculating, but it made sense to him that a raiding party like the one they chased would find this the perfect target. To be determined now was the best plan of action, for there were several. Nestor returned from his scout down the other side of the ridge to report that the Indians had ridden off to the north. Hawk and Conner both looked in that direction, searching for the most likely place for the hostiles to wait. "That's where I'd pick," Conner said, pointing to a low line of hills to the north.

"I agree," Hawk replied. "It's half again closer to that ranch than we are right here and it looks like there's plenty of cover."

Now, assuming he and Hawk were right, and the hostiles were hiding in the hills, Conner had to decide how to proceed—to go at them right away and try to flush them out into the open, or wait until dark and try to fight them when they attacked the ranch. Or should he march his troop into the ranch right now to defend it, thereby discouraging the Indians from even considering an attack? After all, his first responsibility was to protect the ranchers. But if he chose that plan, the Sioux party would most likely choose to flee and look to raid someplace else. This plan was not especially favorable to him because the purpose of his patrol was to capture or kill the Sioux raiders to stop the raids, Still undecided, he said, "That's a long line of hills. I wish I knew exactly where they're holed up."

Hawk studied the hills, partially covered with trees with many open meadows between. He looked back the way they had just come. "I might be able to get a look at 'em if I circle back around this ridge and can get to the lower end of those hills without them seein' me."

"That might be kinda dangerous," Conner said. "I sure as hell wouldn't order you to try it." When Hawk merely shrugged in response, Conner couldn't suppress a guilty smile. "It would surely tell us where and how to hit them, and keep the fight away from the house."

"Reckon so," Hawk allowed, and waited. After a long pause, he asked, "Is that what you wanna do?"

"Yep," Conner replied right away. "But, you be careful. If you find you can't get close enough to see them, turn around and get your ass back here."

"That I will, make no mistake," Hawk said, and climbed into the saddle.

Conner watched him as he descended the back side of the ridge. Turning to Johnson, he remarked, "He's as good as having one of the Crow scouts along."

"He oughta be, he's lived with the damn Injuns long enough." This came from the gruff voice of Roy Nestor, who had walked up to stand behind them. "He's liable to get his ass shot off."

Hawk pulled up at the northern end of the ridge he had just descended to study the terrain between himself and the easternmost tip of the line of hills that ran east to west before reaching the river. A shallow draw stretched most of the way to the first in the line of hills, a distance of perhaps three hundred yards. Although shallow, he felt it was deep enough to give him and his horse cover, so he prodded Rascal forward. He'd decide what to do when he got to the end of the draw, if he got to the end of the draw. With that part of the plan completed without incident a few minutes later, he halted at the end of the draw and considered the open stretch of grass prairie between him and the low hills. *Maybe this wasn't such a good idea after all,* he thought. *What the hell, I've come this far.* He reasoned that the hostiles would more likely be watching the ranch and not the hills behind them. So he gave Rascal his heels and the big buckskin knew what he wanted. Up out of the draw they sprang and charged across the open grass. Lying low on Rascal's neck, he was ready to veer off and run for his life at the first shot. But there was no shot fired and he galloped safely into the ring of trees at the base of the hill.

Wasting no time, he dismounted and led Rascal deeper into the trees until reaching the start of the incline. He wrapped the horse's reins on a branch, tightly enough so Rascal would stay, but loosely enough for him to easily break away. This was in the event he failed to return. He didn't like the idea of the buckskin being tied to a tree if no one came to find him. He pulled his rifle then and made his way up the hill on foot. Over the top of the first hill, he descended to cross a saddle between it and the second hill, circling around through the trees whenever he came to an open meadow. Moving quickly, but cautiously, he worked his way to the fourth hill in the chain before he suddenly froze when he heard a horse whinny. He dropped to one knee and listened, his rifle held ready to fire. Then he heard another whinny. This time, he determined the direction from which it came. On his feet again, he crept carefully through the branches of the trees to discover a ravine just ahead of him. Dropping to his knees at once, he crawled to the edge of the ravine to discover eight Indian ponies gathered at the bottom. Two of them were without saddles of any kind. *That makes it six,* he thought. *Now, where are they?* In answer to his question, he heard the sound of a man's voice coming softly but clearly on the opposite side of the hill from the ravine.

Moving along the rim of the ravine as quickly as he could without making a noise, he made his way to the top of the hill before dropping down on his knees again. An inch at a time to avoid any noisy cracking of a pine bough, he moved slowly forward until he suddenly froze again. Halfway down the slope an Indian crouched, his back toward him. Hawk slowly lowered himself to lie flat on the ground. A lookout? He wondered, then a voice called out somewhere from below the crouching Indian, followed by the sound of laughter from several others. In response, the crouching man called back. The language was definitely Sioux although Hawk couldn't catch enough to know what was said. At that point, he really didn't care. He knew what he had come to find out. They were Sioux, there were six of them, and they had holed up in a wooded pocket on the back side of a ravine that ran up the fourth hill.

He could have easily shot the one hostile he had seen, but had he done so, the other five would have undoubtedly escaped because he couldn't really see them. And there was no guarantee he could outrun them back to the place where he left his horse. So as cautiously as he had come up, he backed slowly away. He was almost back to his horse before it occurred to him why the Indian was squatting on the side of the hill.

CHAPTER 3

"Maybe when we kill these white men, they will have some more of those beans you like, Crooked Leg," Kills Two Bears called out again. His remarks were once again met with laughter from the other four sitting around the fire. "Maybe you can eat some of these berries now," he said, referring to the thicket of serviceberry bushes that lined a tiny spring that ran through the pocket.

"Augh," Crooked Leg groaned painfully and called back. "Spotted Pony ate from the same pot. Why is he not in pain?" Spotted Pony had dipped into the pot of meat and beans they had found outside the shack where they killed the white man. It had obviously been left there for some time, but the taste was not rancid. So Crooked Leg had finished it off when the others had declined to chance it. To make matters worse, he had chided them about their dainty appetites. Now he was paying for his playful sarcasm as his insides churned in an effort to process the spoiled mixture of beans and rabbit.

On a more serious note, Spotted Pony, who was Kills Two Bears's brother, was moved to speculate, "If he does not rid his belly of the white man's dirty food by the time it becomes

49

dark, we will have to leave him here. He will be of no use to us."

Kills Two Bears shrugged indifferently. "We can attack the white man without him. We have counted no more than four men the whole time we have been watching the house and barn. Two women and two small children are the only others. I think we could have easily killed them all already, instead of waiting for darkness."

"What you say is true," Buffalo Heart replied. The oldest of the six warriors, he was always the most practical and patient of the young Sioux. "But it will be easier to strike after dark when the white men are inside eating and we will be less likely to be shot. Our plan is good and if Crooked Leg is still unable to ride, it will still be easy to kill them all." Their plan was simple. If there was any lookout watching the ranch, he would be killed. Then they would sneak in and let the horses out of the corral. When the white men ran out to save their horses, it would be a simple thing to shoot them down with warriors positioned at the front and back doors of the house, as well as the door of the bunkhouse. "It will be a simple matter to kill the woman and the children then and burn the house." He was also conscious of the glory they would earn by stealing the many horses in that corral.

Crooked Leg stumbled back to the campfire and slumped down on the ground. "It is your turn to go back up to watch the house," Running Bird said to him. "Many Scalps has been watching the house for a long time. Can you do it?"

"I can do it," Crooked Leg mumbled, but suddenly held his stomach when he tried to get up, trying not to retch.

"I will do it," Buffalo Heart said, this time with some degree of disgust in his tone. He rose to his feet. "It will still be a little while before the sun goes down. Maybe you will be well enough to join us by then."

Lieutenant Conner walked to meet Hawk when he rode back up the ridge, eager to hear what he had discovered. "Yep," Hawk said, answering his question before it was asked. He threw a leg over and stepped down from his horse. "They're sittin' up there in those hills. Couldn't be much else on their minds but attackin' that ranch. Just waitin' for dark, I expect." Conner nodded. "Did you decide how you're gonna go after 'em?" Hawk asked.

"I'm still thinking about it," Conner said. "Are there any more of them than we figured?" He was hampered by the open prairie land between where his soldiers now stood on this ridge and the ranch house by the river. He would prefer to have been hidden at the ranch so as to surprise the hostiles when they attacked, but there was no way to ride from this ridge to the ranch house without being seen. Perhaps Major Brisbin would prefer that he should take no chances on endangering civilian lives and advise him to march his patrol directly to the ranch right now. Their mere presence would frighten away a raiding party of six warriors, but Conner was set on stopping the hostiles from preying on anyone else and not just scaring them away.

"Six warriors with eight horses," Hawk said, answering Conner's question. "One of 'em with a case of the shits"—he paused—"a warrior, not a horse."

Conner puzzled over Hawk's remark for only a second, his mind still churning over his best plan of action. "Johnson," he commanded, "get the men ready to mount up. Check your weapons, fully loaded and ready to fire. We're gonna move outta here in fifteen minutes. Johnson immediately obeyed and when he ran to carry out the order, Conner turned back to Hawk. "I'm not waiting till dark to give those devils a chance to sneak in there and lob a few fire arrows into that man's roof. How close do you think we could get before they discovered us, if we went the way you did?"

"Don't know, Lieutenant. Right on top of 'em if they don't set a lookout on that end of the hills. If they do, they'll likely spot you when you're about a hundred yards from that last hill. You'd play hell catchin' 'em then. But like I said, they didn't have anybody watchin' their backs when I went up there."

Conner hesitated a moment. "Well, we'll just roll the dice and hope we're lucky. I'm going after them while they're still lying around in those hills. Now tell me how to catch them napping."

Using a stick to draw a diagram on the ground, Hawk tried to show him how the fourth hill in the chain stood up higher than those on either side. He indicated the ravine where the ponies were and the approximate location of the pocket where the Indians had built a fire. "I ain't sure exactly how that pocket lays out," he said. "Because of that buck squattin' above it on the hill, I couldn't get close enough to see down into it."

Not happy about being left out of the planning of the attack, Nestor felt compelled to remark. "It woulda been a helluva lot better if you'da scouted the front side of that hill, too, so we could cover the front door and the back door."

"Too bad you weren't with me, Nestor," Hawk couldn't resist replying. "I coulda given you that job. Or I coulda just hollered, 'Hey, look at me, Injuns. I'm scoutin' your little hideout.' That woulda done just as much good."

"Why, you smart-mouth son of a bitch," Nestor retorted. "You're gettin' a little too big for your britches. Somebody needs to trim your wick for you."

"You, I suppose," Hawk shot back.

"That's enough, damn it!" Conner ordered before it progressed beyond name-calling. "I'm trying to mount an attack on a hostile Indian party. I don't have time for any schoolyard catfights between my scouts. If you two want to cut each other's throat, you'll have to wait till we get back to Ellis. Then if you still wanna do it, why, hell, we'll all gather around to watch the fight. But until then, you'll behave yourselves and take my orders, or I'll see you never scout for another army patrol again. Is that understood?" He glared at each of them until he got a simple "yes, sir" from both of them. "Now, Mr. Hawk, let's go over that layout again."

"Yessir," Hawk slurred. "Like I said, it's gonna depend on whether or not we can move your men up the backside of that hill before they know we're behind 'em. If we do, we'll be above 'em in that little pocket they're holed up in and they won't have any choice—either surrender or get shot."

"All right, let's get started and hope for the best," Conner said. Then he turned and barked, "Johnson!"

"Yes, sir," Johnson replied. With no need to wait for the order, he immediately went to get the men mounted, and the patrol was under way. Hawk thought he could feel Nestor's eyes on his back as he passed by him on his way to take the point. He had no real desire to fight the belligerent scout. He would be happy just to avoid him in the future.

"Someone is coming from the house!" Buffalo Heart exclaimed, immediately alerting the warriors sitting by the fire. Scrambling at once to grab their weapons, all of them, including the suffering Crooked Leg, ran to follow Buffalo Heart back to the lookout point at the top of the hill. "See!" he said excitedly, and pointed to a pair of riders leaving the barn and heading toward them.

"They are coming right at us," Spotted Pony declared as the two riders held their horses on a line that would take them to the foot of the very hill the warriors stood on. "If they don't turn soon, they will ride right up to our feet." The warriors watched anxiously, waiting to see if their plans for a surprise night attack were going to be ruined. "If they keep coming, we will have to kill them and that will alert everyone else there of the danger."

"And that will ruin our plan to steal the horses and burn the house," Kills Two Bears finished for him. "I say we should get to our ponies now and kill these two."

"If we do that, then we might as well go ahead and attack the house," Running Bird said. "Maybe they will not have time to defend themselves." The prospects of gaining a sizable herd of horses and killing everyone at the ranch, having suddenly been compromised, there was now confusion among the warriors.

"They are still some distance yet," Buffalo Heart said when the riders were a good two hundred yards away. "Maybe they will turn and go in another direction. If they do, then all is well. Our plan will not change. But I think we must get our ponies and be ready to kill them if they come to this hill." His words were met with nods of agreement, for no one could offer a better strategy. It was a disappointing change to their original plan, but they could at least kill two of the white settlers. "Then we can make one sweep through the buildings and maybe catch some of them outside before they have time to run for their weapons."

"One of them is a woman," Many Scalps announced. He had never taken his eyes off the approaching riders while the discussion of what to do went on.

"Good," Spotted Pony said. "That will make it easier." They hurried to ready their horses.

The six Sioux warriors were not the only ones who spotted the two riders leaving the barn. The column of soldiers making their way along the shallow draw caught sight of them, too, as they approached the eastern end of the hills. Nestor was the first to spot them. "Well, look at them damn fools," he said, as if they should know the hostiles were in the hills.

"Oh, good Lord, no!" Lieutenant Conner exclaimed, and signaled for the column to halt. He motioned for Hawk to fall back to talk.

"Damn" was all Hawk could say upon first seeing what Conner was pointing to. This unexpected development would effectively change everything and definitely defeat Conner's intention of preventing any contact between the ranch and the Sioux raiders.

"We're going to have to abort our original plan to catch those hostiles by surprise," Conner said. "I'm gonna have to swing the column around and get between those people and the hostiles. That will probably cause the Indians to sneak away on the backside of these hills, but I don't want to risk the lives of those two people."

Hawk was thinking fast. It looked like Conner was right, unless something else might work. "There might be another way to keep those folks from gettin' shot and maybe keep the Indians from runnin'." Conner was all ears, anxious as he was to inflict punishment upon the Sioux raiders, so Hawk continued. "I can cut that pair off before they get a hundred yards from the hill. I'm thinkin' there's a good chance those Indians won't think anything suspicious about one person meeting those two and then riding off in another direction. It sure as hell shouldn't spook 'em and cause 'em to run."

Conner hesitated while he considered it, then said, "You'd be putting yourself out there in the open in easy range of a rifle."

"I know, but I think these bucks are hopin' to wait till dark, so they can score a big raid," Hawk said. When Conner hesitated again, reluctant to put him in harm's way, Hawk reminded him, "They're gettin' closer."

"All right, go," Conner said. "I'll hold the column here at the foot of the hill in case we have to come quickly." Hawk was off at once.

Rascal responded to the task as Hawk expected of him, but the pair of riders from the ranch were closer to fifty yards from the face of the hill when they saw him riding to intercept them. Puzzled, they pulled up to wait for him. "Howdy, folks," he greeted them as casually as he could affect when he realized one of them was a woman. "I'm gonna need you folks to turn and ride with me back toward the house."

"Who the hell are you?" the man asked, suspicious of the stranger.

"I ain't got time to introduce myself," Hawk replied. "There's a column of cavalry behind me and they're hopin' I can keep you from ridin' into a Sioux war party hidin' on that hill in front of you. So I'd be much obliged if you'd just trust me and we'll ride off together real easy-like, so those Indians don't think we know they're there and we're runnin'."

"Listen to him, John," the woman instructed when her husband hesitated, then she turned her horse. She had made a quick judgment and could see no dishonesty in the rugged man's face. Her husband immediately followed suit and the three of them casually loped off together.

On horseback now, and gathered in the cover of the trees at the base of the hill, the six warriors watched with anticipation of a sudden engagement, only to hold up when the lone rider had suddenly appeared. A man, tall in the saddle, wearing a buckskin shirt and a flat-crowned hat with a feather stuck in the hatband, appeared to be an acquaintance of the two he met. "Where did he come from?" Buffalo Heart asked.

"There may be more," Running Bird said, "maybe on the other side of these hills."

Suddenly a cloud of uneasiness descended upon the war party, prompting Spotted Pony to say, "I think someone had better scout the hill behind us. You might be right, there may be more where that one came from. I will go." He turned his horse and started back up the hill, not waiting for anyone else to join him.

When he reached the top, he started out along the tops of the other hills as fast as he could until he made his way back to the easternmost hilltop. The man with the feather had come from that direction, so he sought to scout the plains beyond the line of hills. He was about to descend to the band of pines that circled the base of the one he was now on, but was stopped by the sight of something moving in the trees. Reacting automatically, he reined his horse to a stop and jumped off his back. Anxious to see what had caught his eye, he quickly made his way down through the trees until he could see a little better. The sight that met his eye almost made him grunt in surprise. There, on the other side of the trees, he saw a column of mounted soldiers, waiting no doubt for him and his friends to make their move. Very slowly, he backed away until reaching his horse. Then he led the pony back up to the top of the hill before jumping on his back and racing back to tell the others.

"What did you find?" Buffalo Heart exclaimed when Spotted Pony's horse slid to a stop just short of plowing into the other horses gathered there.

"Soldiers!" Spotted Pony blurted. "They are hiding behind the hill, waiting for us to attack the man and woman. They hope to trap us, I think!" His report ignited an explosion of excited voices, all wanting to be heard at once.

"Hear me!" Buffalo Heart raised his voice. "I don't think the soldiers knew the man and the woman were going to ride to this place. And that is why they sent the man to turn them away. I think the soldiers were hoping to attack us from behind. We must decide what to do." When they quieted down to hear him speak, he asked, "How many soldiers are there?" Spotted Pony told him there were fifteen plus an officer and a guide. "And Feather In His Hat," Buffalo Heart said, reminding them of the man who had intercepted the couple. "I think that is too many for us to fight, but that is just what I think."

"Buffalo Heart is right," Crooked Leg said, his gut still churning violently. "My belly won't let my eyes see without spinning everything around.

"Maybe so," Kills Two Bears spoke up. "But I don't want to give up without taking one white life. We are out of food and I had thought we would get food here at this place."

"There are too many," Running Bird said. "I agree with Buffalo Heart. It is best to leave this ambush the soldiers have made. I also think Kills Two Bears is right. I, too, don't want to run without killing at least one white man. So I say let us ride out this side of the hill while the soldiers hide on the other side. There are two white men and one woman still between us and the house. We can kill them and head for the river, long before the soldiers can come after us."

His suggestion was met with quick approval, especially in their pressing position. "There is only one man now," Many Scalps announced, his eye still on the three riders. "The man and the woman are returning to the house, but Feather In His Hat has turned around and is coming back."

"No matter," Buffalo Heart said. "Feather In His Hat has big medicine, I think. To kill him will be a great thing for us all." When his words were met with nods of approval, he said, "We go, then. It will be a good day after all."

It was anybody's guess what the Indians would do now. Hawk was just thankful that they had decided not to shoot at the couple from the ranch when they were in easy rifle range. He had spoiled a young couple's outing to pick serviceberries on the mountainside, but they were not reluctant to change their plans when he told them a party of Sioux warriors had beaten them to the patch. In fact, he had to caution them to ride back home leisurely, so as not to alert the Indians. He told them to tell everyone to get their weapons ready to defend their home. Although he thought the soldiers would prevent the hostiles from attacking the house, it was always better to be prepared. "We'll most likely check by with you after whatever happens," he had told them.

Now he was wondering if he might be able to ride back to join the patrol, that is, if his meeting with the couple from the ranch was casual enough to convince the hostiles that their presence had not been discovered. It was either that, or follow the couple to the house. He decided he'd rather chance rejoining the patrol, so he nudged Rascal to a comfortable lope and started back across the open prairie. Although his senses were sharp and alert, he was nevertheless startled by the sudden attack that exploded out of the trees at the foot of the largest hill.

All at once, he found himself in a swarm of lead snapping all around him like angry hornets as the Sioux war party charged out of the trees, firing wildly. His initial reaction was to run, knowing the only reason he had not been hit was because of the distance and the difficulty of firing accurately while at a full gallop. It was only a matter of seconds before one of those shots found purchase in him or his horse, or both. So he hauled back on the reins long enough to draw his rifle and jump out of the saddle. As soon as his feet were on the ground, he gave Rascal a sound slap on the rump, and the big horse galloped away, leaving Hawk to sprint for one of a series of hummocks on the open grassland. With no time to be picky, he dived behind the first one he came to and cranked a cartridge into the rifle's chamber. Lying flat on his stomach behind the low mound, he tried to find the best position to fire from.

The hostiles were driving their horses straight at him, no farther than seventy-five yards away and closing fast. Their shots were more accurate at this distance and he could hear the constant sounds of impact as the bullets hit the front of his hummock. *I wish I'd picked a bigger mound,* he thought. They could not see him behind it, so most of their shots were aimed at the center of the mound, so he slid his body to one side and brought his Winchester to the party. Taking his time to take dead aim, he laid his front sight on the leading hostile and squeezed the trigger. Buffalo Heart was the first to fall, knocked backward off his pony to land hard on the prairie floor. Those behind him jerked their horses hard to avoid his body. Hampered with the task of leading the two horses they had captured, Many Scalps straightened up, offering a better target for Hawk's second kill. With a cry of shock, the surprised Indian slid off his horse when Hawk's shot smashed the center of his chest.

"Soldiers!" Kills Two Bears cried when the patrol of fifteen troopers suddenly appeared, charging full force, carbines blazing away. He veered sharply to the right. The others followed, no longer concerned about the lone man behind the mound. On ponies fresh from their long rest, the four surviving warriors galloped toward the river.

The brief battle over, Hawk got to his feet to send one last round after the fleeing Indians, but missed. He stood there awaiting the patrol and when they came up to him, Lieutenant Conner halted them briefly to make sure he was all right.

"Yeah," Hawk said in reply to Conner's question. "I'm all right. Keep after 'em." He stepped back to avoid being knocked down by one of the horses and watched them gallop off after the fleeing hostiles, who had already reached the river. His concern then was the health of his horse, but first he decided he'd better check on the condition of the two warriors he had shot. With another cartridge cranked into his rifle, he walked to each one, ready to fire if the hostile was playing possum. After confirming both men dead, he looked around for his horse. Seeing the buckskin standing some fifty yards away, he whistled, and Rascal immediately trotted toward him.

Looking out toward the river, he saw the soldiers riding hard up the other side, already almost a mile away. And the thought struck him—*if you ain't caught them by now, I doubt you'll ever catch them*. His money was on the fast Indian ponies in a life-or-death race against the heavier cavalry horses. He turned around and looked back toward the ranch house. *Might as well ride on in and tell them what happened,* he thought.

Lieutenant Conner found Hawk sitting on the front porch of the ranch house, working on a cup of coffee, an empty plate and a fork on the floor beside his chair. Garland Davis, the owner of The Double-D, got up from his chair and went down the steps to meet the lieutenant. "Welcome, Lieutenant. I'm mighty glad you boys came along when you did. From what Mr. Hawk tells me, we mighta been in a whole heap of trouble. I don't reckon you caught up with those Injuns."

"Thank you, sir," Conner replied. "No, we didn't catch up with them."

"Right," Davis replied. "Hawk said you wouldn't."

Conner cast a knowing smile at Hawk, then replied. "I doubt they'll be back here to cause you any trouble, though."

"That's what Hawk said," Davis remarked, then led him up on the porch to meet the rest of his family. "This is my wife, Amanda, and this is my son, John, and his wife, Lucille. John and Lucille was headin' out to that spring in the hills over yonder to pick some berries till Hawk turned 'em around. We got two hired hands here on the place and one more up at the line shack. When John told us what Hawk said to do, why, we got our guns and we was ready for 'em."

"I expect you were," Conner said. "I'm glad you didn't have to use your guns." He glanced over to catch Hawk's eye. Understanding, Hawk slowly shook his head, so Conner broke the news. "About that man of yours in the line shack, I'm

66

sorry to have to tell you that the Indians killed him and burned down the shack. We buried him, of course."

His news caused both women to gasp in horror. "Oh, that poor man," Lucille lamented. "We didn't even know his name."

"It was Ed somethin'," John spoke up.

"That's right," Garland said. "We didn't know much about him. He drifted in here about two months ago, lookin' for a grubstake. So I told him I'd use him up at the shack. That's sorry news, though. I hate to hear it." Talk was interrupted then by the arrival of the patrol, led up in the yard by Corporal Johnson, the horses having been watered at the river. "I expect your horses are pretty tired, Lieutenant," Garland said. "And your men, too. You're welcome to camp here tonight if you want. Matter of fact, I'll have one of the boys cut out a steer and we'll feed your whole outfit with some fresh beef." He turned to his wife. "Mother, have we got enough coffee to take care of these boys?"

"I think so," his wife replied cheerfully. "I'm sorry we don't have any pie for them. Mr. Hawk got the last picce of that."

Conner raised an eyebrow and gave Hawk another sly smile before accepting the invitation. The fresh beef would be enjoyed by his men, especially since they were already short of rations. "That's mighty hospitable of you folks," he said. "I know my men will certainly appreciate it. I'll have the men move on over to the other side of the barn to make camp." He turned to go down the steps just as Hawk did. "What kind of pie was it?" Conner whispered aside.

"Apple," Hawk replied, grinning.

Seated on his horse, sullenly witnessing the introductions, Roy Nestor felt a now-familiar pang of jealousy from the special treatment received by Hawk. It galled him to know that while he was riding hard after the Sioux, Hawk was having pie and coffee on the front porch. *The damn Indians,* he thought. *Not a one could hit the son of a bitch, and him right in the middle of the prairie.* He had considered throwing a shot at Hawk when they rode by him, but was afraid he wouldn't get away with it. He wished now he had done it.

Conner was certainly right when he told Davis his men would appreciate the fresh beef. Before they gathered around a fire pit built for the purpose of roasting meat, Corporal Johnson assigned some men to pick up the bodies of the two hostiles Hawk shot. Under the corporal's supervision, a shallow grave was dug at the base of the hills. With nothing more of a serious nature to occupy their time, the men enjoyed the rare respite. And for a change, everyone went to bed with a full stomach. The next morning, the patrol headed back to Fort Ellis with only a short day's march before them.

It was early in the afternoon when Conner led his patrol back into Fort Ellis, just south of the Gallatin River. He ordered his men to take care of their horses while he reported directly to Major Brisbin. Hawk and Nestor accompanied Conner, and Lieutenant Meade, who was in charge of the scouts, came in to hear their report as well. Afterward, Conner dismissed the scouts, then remained to discuss the performances of the two assigned to him for this particular patrol. "Are you saying Hawk and Nestor didn't work well together?" Brisbin asked.

"I guess I'm saying those two seem to have a natural hatred for each other," Conner answered. "Hawk not so much, but Nestor seems to have a need to disagree with everything Hawk says. I don't know, it just works out that Hawk is right about ninety-nine percent of the time and I think that riles Nestor no end. So it causes a friction that a commander can do without on a patrol like this one. You need to have your scouts helping each other instead of disagreeing on everything that comes up."

"I see what you mean," Brisbin said. "And from what you tell me, you prefer Hawk on your patrols. Does Hawk have trouble with other scouts?"

"Not in my experience, and he's ridden with

me on numerous patrols," Conner replied. "In my opinion, he's the best scout in the regiment."

Brisbin glanced in Meade's direction and the lieutenant remarked, "I'd have to agree."

"Then I suggest you need to have a talk with Nestor," the major said. "We might be better off without him if he's a source of friction like Lieutenant Conner says. This is not the first trouble we've had with this man and it makes me wonder if he should have been fired after that incident six months ago." The major was referring to a raid on a Sioux village where some Lakota horse thieves were thought to be hiding. Nestor had been the only scout on that mission and he had shot a Sioux woman and her baby he found hiding in a gully. He claimed the woman was about to shoot him, but there was no weapon found near the bodies. In Conner's opinion, Meade should have fired Nestor then, but he gave Nestor the benefit of the doubt. His reasoning was that there were nearly always deaths and injuries to noncombatants in the course of a hot firefight.

The problem with Roy Nestor would solve itself, as far as the military was concerned, however, for Nestor decided after this last patrol that he was no longer inclined to ride for the army for the meager wages they paid. He was confident that there were any number of ways for a man to make good money without working for it. He was already kicking around an idea in his mind he had been thinking about for some time. Now was a good time to give it a shot. *Hell,* he thought, *I can do it just as good as anybody else. Lieutenants Conner and Meade, the other scouts, especially Hawk, could all go to hell.* That thought triggered another in his mind. He wished to hell he had taken that shot at Hawk in the confusion of the chase after the fleeing Indians. *I won't pass it up the next time, if it ever comes around again.*

"There you are," Lieutenant Conner said when he walked into the stable. "I thought you might be here."

Hawk interrupted the packing of his saddlebags to greet him. "Lieutenant," he acknowledged. "What can I do for you?"

"Lieutenant Meade said you told him you were gonna give up scouting for the regiment," Conner said. "I thought I'd like to know what you're thinking about doing instead. Hell, man, you were born to do what you're doing. I hope to hell you're not letting Nestor run you off."

Hawk had to laugh. "Is that what Meade told you? I didn't tell him I was quittin' scoutin' for good. I need the money, as stingy as it is. No, sir, I told Meade I was takin' a little vacation for a while 'cause I need to do a little work on my cabin up on the Boulder River. We've been goin' hot and heavy for a long spell and I've got to see if my place is still standin', or if somebody has moved in on me." He laughed again. "Nope, you're not gettin' rid of me that easy. I'll be back, if for no other reason, so I can aggravate you. Besides, you've got a good man in Roy Nestor to scout for you."

Conner was visibly relieved. He ignored the remark about Nestor. "Well, you do aggravate better than most, I have to admit," he said, and Hawk laughed with him. "You'd best watch your scalp back in that wild country. Come to see me as soon as you get back." He turned and walked away.

"I'll do that," Hawk called after him.

CHAPTER 4

"Don't move." The command was soft, but deadly, striking Monroe Pratt with an immediate sense of danger and stopping him in his tracks. Not sure where the voice had come from, he scanned the almost solid bank of berry bushes on the other side of the small stream before him, but saw no one. About to speak, he paused, suddenly apprehensive when he caught sight of a rifle barrel, protruding from the bushes and pointed his way. Due to the thickness of the branches, the barrel was all he could make out. Thoughts of diving for cover in the stream crossed his mind, but the bank was not high enough to give him any real protection. And it would be foolhardy to try to retreat back to the pines some twenty yards behind him. He would never make it. It seemed obvious to him that he had blundered into an open ambush as he had made his way carelessly through the heavily forested riverbank to this clearing where the stream emptied into the river.

For long seconds, he stood frozen with no sound now except that of the gentle breeze rustling through the pines behind him. *Well, I'm not going to just stand here to be executed,* he decided, but his decision to draw the Colt .44 he wore came too late. The rifle suddenly split the stillness of the forest with a sharp report and the snap of the bullet sounded only inches from his head. Shocked, he dropped to one knee and fumbled in his panic to defend himself, feeling it a miracle that he had not been hit. When he finally freed his reluctant .44 from his holster, he prepared to fire at the berry bushes where he had seen the rifle barrel, but stopped, uncertain, when he heard something in the pines behind him. Thinking he was caught between two assailants, he turned to defend against the attack from behind, only to discover a deer thrashing about in a helpless effort to run. Captured in a sudden paralysis of confusion, Monroe watched the wounded animal stumble a half-dozen yards before collapsing. He regained his wits then and whirled back toward the berry bushes in time to see them part and a tall man emerge, wearing a buckskin shirt and a flat-crowned hat with a hawk's feather stuck in the band.

"I've been waitin' for that buck to come for his supper berries for half an hour," the man said. "He started hangin' back when he heard you come crashin' through the bushes like a herd of buffalo. But he didn't hang back far enough to keep from gettin' shot."

It took a moment before Monroe could realize that he had not been the target. When he did, he was not happy about the situation he had been in between the man and the deer. "God A'mighty, man!" he blurted. "You almost shot me! I heard that slug snap right beside my ear!"

"Not hardly," the man said, maintaining his low, casual tone. "I shot a good foot to the right of your head. Plenty of room, but I druther you hadn't stepped right in my line of sight. If you'd come a few steps closer, I mighta had to pass on deer for supper." He gave Monroe a quick look up and down as he walked on by him and went to put the deer out of its misery. When he had finished, he wiped the blood from his knife, replaced it in the scabbard he wore on his belt, and turned to Monroe again. "What are you doin' wanderin' around in the woods here? Did the army send you out lookin' for me?"

Not comfortable with the deer hunter's seeming unconcern for the closeness of his shot, Monroe answered, "I'm lookin' for a man named John Hawk. I was told he had a cabin near this creek."

"He does," Hawk said. "Whaddaya lookin' for him for?"

"I reckon that's something for Mr. Hawk and myself to discuss," Monroe replied, irritated by the man's abruptness. He felt compelled to make the remark even though he had a suspicion that he was talking to John Hawk. Based upon the description he had been given of the sometimes army scout, it was easy to assume the rugged-looking individual who stood at least a couple of inches taller than he, was the man he searched for. The hawk feather stuck in his hatband was enough to confirm the identification. In response to Monroe's remark, the man simply shrugged, seeming to have no interest in the matter. "Are you John Hawk?" Monroe finally pressed.

"I am," Hawk answered, then repeated the question. "Whaddaya lookin' for me for?"

"Major Brisbin at Fort Ellis told me you'd be the best man for the job I've got to do. He said you know the mountains on both sides of the Yellowstone better than any man hiring out as a scout or guide. Are you interested in a job?"

"Depends," Hawk said. "What's the job?" He looked back toward the berry bushes and whistled softly. After a few seconds, a buckskin horse pushed through the bushes, plodded slowly up to Hawk, and stopped a couple of yards from him. Without waiting for Monroe's answer, Hawk grasped the front legs of the deer and pulled it up high enough to get his shoulder under its belly. He let the body fall across his shoulder, then lifted it off the ground. Once the carcass was draped solidly across his shoulders, he proceeded to unload it onto the horse.

Feeling slightly irritated by the stoic scout's apparent lack of interest, Monroe waited until Hawk returned his attention to him before continuing. "It's a very serious matter," he said. "And one I hope you would consider a Christian duty."

Hawk paused at that, shifted the carcass slightly to one side to center it, and turned to study Monroe. "I don't consider much of anything I do as my Christian duty. I might, though," he said, "dependin' on if you'll get around to tellin' me what you're wantin' me to do."

"I want you to find a white man and woman who went missing around the first of June. The man is my brother and the woman is his wife."

Hawk took a moment to reflect before replying. "Up toward Helena, on the Mullan Road?"

"That's right," Monroe said. "You heard about it?"

"Yeah, I heard about it—heard the army sent out a patrol to look for 'em." He cocked his head to one side and scratched his chin to help him think. "But that was a couple of weeks ago and if I recollect properly, they didn't find hide nor hair of 'em."

"You remember correctly," Monroe said. "And the army called off the search."

"But you didn't."

"He's my brother," Monroe replied, thinking that should be reason enough.

"What makes you think I'd have any better luck than a cavalry patrol?"

"I don't know about luck, but Major Brisbin told me that if there was anyone who could find them, it would be you." He waited a few minutes while Hawk appeared to be thinking it over.

"Dead or alive, I want to find out what happened to my brother and his wife. All the army found was his wagon, left on the side of the trail with a broken axle. They found no trace of them, and the horses were gone as well. Whether they went on, on horseback, or they were attacked by Indians, it's hard to say. But there were no bodies found, so that means there's a chance they're still alive. What do you say? Will you help me?" He paused then to watch the scout's reaction, waiting for his response.

"I ain't sayin' I will and I ain't sayin' I won't," Hawk said. "You're talkin' about a long search, a lotta time spent, and you've got a good possibility of comin' up empty-handed. Your odds ain't too good."

"I know that," Monroe responded right away. "But he's my brother," he repeated. "If you're worried about the money, I'll pay you one hundred dollars to look for them and I'll double it if we find them, dead or alive. Plus, I'll pay all your expenses for ammunition and supplies."

That perked Hawk's interest more than a bit. That was about four months' pay when scouting for the army. "It's about a three-day ride from here to Helena before we even get started," he said, just to make sure Monroe understood the expenses to be encountered. "You ain't told me where your brother was headed when he joined that wagon train."

"He was heading for Missoula and our ranch in the Bitterroot Valley," Monroe said.

Hawk let that sink in for a few seconds. "I heard that train didn't go any farther than Helena, so your brother went on by himself, I reckon." He paused to stroke his chin while he considered that. "Just him, his wife, and their wagon, headin' out on a trip over a hundred and twenty miles away, through country that two or three Indian tribes claim." He shook his head and commented, "Mister, if I was dealt that hand in a poker game, I'd throw it in."

"I suppose so, but Jamie drove that wagon all the way from the Bitterroot Valley to Minnesota to get Rachel and her things, and he's never been one to fear anything or anyone. So I'm not surprised that he didn't hesitate to drive the rest of the way with just the two of them," Monroe said, and still pressed for an answer. "Will you take the job?"

Hawk snorted a small laugh. "I reckon. I've got a few things to do before I go, though. One of 'em's to skin and butcher this deer. I reckon we'll be eatin' it on the way to Helena. You got a horse tied up somewhere on the other side of the creek, or did you walk all the way from Fort Ellis?"

Monroe laughed. "No, I've got a horse tied up back there in the pines." Unable to resist a little sarcasm, he added, "I left my horse and came on foot when I heard you thrashing around in those berry bushes like a herd of buffalo." Hawk chuckled to show his appreciation for Monroe's sarcasm. "How soon can you be ready to leave?" Monroe asked.

"Like I said, I need to butcher this deer and smoke a good bit of it to eat on while we travel. I'll close up my cabin, put a few things in a little cache I've got hidden back up the hill, and that's about it. I'll be ready to leave tomorrow afternoon. It's about forty miles from here to Bozeman, so we'll need to rest the horses before we start out from there to Helena."

"I figured it a little farther than forty miles to get here," Monroe said. "I left Fort Ellis early yesterday morning and already it's getting dark between these mountain ranges today."

"Most likely you had to ride east to the Yellowstone, then follow it to strike this river, then follow it to the pie-shaped boulder Major Brisbin told you to find, right?" Monroe nodded and Hawk continued. "We won't go that way goin' back. We'll cut across through some mountain passes that'll shorten the trip. You got all your possibles with you?"

"No," Monroe replied. "I've got my bedroll, but I left a packhorse back in the stables in Bozeman—didn't think I'd need it till we start back in that direction. I was thinking we can ride back to Bozeman tomorrow and stay there overnight. Then the horses will be rested and ready to go. Does that suit you?"

"Suits me fine," Hawk replied. "I'll wait here while you go get your horse, then I'll lead you to my cabin." He stood there, holding the buckskin's bridle, watching Monroe walk back into the pines. *Seems like a reasonable man,* he thought. *I hope we can find his brother and his wife, but there ain't much chance of it.* "We can sure as hell use the money, though," he said to the buckskin.

The first evening the two new partners spent together went well enough. Monroe was eager to help in any chore Hawk had to do before leaving—mostly helping with the smoking of the fresh venison. While they worked, Monroe told about all the events that led his brother, Jamie, to be missing. "Jamie had been writing letters back and forth with a friend of one of our cousins in Minnesota. One thing led to another till Jamie got around to asking her to marry him. She said yes, so he drove a wagon back to get her and her things. The last word we got from him was that he was on his way home to the Bitterroot Valley at Missoula with a wagon train following the Mullan Road to Walla Walla in Washington Territory. They never showed up when they were supposed to, so I left Missoula and backtracked along the Mullan Road, hoping to meet the train. Come to find out, the fellow leading the train left them all high and dry just short of Helena and the other folks on the train decided not to go any farther. Roy Nestor was the wagon master's name, supposed to have been an army guide. I ran into Nestor in Helena and he told me that Jamie and his bride went on alone from Helena. And like I said, I never met them on the Mullan Road anywhere between Missoula and Helena. I'm hoping you can pick up their trail somehow. I need to know what happened to them."

"Nestor, huh?" Hawk responded, still stunned by the news that he had been hired as the wagon master. "So he was out in Minnesota. I wondered what happened to him after he quit scoutin' for the army." He refrained from sharing his opinion of Roy Nestor with Monroe—that he doubted Nestor could have found his way back from Minnesota if the army hadn't built the Mullan Road for him to follow. It didn't sound like he turned out to be any better as a wagon master than he had as a scout. "You say he quit the train?"

"That's what I was told by one of the men who had been a member of the wagon train," Monroe replied. "Of course, Nestor had a different version of the story. He said the folks in the train decided not to go any farther after they saw the available land around Helena. But according to this fellow who had a wagon in the train, they didn't decide to stay until after Nestor convinced them it was too dangerous to continue, due to Sioux war parties between Helena and Missoula."

"Is that a fact?" Hawk responded. "I ain't heard there was any increase in Sioux raidin' parties along that road this summer so far. You said you rode the road from Missoula to Helena. You see any sign of Indian activity?"

"Obviously not," Monroe replied, "or I wouldn't be standing here."

"That's what I was thinkin'," Hawk said. "If I was to guess, I'd say those folks never got any of their money back."

"You'd be guessing right," Monroe said.

It was a good thing Hawk had waited to take Monroe to his cabin. Otherwise, Monroe was not sure he would have found it if left on his own. It was located on the stream, about three hundred yards from where it flowed into the Boulder River. Nestled back under the overhang of a ridge above it, it almost looked to be part of the ridge. Monroe had to give the rough-edged scout credit for building a solid cabin with a fine-working stone fireplace. Although it was still in the middle of summer, the night air chilled the valleys and ravines considerably, but a small fire in the fireplace kept the cabin comfortable. When the chores were finally done in preparation for leaving, Monroe slept solidly until awakened by Hawk early the next morning.

"There's still a few things to do before we can go," Hawk said. "There's coffee boilin' in the fireplace. Help yourself. I'm gonna go put some things in my cache, then I'll be right back to saddle up and load my packhorse." He picked up a large pack and went out the door. When he returned, he busied himself closing up his cabin while Monroe finished his coffee. "We'll stop after a while when we rest the horses and fix a little breakfast," Hawk said when he was ready to start out.

As Hawk had said he would, he led them across the river and followed a series of game trails that took them through the rugged mountains before striking the Yellowstone at a point about twenty miles southeast of Bozeman. This was where they stopped. After resting the horses and eating some of the fresh venison, they were in the saddle again, arriving in the settlement of Bozeman in the afternoon. "I'll leave it up to you," Hawk said as they walked their horses slowly up the one street toward the stables at the far end. "There's still some daylight left, so if you want to, we can start out for Helena today after we rest the horses."

"No, I think I'd rather wait here and start out in the morning, like we planned. By the time I pack up my stuff and check out of my room at the hotel, get my packhorse loaded, it'll be getting along toward sunset. Besides, we might wanna take the opportunity to have a good supper and a drink of whiskey before we start riding again."

"Whatever you say," Hawk said, although he would have expected Pratt to insist upon starting as soon as possible. "We're ridin' on your dollar." They continued on to the stable.

"I see you found your man," Lem Birchfield greeted Monroe when they pulled up by the corral. He looked Hawk up and down when he dismounted. Offering his hand, he said, "Lem Birchfield."

"John Hawk," he returned, taking his hand.

Although never having met the man, Lem had heard of him. The feather in Hawk's hatband should have given him a clue and at first glance, he looked worthy of his reputation. Back to Monroe then, he asked, "You fixin' to leave your horses here?"

"Yep, we'll leave mine and Hawk's here for the night. We're heading out in the morning, so I reckon a ration of oats might be a good idea for all four of 'em." Hawk nodded in agreement. If Monroe hadn't suggested the oats, he would have. His buckskin didn't often get grain, so whenever Hawk had occasion to stable the horse, he usually sprang for the extra treat. When Hawk asked Lem what he would charge for him to sleep in the stall with his horse, Monroe interrupted. "You can stay in the hotel—bunk in with me if you want to, or I reckon I could pay for another room if you'd rather."

"Thanks just the same," Hawk said. "But I'll just bed down with my horse, here, if Mr. Birchfield don't mind. Sometimes those hotel beds are too soft, and I end up on the floor, anyway. Seems like a waste of money." He looked at Lem. "How much?"

"I usually charge an extra two bits for a man to stay with his horse," Lem said.

"Ought not charge anything since I'm payin' to board four horses," Monroe commented. "Hawk's not likely to eat any oats or hay." Lem shrugged and complied. Hawk grinned, thinking that Monroe was not as loose with his money as he had at first appeared to be.

Hawk piled his saddle and packs in a corner of the stall Lem suggested, pulled his Winchester 73 from the saddle sling, then joined Monroe in the short walk to the hotel. When they came to Grainger's Saloon, next to the hotel, Monroe said, "No sense in you having to go up to the room with me. Why don't you go on in Grainger's here and have a drink? And I'll be back in a few minutes." There was no argument from Hawk. He paused a moment while Monroe continued on to the hotel, then stepped up on the board stoop in front of the saloon.

Grainger's was fairly busy, although it was not yet into the evening hours. Hawk walked through the open door into the dimly lit barroom and stood for a moment looking around the room for a table. There were several open along the far wall and while he paused to decide which one he preferred, he heard a voice from the bar. "Hawk." There was no mistaking the undisguised contempt in the low, slurred delivery.

Hawk turned toward the bar, where a small knot of men was gathered around the end, talking to the bartender. His gaze settled upon a broad-shouldered, heavyset man in the center of the four men. "Hello, Nestor," Hawk said, not at all pleased to see the irritating man. "I heard you were up in Helena."

"You did, did you?" Roy Nestor replied.

"Yeah, fellow told me you were in the wagon train business, guidin' settlers to Washington Territory," Hawk said. "Whaddaya doin' back here in Bozeman? You plannin' on scoutin' for the army again?"

"Hell, no," Nestor shot back. "I ain't wastin' my time on no twenty-five-dollar-a-month job nursemaidin' a bunch of dumb soldiers." He sneered when he added, "I reckon you're still scoutin' for 'em."

"Whenever they need me," Hawk said, and turned his attention to the bartender, wanting no further conversation with the loudmouth blowhard. His history with Nestor was short, but of conflicting issues from the start. The first involved the cruel treatment of a horse that Nestor was trying to saddle-break. Hawk didn't approve of beating a horse into submission and he didn't hesitate to tell that to Nestor. It was just before turning into a fight when Lieutenant Meade stepped in to stop it and threatened to fire both of them. After that, the lieutenant made an effort to keep them apart whenever possible, but when the company was in the field, it was not always easy to do. The last time they were paired together was on a patrol under Lieutenant Mathew Conner's command. It was shortly after that patrol that Nestor quit. His sudden resignation came as a welcome surprise, graciously accepted by Meade, for he had already made up his mind to fire the belligerent scout. As for Hawk, he didn't concern himself with Nestor, one way or the other. He figured he took army pay to do a job, so that was his primary interest. He never sought Nestor out, but neither would he back away to avoid him. Just as he would when encountering a rattlesnake, he would step aside if convenient. But if the snake was prone to attack, he wouldn't hesitate to kill it. He didn't have time to settle himself at a table before he was caused to wonder if this was going to be one of those occasions when it was going to be hard to avoid the snake.

"What's your poison, mister?" Fred Grainger asked.

"I reckon I'll have a glass of beer," Hawk said, and fished in his pocket for a coin.

"You're lucky I've got some," Grainger said. "First I've been able to get in about a month." He poured the beer from a barrel under the bar and set it on top. Hawk picked it up and started toward a table against the wall.

"Thought you might drink with us at the bar," Nestor mocked. "Have a shot of whiskey, like a man." He looked around him at the men standing with him, smirking. "Reckon you'd rather set down at a table and drink your beer like a woman." He was rewarded with a few chuckles from those standing with him before the room became silent with the patrons suddenly becoming aware of a possible fight.

Hawk smiled, not at all surprised by Nestor's baiting. It was the nature of the man to blow and bluster when he had an audience. It was the main reason he had not gotten along with the other scouts who rode for Lieutenant Meade. "Why, I appreciate your kind invitation, Roy," Hawk replied, ignoring the intended insult. "But I'm waitin' for a fellow that'll be here in a few minutes, so I'll just wait for him to show up. Thanks just the same."

"Who is it, your big friend Lieutenant Conner?" Nestor went on. "You two always were thick as thieves." Hawk ignored the remark and heard the derisive grunt behind him as he continued on to the table. He ignored the grunt as well. Disappointed, the other patrons resumed their noisy drinking.

He had not finished his glass of beer by the time Monroe came in the door. He stood just inside, looking the barroom over until he spotted Hawk seated at the table, and strode straight toward him. "What are you drinking, beer?" Monroe asked as he pulled a chair back. "I was thinking of something with a little more bite than beer."

"Me, too," Hawk said. "But I thought I'd wait for you. Whaddaya want?" Monroe expressed a preference for rye whiskey, but said he'd settle for corn if that was the only choice. "Set yourself down," Hawk said, "and I'll get us a bottle."

When Hawk went to get the whiskey, it momentarily silenced the loud conversation between the four men at the bar. Nestor didn't say anything at first while he stared at Monroe sitting at the table. He was sure he had seen him before, but his memory was clouded by the alcohol he had consumed, so he returned his attention to Hawk. "You sure you're man enough to handle that stuff?" he said when Hawk picked up the bottle Grainger placed on the counter.

Hawk didn't respond at once, waiting until he picked up the two shot glasses the bartender set out. He locked eyes with the obviously drunken belligerent and said, "Nestor, I don't normally take advantage of a man too drunk to keep his mouth shut, but I reckon I've heard enough outta you. I don't know what your problem with me is and I can't say as I really give a damn. So you just mind your own business and I'll take care of mine." He turned and walked back to the table where Monroe sat, astonished by the confrontation between the two.

"You better turn your back and walk away," Nestor bellowed after him. Hawk ignored him.

"That's that Nestor fellow, that wagon master," Monroe said when Hawk sat down. "What's he raving about?"

"Nothin'," Hawk replied, and filled the two glasses. "It's just the whiskey workin' on what he calls a brain." Eager to change the subject, he said, "Corn whiskey's all the bartender's got. Sorry he didn't have any rye."

"That's all right," Monroe said. "I'm sure it'll do the job. I'm not in the habit of drinking too much, anyway."

"I reckon that's something we've got in common," Hawk allowed. "I never wanted to drink so much that I didn't have control over my actions."

"Like that fellow over there?" Monroe asked.

"Yeah, like him," Hawk replied. He filled the shot glasses a second time. "Damn, that stuff burns pretty good, don't it?" He chased it with a swig of beer, then pushed the glass over toward Monroe. "Help yourself. Maybe there's enough left to put out the fire."

"I appreciate it," Monroe said, trying to laugh while grimacing from the first drink. They both chuckled over their reaction to the stinging liquid. "I don't believe I'm gonna need more than two drinks before we go get some supper. That stuff's hard on an empty stomach."

"We'll take the bottle with us," Hawk said. "It'll be good for snake bites or bullet holes, or anything else we run into that needs killin' or skinnin'."

They both pushed their chairs back and got up, but their departure was not going to be that simple. "Uh-oh," Monroe murmured when he turned to see Roy Nestor push away from the bar and stride on wobbly legs to stand in their way. He glanced at the grinning faces of the men still hovered around the end of the bar before taking a quick glance in Hawk's direction to see his reaction. Seeming not to even notice Nestor's outright challenge, Hawk walked right by him to pay Grainger for the bottle in his hand.

Enraged to be so coldly ignored, Nestor turned to again block Hawk's path, causing the rangy scout to inform him, "I ain't got time to fool with you right now, Nestor. You're standin' between me and supper."

"You smart-mouth son of a bitch," Nestor

blurted. "I'm callin' you out. You've been stuck in my craw ever since that patrol on the Yellowstone."

"You mean when you went ridin' off up the river chasin' after that Sioux war party you couldn't find?" Hawk responded.

"Damn you!" Nestor bellowed, his hand hovering over the handle of the .44 he wore on his hip. Even as inflamed as he was, however, he hesitated to draw it. He was not so drunk that he thought he could draw his weapon before Hawk cut him down with the Winchester he already held in his hand. His vision, although somewhat fuzzy from the alcohol, was sharp enough to see that the hammer on the rifle was cocked and Hawk's trigger finger rested lightly on the trigger guard. Nestor prided himself on his reputation as a fast gun, but nobody was that fast. "You're wearin' a six-gun on your hip, so hand that rifle to your friend, there. I'm goin' out in the street and wait for you to come out and face me. If you ain't out there in five minutes, you're nothin' but a low-down yellow bastard, and I'll come back in here to get you."

"All right, Nestor," Hawk replied. "I'll be right out as soon as I pay Mr. Grainger for this bottle of whiskey."

Nestor tossed an arrogant smile in the direction of the drinking partners he had been performing for, then spun on his heel and marched toward the door. From having ridden on patrol with Hawk before, he was smug in the knowledge that the rugged scout was not one to practice with a handgun, the rifle being his preferred weapon. He, on the other hand, considered himself quite adept at handling the Colt .44 he carried. Consequently, he was quite confident that he would win any duel with pistols between them and it would go a long way in establishing the reputation he coveted. The fact that he had consumed an impressive amount of Fred Grainger's liquid fire did not worry him in the least. If anything, it bloated his estimation of his ability as a gunman.

Finding it hard to believe what was actually happening, Monroe shook himself out of his temporary paralysis in time to step up to the bar where Hawk was busy negotiating a price for the bottle of whiskey. "Here, I'll pay for that," Monroe volunteered. "That comes under the heading of supplies."

"Much obliged," Hawk said, and stepped aside. "I was just tellin' Grainger, here, that the bottle wasn't quite full when we bought it, so we oughtn't have to pay for a full bottle."

Monroe ignored the comment and slapped some money down on the counter, his thoughts on a matter he considered of more importance than the price of the whiskey. He had not known Hawk long enough to judge his reaction to an outright challenge that might possibly end his life. Monroe was greatly concerned about the threat issued by Nestor and he turned to confront Hawk while Grainger eagerly counted out the price for an unopened bottle. "Are you planning on going out in the street to face that man in a duel?" Monroe paused for a few seconds until Nestor's friends filed out the door, eager to watch the showdown, the smiles of anticipation still plastered on their faces. A thought occurred to him that he might be losing his guide if this thing didn't turn out in Hawk's favor.

In answer to Monroe's question, Hawk said, "No, you and me are fixin' to go to the hotel to eat supper. You ready? I know I am. I ain't in the mood to waste time with loudmouths like Roy Nestor."

Baffled by Hawk's seemingly casual ignoring of a man waiting for him with the express purpose of shooting him down, Monroe questioned, "How are we gonna get around him? He's standing in the middle of the street and we'll have to go by him if we're really going to the hotel."

"We're not goin' around him. We're goin' through him. You ready to go?" Without waiting for an answer, he started for the door, cranking a cartridge into the chamber of the Winchester as he walked. "Just follow me." Monroe hurried out behind him, followed close behind by Grainger, who didn't want to miss the show.

Outside, Hawk paused just a moment to survey the scene. A sizable group of spectators had gathered even in that short time, a testimony to the quickness with which word of a possible gunfight could spread. He returned his cool gaze to focus on Nestor, some forty yards away in the middle of the street. He was standing with feet widespread and knees slightly bent, as if ready to spring into action. Hawk glanced at a tiny dust devil skipping along the dusty street, then looked at the flag on the short pole by the post office just to verify the direction of the slight breeze. Satisfied that it was not enough to make him overly cautious in his aim, he stepped off the board stoop.

The first shot startled everyone on the street, though none so much as Roy Nestor when the rifle slug kicked up a puff of dust between his feet. Stunned, Nestor was still confused when a second shot, then a third, ripped into the dusty street close around his feet, causing him to jump backward. On a straight line, walking toward him, Hawk fired shot after shot around Nestor's feet, each one seeming closer than the one before. Frantic, Nestor pulled his .44, although he was hard pressed to take aim, what with the bullets plowing up the street at his feet. When he finally fired one harmless shot that went through the window of the saloon, Hawk shifted his aim to send a slug through Nestor's boot. Nestor emitted a loud howl and hobbled for the safety of the general store, which was the closest port of cover. Two spectators standing at the entrance to the store scampered away, fleeing the path of the apparent maniac.

"Step lively," Hawk cautioned Monroe. "We need to get outta range of his handgun before he decides to come out of the store."

It was a wise but unnecessary precaution, due to the panic that now possessed Nestor. Suffering the pain in his foot and the tempest swirling in his stomach from too much alcohol, he lurched drunkenly into the store only to empty the contents of his gut onto the floor. His anger now reaching a boiling point, he straightened up to confront an eight-year-old girl who stared at him with eyes open wide in amazement. It was only for a moment, however, before the child's mother grabbed her hand and snatched her behind the counter. Suddenly feeling the humiliation of vomiting on the floor, Nestor turned to meet the astonished face of William Bates, the owner of the store. "What the hell are you gapin' at?" Nestor roared at Bates. The terrified store owner was too stunned to answer. Nestor tried to regain some measure of dignity, but he was unable to ignore his throbbing foot as he limped to the window. Hawk and Monroe had already disappeared. Left with the feeling that he had been buffaloed, he mumbled a vow to kill

Hawk, holstered his .44, and went to the door.

Bates, no longer fearing the loss of his life, managed to utter a parting remark. "Looks like you're gonna be needin' some new boots. I've got several styles that oughta fit you." Nestor paused for a moment. His first reaction was to turn around and shoot the store to pieces, but he had been shamed enough by the mess he had made on the floor. To him, that might have been taken as a sign of total cowardice by Bates, thinking he had become sick with fear. He swore to avenge himself, but the throbbing in his foot caused him to think about a doctor first. The closest thing to a doctor in Bozeman was the barber, so he limped down the street to his shop, waving his pistol at anyone on the street stopping to stare at him.

While Nestor had suffered the humiliation of emptying the contents of his stomach on Bates's floor, Hawk and Monroe had plenty of time to reach the hotel. Monroe needed to avail himself of the hotel's outhouse before eating, so he told Hawk to go on to the dining room and he would join him there. The happenings in Grainger's Saloon were not the norm for him and he thought it would be good for him to consider the possible consequences to follow.

CHAPTER 5

Monroe Pratt was rapidly learning that the guide he had hired to help him track down his brother was like no other man he had ever met. When Hawk had started firing his rifle Monroe naturally thought he planned to murder Nestor at long range, with no intent to face him in a duel. To the contrary, the rangy rifleman appeared to have no desire to kill Nestor, because every shot he fired traced a neat little pattern around Nestor's feet, moving him backward, like herding cattle. Monroe didn't think to count the shots, but he guessed that Hawk must have almost emptied the magazine, and every shot, one of pinpoint accuracy. There was little doubt that he could have placed a fatal shot, had he so desired, but he settled for a wounded foot, just to rid himself of an annoyance. The only worry that occurred to Monroe was whether or not Nestor had sense enough to know his life had been spared and to count himself lucky to still be walking around. Or was Hawk, and maybe himself, now in danger of being shot in the back? He knew one thing for certain—he was not going to rest easy until they had left Bozeman behind them, and that would not be until morning.

These were the thoughts that occupied Monroe's

mind when he walked into the hotel dining room to find Hawk seated at a table with his back to the wall, waiting for him. He noticed the rifle propped against the wall beside Hawk's chair as he unbuckled his gun belt and left his Colt on the table just inside the door. He questioned Hawk about it when he approached the table. "How'd you get away with holding on to your rifle? The hotel's pretty strict about their rule of no guns in the dining room."

"Yes, they are," Hawk replied. "And a good rule it is, too, but the woman runnin' things here agreed that it might be a good idea to have a little bit of protection while there's a mad dog with a sore foot runnin' around town. I reckon she heard all those shots fired in the street earlier—mighta spooked her a little. She—I think her name's Sadie—told me to leave it by the door at first, but she let me keep it as long as I promised not to shoot her cook if I didn't like the food."

Monroe nodded. He could well imagine that Sadie might have even witnessed the altercation having just taken place outside on the street. With that thought in mind, he pulled out a chair on the side so as not to have his back to the door as well. "It's been pretty good eating here for the couple of days I've been in town," he said, mostly for the benefit of the woman approaching the table with a coffeepot and an extra cup for him.

"You eatin', too?" Sadie asked Monroe.

"Yes, ma'am," he replied. "What is the special tonight?"

"Beef stew," she answered. "Same as it is every Wednesday night."

"Right," he came back quickly, as if he should have known. He had tried on prior occasions to make polite conversation with the stoic woman, but she seemed either incapable of small talk or simply saw no future in knowing him any better. She filled their cups and returned to the kitchen to prepare two plates.

In spite of Sadie's lack of cheer, the food was good and the servings were generous. They ate their supper without interruption save that of the somber woman with her coffeepot. Although Hawk had taken precautions against a sudden visit from Roy Nestor, he had felt that there was little danger of an attack in the hotel dining room. He figured Nestor to be more inclined to hide someplace across the street from the hotel, wait for him to come out, and try for a shot in the back. They ate their supper and made their plans to get started early the next morning before breakfast. Because neither man had any strong need, nor desire, to visit a saloon after supper, and because of the early start scheduled the next day, they said good night when the meal was finished. After Monroe went upstairs to his room, Hawk stuck his head in the kitchen door to tell Sadie he thought the stew was the best he'd ever eaten. It wasn't, but he made it a habit to always compliment the cook. His comment served to replace the ever-present scowl on her face with an awkward smile. "You come back to see us," she said as he went out the back door to make his way behind the buildings on his way to the stable. He had advised Monroe to take the same route in the morning, just to be safe.

Like the night just past, morning came without further incident. Hawk was saddled up and his packhorse ready to go by the time Monroe appeared at the stable door. "I saddled your horse," Hawk said. "You can check that cinch to see if it suits you."

"Much obliged," Monroe said. "I reckon we're ready to get started, then." Since Lem Birchfield had been paid in advance, they stepped up into the saddle and walked their horses out into the early-morning light. Hawk peered down the empty street, his focus moving from storefront to storefront, seeking to catch any irregularity in the normal outlines of the structures. Satisfied that Nestor had no plans for an early visit, he waved Monroe on and pushed his buckskin to a steady lope past the hotel and saloons.

Once they were out of town, they followed the wagon track northwest along the Gallatin River to a point about twelve miles east of Three Forks. They left the common wagon track at that point

102

and veered off up the valley to the north, riding another ten miles or so before stopping to rest the horses and eat their breakfast. Pushing on, they continued up the broad valley, west of the Big Belt Mountains, stopping to make camp on the Missouri River with a little over a day's ride left to reach Helena. Hawk had caught no sign of anyone following them all through the day, but he reminded himself that Nestor had worked many years as a scout and tracker, so he was careful in choosing a campsite. There was never any reason to be careless, he told himself, whether anyone was chasing him or not. But by the time they were sitting around the fire eating the venison Hawk had killed two days before, concern about Roy Nestor was all but forgotten. Their talk centered more on Jamie Pratt. Hawk was interested in knowing more about Monroe's younger brother, thinking the more he knew about him, the more he might be able to mentally walk in his boots if it came to the point of guessing what might have happened to him. There was not much Monroe could tell him, however, that would provide any help in tracking him. Most of what he learned was about the Pratt ranch in the Bitterroot Valley. From what he gathered, Monroe, the oldest brother, made the decisions since the death of his father, but nearly always after conferring with Thomas, the middle brother. According to Monroe, Thomas was married to the land and the cattle, and worked harder than anyone else to develop the Pratt brand. Jamie, on the other hand, was never one to embrace the business of the ranch. It was welcome news to his brothers when he began exchanging letters with Rachel White, at last showing the interest in the family ranch his brothers shared. A separate cabin was already being built for Jamie and his wife to start their family. *Kinda sad when you think about it,* Hawk thought, and took the last swallow of his coffee.

"Might be he knows we're on his tail," Walt Keenum suggested. The three men stood over the hoofprints leading away from the common trail.

"Maybe," Nestor conceded, "but I doubt it." He held on to his saddle horn in an effort to relieve the weight on his right foot. The bullet that had smashed three of his toes had required no removal by the barber since it had gone right through the boot. But the swelling in his foot had rendered his every step painful—this in spite of the enormous wad of bandaging that forced him to walk on his heel and made it impossible to place his right foot in the stirrup.

"These tracks mighta been left by somebody else," Shorty Doyle suggested. "How do you know these tracks are his?"

" 'Cause they're the same damn tracks we've been followin' ever since we left Bozeman,"

Nestor replied curtly. "And they're the only fresh tracks on the whole damn road."

Shorty paused to consider that, then asked, "Reckon why he didn't just stay on the road to Helena?"

"Hell, I don't know," Nestor replied. His impatience with the two partners he had enlisted was growing with each mile. On another occasion he might have been oblivious to Shorty's inane remarks, but after his humiliation the night before, he was in no mood to be tolerant. "Maybe he thinks it's a shorter distance ridin' straight up the valley."

Keenum and Doyle were two of the three men who had been drinking with him the night before when Hawk walked into Grainger's. Both men were drifters, Shorty wanted in Nebraska for bank robbery, Walt in Texas for stabbing a dance hall woman. Between the two, there weren't enough brains to fill the head of a lizard, but they provided Nestor with two extra guns and they agreed to ride with him for a split of the money they found on the two bodies. With no idea if it was true or not, Nestor told them that Monroe was carrying a great sum of money. He figured that after the job was done, he'd be inclined to pay Shorty and Walt in lead and continue on to Helena alone, where he was not well-known. "We need to hang back a little farther," he said. "I don't wanna take a chance on them seein' us.

I don't wanna catch up to 'em before they've already set up for the night. If we catch 'em in their blankets, it'll be like shootin' fish in a barrel."

"That's the way I like it best," Shorty said, a foolish grin spreading his whiskers. Matching Shorty's grin, Walt agreed, and they stepped up into the saddle and followed Nestor over a low rise beside the road in the direction the tracks led. Unseen by Nestor, his two partners exchanged winks at the sight of his one bundled foot dangling beside his right stirrup. They were not above enjoying a bit of amusement watching him grimacing and cursing his sore foot, but they took care to hide it from him. Nestor was in no mood to endure ridicule or japing at his expense.

After a ride of about two hours, they came upon the ashes of a small fire beside a tiny stream. "That's about what I figured," Nestor said. "I figured they oughta been stoppin' pretty soon to rest their horses and this was the place."

"That's what I figured, too," Walt said. " 'Cause it was gettin' about time to rest mine."

They dismounted and Shorty went immediately to inspect the ashes of the fire to see if there were any with a little life left to make it easier for him to start another one. "Hell," he cursed. "They threw water on the fire." He looked around him. "There ain't nothin' close enough to worry 'bout startin' a prairie fire."

"We ain't gonna be needin' to build a big fire, anyway," Nestor muttered, really no more than speaking his thoughts aloud. "We ain't gonna be here long." He looked at the sun, already well past midday, thinking he wanted to catch up to Hawk before hard dark. His concern was that the rangy scout might hide his camp so well that he wouldn't be able to find it after dark. He hoped that Hawk didn't expect him to come after him, and so far, there seemed to be no real effort to hide his trail. But he wasn't willing to discount the possibility that the wily scout might try to lead him into an ambush. So in spite of his urgency to settle the score, he forced himself to be cautious.

"I hope we're gonna be here long enough for a cup of coffee," Walt declared. "I can't go all day without somethin' to keep the sides of my belly from rubbin' together." He pulled a frying pan out of his "war bag" and some salt pork to slice. That was enough to encourage Shorty to start searching the underbrush for kindling. It was not long before Walt's coffeepot was boiling over in the fire and there was bacon sizzling in the pan. It was difficult for Nestor to keep from brooding over the two brainless partners he had to rely on to help him settle the score with Hawk. Watching them, he was reminded of a Sunday school picnic at least what he imagined one would be like. He would have no trouble shooting both of them as soon as Hawk and Pratt were dead. He had no real quarrel with Monroe Pratt, but he didn't plan to leave a witness, either.

It seemed longer to Nestor than the hour he had allowed to rest the horses, but when it was finally time to mount up, he wasted no time arousing his partners. Both men had taken advantage of the time after their stomachs were content to take a nap. So with a bitter spleen and an aching foot from bearing his weight while he used his good foot to kick both of them awake, Nestor started out again, his hired gunmen following.

It was close to twilight by the time the three would-be assassins reached the Missouri River. Nestor had planned his time just right. He had figured Hawk would camp at the river and in the dusky light of evening, the tracks he followed could still be seen. He pulled up when they were within about one hundred and fifty yards from the cottonwoods lining the river. Shorty was the first to spot the smoke. A thin gray ribbon of smoke was barely discernable drifting up through the branches of the tall trees. Nestor was satisfied that the timing was just as he had planned. In another hour, the smoke would be invisible and it might have been much harder to locate the camp. "Reckon it's them?" Shorty asked.

"Who the hell else would it be?" Nestor replied. He could feel his heartbeat quicken with the prospect of having the opportunity to leave Hawk for the buzzards to feed on. "As long as nobody don't make a move till I tell 'em," he said, finishing the thought out loud. Looking around them, he spotted a low grassy swale a few yards away. "All right, we're gonna set awhile over there and let those boys bed down for the night. Then we'll move in closer and see what's what before we start shootin'. I don't want nobody gettin' outta there alive."

"You got nothin' to worry about, Roy," Shorty responded. "Me and Walt know how to handle a gun. Reckon how much money that Pratt feller is totin'?"

"I hope he's totin' as much as you said he was," Walt said.

"He is," Nestor assured them. "Don't you worry about that. He came all the way over to Bozeman to find Hawk and Hawk ain't about to lift his hand lessen he gets paid for it." They rode over to the swale and dismounted and Nestor cautioned them, "You can let them horses graze, but hold on to them reins. I don't wanna be chasin' no horses when I'm ready to move in closer to that river." There were no trees close to the swale to tie the horses to and Nestor wasn't even willing to hobble them for the hour or so they would be there.

The time ticked away at a snail's pace for Roy Nestor, his mind filled with the hatred he felt for

Hawk. He would never think to admit it, but that hatred was fueled by a huge dislike for anyone who was better at his craft than he was. *And now the son of a bitch has shamed me, made a fool of me, in front of a whole town.* The thought of it triggered a wave of pain in his right foot. He would kill him and leave this part of the country, go someplace where nobody knew him, and he would leave no witnesses behind. As he thought it, he looked over at Shorty and Walt, exchanging tall tales like two simple children. *No witnesses,* he repeated to himself.

Finally it was time. A dark moonless sky settled over the prairie. All three men checked their rifles to make sure they were fully loaded before climbing into the saddle. Nestor led them at a slow walk to a point almost a hundred yards upstream of the camp. They tied their horses there, lest they might alert Hawk's and Pratt's horses. Hobbling painfully on his heavily bandaged foot, Nestor led them through cottonwoods and bushes until they reached a point where they could see the slowly dying fire through the trees. Nestor paused there only a moment before cautiously moving closer until they spotted the horses by the water's edge. At first, the two men were nowhere to be seen, causing Nestor to be more cautious. There were no bedrolls or blankets close by the fire. Thinking he may have been tricked, he hesitated, suddenly afraid he was about to walk into an ambush. *What if the son of a bitch is circling around us?* he thought, and unconsciously looked behind him. But there was nothing behind him except the two anxious faces staring back at him. *He never spotted us,* he reassured himself. He was certain of that.

"Yonder they are," Walt suddenly whispered, "just outside the firelight. Their fire's died down some. That's why we didn't see 'em right off."

"I see 'em," Shorty whispered. "Let's get the job done."

"Hold on!" Nestor cautioned. He could see the two blanket rolls just outside the light of the fire, but they didn't look big enough for a man Hawk's size. *He knows we're following him!* The question he asked himself now was, what would he do if he was in Hawk's place and didn't want to bed down where anyone could surprise him in the open? He took another long look over the clearing and the campsite. There were no high bluffs to hide under at this point in the river, except for one spot where the channel had cut off one side of a low hummock. His attention was immediately drawn to it. A slow grin spread across his face. That was where they were hiding, and anybody who came charging into the camp, looking to catch them asleep, would be sitting ducks. They could pop up from behind that hummock and blast away. He couldn't help but

111

chuckle to have seen through the trap Hawk had prepared. He was especially amused by the added touch Hawk had gone to, placing the two blanket rolls just outside the light of the fire. By doing so, it would appear that the two men felt they were hidden while they slept. It was an old trick and Nestor was onto it. He looked again toward the hummock. They would be well protected from anyone slipping up on them from either side. *But not from anyone on the other side of the river,* he thought. "I've got 'em," he whispered. "Follow me, we're gonna cross over."

"Cross over?" Walt questioned. "What for? Hell, we're close enough to pick 'em off from right here."

"That ain't them," Nestor explained. "They just want you to think it's them. They're hidin' behind that hump over there by the river, so we've got to get behind them."

"Oh," Shorty muttered. "They thought they was gonna outsmart us."

They backed slowly away from the edge of the clearing until well out of sight, should anyone in the camp happen to be looking their way. Hobbling as fast as he could manage, Nestor led them into the water and started across. His two partners followed, but not without complaints, most of them from Shorty when the water reached up to his armpits before gradually becoming shallow again. "If I'da knowed we was plannin' on takin' a bath," he joked, "I'da brung me a bar of soap."

"Hell, you don't own a bar of soap," Walt chided.

"Keep your voice down!" Nestor scolded, and started back downstream along the bank, almost ignoring the wet bundle that served as bandage for his right foot now, as he anticipated the pleasure of catching Hawk with one of his own tricks. When they reached a point opposite the hummock he had spotted, he crawled down halfway to the water's edge, straining to make out details in the dark bluff created by the river in times of high water. The smug smile returned to his surly face when he began to make out the shapes of the two sleeping campers snuggled up under the bank. He had ridden on patrols with Hawk, enough to know some of his tricks. *Well, this ol' dog knows some tricks, too,* he thought. "Yonder," he whispered, and pointed.

"I see 'em," Walt whispered back, and moved up beside Nestor, trying to get a clear line of fire. "Might have to get down closer to the water to get a better angle, though."

"I got 'em now," Shorty almost blurted out, "right there under that bluff, sleepin' like a couple of babies." He scrambled down closer to the water beside Walt, then looked back at Nestor when a random thought occurred to him. "How can we tell which one is Hawk?"

"It don't make no difference, dummy," Walt said. "We're fixin' to shoot both of 'em."

"Oh, okay then," Shorty replied, thinking that he might have thought of that, given enough time.

"Take dead aim and wait till I shoot, then pump enough lead into them two bodies before they get woke up enough to know what hit 'em," Nestor said. "I'm puttin' my first shot into that one on the left." He wasn't sure why, but he somehow sensed that the body lying closer to the edge of the depression was Hawk because it was in a position to return fire quicker than the one back up under the bank. *Only, there ain't gonna be no time to return fire,* he thought. "Everybody ready?" He squeezed the trigger that released the first round of .44 slugs to descend upon the hapless victims like a blanket of relentless fire.

The peaceful riverbanks were turned into a hailstorm of lead as Nestor's wishes were fulfilled, with the continuous barking of the three rifles and the screaming of the frightened horses. The attack was so intense that there had been no opportunity for return fire. The body that Nestor had assumed to be Hawk had finally rolled out of the hollowed-out depression and lay still by the water's edge. "That's enough!" Nestor finally had to shout to stop his two partners caught up in the sensation of killing. "They're done for. You're just throwin' away cartridges now."

It was deathly silent again until Walt released

a joyful oath. "Hot damn," he drawled, which prompted Shorty to perform his imitation of a howling wolf. It was cut short by the impact of a rifle slug between his shoulder blades, causing him to stagger a few steps forward before collapsing facedown in the water. Confused when he heard the report of the shot that killed Shorty, Walt made the mistake of standing stone-still, making him an easy target. He dropped to the ground, the victim of a bullet in his chest. Quicker to react and lucky to have been standing with Walt between him and the rifles firing from the slope behind them, Nestor hit the ground immediately and rolled as fast as he could into the river. With no cover available to him, he was in no position to return fire, even if he was sure where the shooters were. His only option was the river, so he clawed and crawled his way into the dark water while rifle slugs probed the surface all around him. As soon as he reached water deep enough, he went under, dragging his rifle behind him, the soggy bandage on his foot leaving a tail as it unraveled. The only emotion that registered in his brain was the desperate need to run for his life, so he held his breath as long as he possibly could and swam as best he could, using only one arm. Even in his desperation to escape, he could not release his rifle, so he continued to struggle until the water suddenly became too shallow to swim under any longer.

Knowing he was going to have to wade the rest of the way to the other side, he slowly raised his head above the surface to see where he was. With his knees drawn up under him, he crouched in the shallow water and peered back toward the bank from which he had fled. It was too dark to see anything other than the dark outline of the slope beyond the trees. It occurred to him then that that was a good thing because it meant Hawk couldn't see him, either. Trying to make as little noise as possible, he rose up and started making his way to shore, scanning the bank as he did, in an effort to determine where they had left the horses. He recognized a bent-over tree they had passed, so he left the water and headed toward the tree. Only then did he remember his bandaged foot, when he stepped on dry land and he felt the dull throbbing return. "Damn," he cursed, reminded that he had been outfoxed by Hawk again, and the bitter bile of defeat returned to his throat. He paused for a second to consider another attempt to avenge himself. He didn't like the odds with surprise no longer in his favor, and he was now outnumbered two to one. He looked at his rifle and wondered how much the soaking in the river might affect it. Maybe it wouldn't shoot at all until thoroughly dried out and oiled. The same applied to his pistol. He didn't really know, and it would be bad to find out when it was too late. These were the thoughts that went racing through his brain as he continued to make his way as fast as he could through the bushes where he and his partners had left their horses.

He felt a wave of relief wash over him when he found the horses right where he remembered. He told himself that it would have been impossible for Hawk to have somehow circled around and stolen the horses. Still, it was a thought that had occurred, since everything else had gone wrong. It took precious time for him to untie Walt's and Shorty's horses and retie them to a lead rope behind his saddle, but he was reluctant to leave two good horses and saddles behind. Up in the saddle and ready to ride, he had one more thought. Hawk and Pratt had been waiting in ambush on the other side of the river. Maybe they had come across already and maybe they hadn't. Their horses were on this side of the river. Should he go back and make a try to run their horses off, even possibly steal them? He didn't consider that idea for more than a second or two, thinking it a good chance he might get shot in the process. He turned his horse back the way he had come, intent upon putting as much prairie between himself and Hawk as possible. After a full gallop for about a quarter of a mile, he reined his horse back to a lope, concerned about the possibility of stumbling in the darkness. When he became convinced that he had managed to escape the trap set for him, the intense hatred for the man called Hawk flared up in his veins, fueled by the knowledge that Hawk had bested him again.

Behind the would-be assassin, Hawk and Monroe moved down to the water's edge to check on the two bodies lying there. Hawk took hold of Shorty's boots, dragged him out of the water, and turned him over. "Ain't no question about this one. If the bullet didn't kill him, he likely drowned himself."

"This one's dead, too," Monroe said, staring down at Walt. He remained unmoving for a long moment.

Hawk was puzzled by Monroe's apparent trance until it occurred to him that he was reacting to the realization that he had killed a man. It was plain to see that he had never done it before. "It ain't an easy thing, killin' a man, even one as low-down mean as these two, but they were set on killin' us. We just beat 'em to it this time. Next time it might be our time to catch a bullet."

Monroe blinked a couple of times, as if waking from a dream. Then he finally looked up at Hawk and said, "These were two of the men with Nestor in the saloon in Bozeman. You think he has anyone else with him?"

"I doubt it, unless he left him holdin' the horses. We need to find out what happened to Nestor. I couldn't tell if we hit him or not when he was swimmin' in the river, but I expect that we didn't.

Let's check the bank on the other side. If he made it, maybe we can find where he came out."

Hindered somewhat by the moonless night, Hawk and Monroe searched the riverbank on the other side. They moved with deliberate caution, not sure if Nestor had run, or if he was waiting in ambush for them to follow. Helped by a piece of torn bandage caught on a bush, Hawk was able to follow a trail left when Nestor had broken branches in his hurry to run. "This is where they tied their horses," he said to Monroe when he pushed through the bushes to a small clump of pines to join him.

Monroe looked around him in the darkened pine thicket. "How do you know that? I can't see a damn thing, it's so dark."

"I smell horse shit," Hawk said matter-of-factly.

"Oh," Monroe responded, and took a step backward, thinking not to step in it.

"Yep," Hawk said. "He took off right through those young pines." He pointed to some small bushes, trampled by the horses in their haste. "Took those other fellows' horses with him. I don't expect he's thinkin' much about comin' back for more. I think Nestor has finally had enough." Thinking he knew Nestor pretty well now, he figured he wouldn't make another attempt without a couple of new men for backup.

Hawk took the time to scout the banks of the

river for almost a mile upstream and down, moving silently through the dark cottonwoods and pines that lined it. Satisfied that he could assume that Nestor was not likely to make another try, he returned to the campfire to talk things over with Monroe. He found him, kneeling by the fire, examining his rifle as if seeing it for the first time. Hawk had a fair idea of what he was thinking and figured he had been right in guessing that Monroe had never killed a man before. No matter how heinous the victim, to take another man's life was a portal that few decent men crossed. And everything on the other side of that threshold would never be the same as it had been before. He didn't know how to tell him that. Monroe would have to work that out himself.

There remained always a danger that sometime in the future another attempt might be made by Nestor to settle what had now become a sizable score. But Hawk felt sure that they would see no more of the belligerent would-be murderer in the near future. His normal tendency might be to go after Nestor and bring the feud to a close, but there was a more important job to consider, the task they had first set out to accomplish. Every day that passed would put them farther and farther behind in the effort to find Jamie Pratt and his wife. They could not afford to delay any more than they could help, because the trail was already cold. Still, he felt obligated to warn Monroe.

"I can't say for sure if Roy Nestor has called it quits or not. A man like him don't take to gettin' whupped as bad as he just got. It's me he's out to get, but he'll put you under, too, if he decides to come after me again and you're ridin' with me."

"I appreciate what you're telling me," Monroe said. "But I'm still convinced you're the best chance I've got of finding my brother. And you're right, we can't afford to waste any more time, so I say, to hell with Roy Nestor. Let's keep going at first light."

"You're the boss," Hawk replied, glad to see that Monroe appeared not to have let the recent events get the better of him. "We'll get a couple hours' sleep before we saddle up and should be in Helena before dark. We'd best make our beds down close to the horses just in case. I'll go back and see if there's anything left of the blankets we wrapped around those logs. I expect they're about shot full of holes." He started to walk away, then stopped, turned around, and asked, "Is that okay with you?"

"It's okay with me," Monroe replied, "but I think I could use a drink outta that bottle we bought in Bozeman."

"Might not be a bad idea at that," Hawk said, and started toward the hummock to fetch the blankets, a faint smile on his face and the feeling that Monroe showed enough grit to get the job done.

CHAPTER 6

The night passed peacefully enough with no visit from Roy Nestor. First light found Hawk and Monroe in the saddle, each man leading a packhorse. Crossing the river close to the point of the prior night's attack, they passed by the two bodies lying near the water, their weapons and ammunition packed on the packhorses. They paused for only a moment to look at them, content to leave them there for the buzzards to feed on. Hawk couldn't help thinking that providing food for the vultures was most likely the first useful thing the two bushwhackers had ever done. He nudged the buckskin with his heels and set out at a gentle lope, planning to follow the river north through the Helena Valley. Helena was a good forty miles away, but with one stop to eat and rest the horses, they reached the bustling mining town well before dark. Rapidly on its way to becoming Montana's busiest city, it was still not that far removed from the rough little settlement that evolved around Last Chance Gulch. There were several thriving saloons and a couple of bawdy houses on the main street built along the winding gulch as well as some shops and stores for the more peaceful segment of society.

Thinking to take care of the horses first, they

pulled up at the stable where Monroe had stabled his horses while in Helena. Frank Bowen, the owner, was outside in the corral, but came to meet them. "Mr. Pratt," he called out in greeting. "I see you got back from Fort Ellis. Was the army any help to find your brother?" He latched the corral gate behind him while eyeing the man with Monroe as they both dismounted.

"Maybe," Monroe answered. "There wasn't anything else the army thought they could do. They didn't think it was worth sending out more patrols, but they did send me to find John Hawk."

"I was wonderin'," Bowen said. "If anybody had asked me who this feller was, I woulda guessed he was Hawk." He extended his hand and said, "Frank Bowen, glad to make your acquaintance, Mr. Hawk." He had heard people talk about the scout who wore a feather in his hat.

Hawk shook his hand and said, "Mr. Bowen." He didn't ask how Bowen could have guessed his name. He hadn't done any business at the stable before. "I reckon I'm gonna need to keep my horses here for a day or two until we decide what we're gonna do." As he had in Bozeman, he made arrangements to sleep with his horse after Monroe repeated an offer to put him up in the hotel with him. With that settled, Bowen turned back to Monroe.

"One of the fellers on that wagon train with your brother brought his wagon in to fix his front wheels this mornin',", Bowen said. "He might still be over there at the blacksmith's in case you might wanna talk to him. Maybe he can tell you somethin' to help you out."

"Might at that," Hawk answered before Monroe had a chance to. He figured he was going to need information from any source.

They found Grover Bramble working a new rim onto Henry Denson's wagon. Denson was seated on a stool under a sheet of canvas, smoking his pipe while Bramble worked. The blacksmith glanced up and nodded when they walked in, then paused and stood up when he recognized Hawk. "Hawk," he greeted him. Unlike Bowen, Bramble had occasion to do business with Hawk when his buckskin gelding needed shoeing once before. "What brings you up this way again? Last time I saw you, you were scoutin' for an army patrol, chasin' some Sioux horse thieves."

"Matter of fact," Hawk allowed.

"Whatcha doin' up here this time?" Bramble asked.

"Tryin' to help Monroe, here, find out what happened to his brother," Hawk replied. "Feller over at the stable said this man was on the train with him." He nodded toward Denson. "Thought maybe we'd talk to him."

Hearing Hawk's comments, Denson got up from the stool and came over to join them. He introduced himself, and Monroe told him who he was. "So you're Jamie's brother," Denson said. "He was a fine young man, and his wife was a sweet little thing. We were all disappointed to hear about their bad luck. The army sent a patrol up here to look for them. Did they have any luck?"

"No, sir," Monroe said. "Hawk and I are trying to see if we can find some trace of them—thought maybe you might remember something that would help. I guess it was bad luck for Jamie when the rest of you decided not to go on after you made it here to Helena."

"Well, that ain't exactly the way it happened," Denson said. "We didn't intend to stop here. We were all plannin' to travel all the way to Washington Territory, but our guide quit on us, said he got word that Sioux Indians were slaughtering every wagon train that passed through the mountains west of here. We found out when that army patrol came through that there was no truth in what our guide told us. We just got bamboozled, and he didn't give us any of our money back, either. The lieutenant leadin' that patrol told us we could have followed that road ourselves. We didn't need a guide in the first place." Thoroughly heated up from revisiting the incident, Denson puffed furiously on his pipe, but it had already gone out. He tapped the ashes out on the side of his wagon and continued. "We got a group of us together to talk about whether we oughta load up and start out for Walla Walla again." He shrugged. "But we decided we were pretty satisfied with the land right where we are. I staked off one hundred and forty acres near the river about five miles from town. I figure my wife and my three boys and I can make us a nice farm out of it." He shook his head then and concluded, "I wish I could tell you somethin' to help poor Jamie and Rachel, but all I know is they pushed on by themselves."

"I expect you're fortunate to have come this far, considering the man you hired as wagon master," Monroe commented. "You're lucky he didn't murder any one of you." He went on to relate the dealings he and Hawk had just experienced with their leader.

"My Lord," Denson exclaimed. "I figured he was scum, but I never thought he was that evil."

"Maybe you can tell me where their wagon was found," Hawk said, looking toward the blacksmith. "I'd like to take a look for myself."

"I can," Bramble responded, and nodded toward the back of his shop. "That's the wagon back there. I put a new axle on the front. The soldiers found it on the side of a stream in Mullan Pass." He hesitated before continuing, turning his attention to Monroe. "I reckon you could lay claim to the wagon since it belonged to your brother. I wouldn't give you no argument on it, but if you do claim it, I'd have to get paid for goin' after it and puttin' a new axle on it."

Monroe considered that for a few moments. He hadn't really thought about the wagon one way or the other. "I reckon you can keep the wagon," he finally decided. "I don't want to fool with it right now."

"I 'preciate it," Bramble said. Eager to help then, he described in as much detail as he could where the wagon had been found. "You know where the road cuts through that pass they call Mullan Pass, about ten miles north of here, right?" Hawk said he did. "Just as you come to where the road bends around a flat table rock and crosses a stream, that's where they found the wagon. I saw a helluva lotta tracks around it, and some of 'em was Injun." He looked quickly at Monroe. "I know that ain't good news, but leastways there weren't no bodies." Looking back at Hawk, he said, "That's about all I can tell you."

"Much obliged," Hawk replied. He turned to Monroe. "I reckon we'd best head up that way in the mornin'."

"Reckon so," Monroe said. "Right now, though, I think I could use a little drink before supper. Then I'll see if there's a room available at that place I stayed at when I was here before."

"Where'd you stay last time?" Denson wanted to know. When Monroe said it was the Davis House, Henry said, "That's where I'm stayin' tonight. You picked a good place. Gracie Davis runs a nice clean house, but I reckon you know that if you stayed there before."

"You're staying in town?" Monroe asked. "You're not going home?"

Henry answered with a sheepish grin. "Yep, I told the missus the wagon would take a long time and it'd be too late tonight to start back. Farmin's hard work and a man don't get a chance to howl too often. So I figured I'd get me a little drink before supper, too, without the little woman givin' me the fisheye. Maybe I can join you fellers, if you wouldn't mind."

"Sure," Monroe responded, "be glad to have you." He glanced at Hawk to see if it was all right with him, but he showed no sign to indicate he cared one way or the other.

"Last Chance?" Henry asked, referring to the closest saloon.

Monroe looked at Hawk, who shrugged in response. "Last Chance it is," Monroe said.

"Good. I'll settle up with Grover and I'll be right behind you," Henry said. "Looks like he's almost done with that wheel, so I won't be long." He looked at the blacksmith, and Grover nodded his confirmation.

The Last Chance Saloon, one of the earliest watering holes to open up in Helena, was located in the center of the town. Hawk had rinsed the trail dust out of his throat there on several occasions when passing through on his way to hunt with his Blackfoot friends in the mountains north of Helena. It was not yet sundown, but the saloon was already busy, with most of the tables occupied. Some of them had card games under way and a couple of the saloon's soiled doves were working the gamblers, especially those who were ahead in the game. "Pick out a table while I go get a bottle and some glasses," Monroe said, and headed to the bar. There were only a few tables to choose from, so Hawk chose the only one that was not right next to one of the card games.

Standing beside one of the gamblers in a poker game, Gladys Welch could not help noticing the rugged stranger carrying a Winchester. She paused to consider the chances that he might be a prospect for her services. He was kind of interesting, she thought, with the look of a man born to the wild, but it was a fair guess that he didn't have a lot of money to spend on a woman. While she was still trying to decide if he was worth her efforts, he was joined by another man with a bottle and what looked to be three glasses. Her interest was sparked a bit by that, thinking maybe the third glass might be for a female companion. So she sauntered over to their table just as Monroe pulled a chair back and sat down. "Howdy, gents," Gladys sang out cheerfully. "Looks like you boys are one short of a party.

129

My name's Gladys and I'm good at parties." Being well experienced in her trade, she quickly sized up the man who bought the bottle as a serious, responsible individual. But that didn't necessarily rule out the occasional dallying when away from home and hearth. As for his companion, she was still not sure how to size him up, him with the hawk feather stuck in his hat. He was handsome in a rugged sort of way, more like that of a tawny mountain lion you might admire, but from a distance.

"We're waiting for a friend to join us," Monroe told her. "Then we're just interested in having a drink before we go to supper." He glanced at Hawk to see if he might have other ideas, but he was as somber as ever, making no comment. "I reckon we'll have to pass up the opportunity to visit with you tonight, Gladys," Monroe said, taking pains to be as polite as he could.

"Suit yourself," Gladys said, and returned to watch the card game.

Hawk and Monroe had finished their first drink by the time Henry Denson came in the door, looked over the crowd until spotting them, then walked briskly over to join them. It seemed obvious in his enthusiastic approach that he had been looking forward to this night out away from the farm. "We're one ahead of you," Monroe greeted him, and poured him a drink. "Sit yourself down and we'll wait for you to catch up."

"Don't mind if I do," Henry said, and pulled a chair back. He took the drink just poured and offered a toast. "Here's hopin' you fellers find Jamie and Rachel unharmed." They drank to that, then poured another. "What did they charge for the bottle?" Henry asked. "I expect to pay for my share of the whiskey."

"The whiskey's on me," Monroe said.

"Why, thank you kindly," Henry responded. "It tastes better already." After another drink, he turned his chair at an angle, better to watch the goings-on in the barroom. He seemed especially interested in the painted ladies working the customers. After tossing back another whiskey, he turned back to the table. "Looks like I'm doin' most of the drinkin'," he declared.

"You just go right ahead," Monroe said. "I just wanted to cut the dust a little before going to supper. And I haven't known Hawk but a short time, but I don't think he ever takes more than two drinks." He looked at Hawk, who was idly fiddling with his empty glass. "Is that about right?"

"Most of the time, I s'pose," Hawk answered, surprised that Monroe had had the opportunity to notice. "Special occasions maybe more," he added. He enjoyed a drink once in a while, but he had never actually been drunk but once, and he didn't like the feeling of unsteadiness it had caused. To boot, it left him with a powerful headache and a queasy stomach the next morning. He decided to limit his drinking ever since.

Henry Denson was the opposite. He got drunk any time he had an opportunity, and they didn't come very often, so he took advantage of Monroe's generosity. In the short time it took for Monroe and Hawk to finish their drinks and announce it was time to start for the dining room, Henry was riding free and easy on the effects of Sam Ingram's corn whiskey. "What's your hurry?" he asked when Hawk and Monroe pushed their chairs back. "It's still a little early for supper. Let's have a couple more drinks."

"We'll leave the bottle with you," Monroe said, thinking that was the most likely reason for Henry asking them to stay.

"You are a true gentleman," Henry said grandly, even as he openly gazed in Gladys Welch's direction. His sense of morality having been loosened considerably by the whiskey he had so quickly consumed, he began thinking about something else he could buy with the money he had planned to spend on drink. He got to his feet when Monroe stood up and started to leave. "Maybe I'll see you over at the hotel," Henry said, and took a few unsteady steps in the direction of the door, but stopped when he reached the poker game and Gladys Welch. Tapping her on the shoulder, he said, "I've got almost half a bottle of whiskey back on the table.

I'd like to buy you a drink." Surprised, she turned to give him a looking-over. "You ain't gonna make no money at this table," he pressed when she exhibited no interest.

Hanging back for no particular reason, Hawk got to his feet and picked up his rifle at about the same moment Henry stopped to proposition Gladys. *That ain't a good idea,* Hawk thought. He'd never seen a man get drunk so soon before. *The little woman back home on the farm ought to see her husband now.* Thinking it foolish, but having nothing to do with him, he started toward the door after Monroe. He passed the poker table in time to hear Gladys's response to Henry's proposal. "Maybe some other time, honey," she said.

Count yourself lucky, friend, Hawk thought, figuring she had saved the drunken farmer from losing whatever amount of money he had. She had obviously decided there was potential for more money from one of the card players. Hawk had not anticipated the more serious trouble he now noticed in the face of the man seated close to her. "I'll get your whiskey bottle and you can come on to the dining room with Monroe and me," Hawk said. "You need some coffee and a little food to straighten you out. You drank a helluva lot of whiskey on an empty stomach. Eat some supper. Then you'll have yourself a better time with the ladies." He didn't particularly care to have supper with Henry, but it appeared that the man was going to find himself in trouble if he stayed in the saloon much longer. So he went back and picked up the whiskey bottle from the table.

Unfortunately, it was already too late to avoid trouble. It came in the form of a large, ham-fisted drifter who answered to the name Rafe. Already suffering a losing streak in the card game, he threw in yet another losing hand when the man to his right raised. Hawk could see the look of irritation in the man's face as he scowled at Henry, still standing stupidly at Gladys's elbow. "Come on, Henry, let's get us some supper," Hawk pressed, guessing that Rafe was looking for some way to vent his anger. And Henry looked to be an easy outlet.

"Henry don't want no damn supper," Rafe snarled. "Henry wants to sneak off with my woman. Ain't that right, Henry?" The card game came to an abrupt pause as the players became immediately alert to the possibility of trouble about to happen. After a long moment of silence, one of the men tried to defuse the situation. "Ah, he ain't lookin' for no trouble, Rafe. He's just a drunk sodbuster that don't know what he's doin'."

With an opinion of her own, Gladys spoke up. "I didn't know I was your woman, anyway. I sure as hell couldn't tell it by the amount of money you've spent with me."

"Shut up, bitch," Rafe growled, and fixed the stunned farmer with an accusing eye. "He knows what he's doin', don'tcha, sodbuster? You figure you're man enough to take her from me?" He rose to his feet then and stepped away from the table.

"He ain't wearin' no gun," one of the other players said.

"Well, somebody get him one," Rafe bellowed, "or I'm gonna shoot him where he stands." Henry took an unsteady step backward. Soaring high just moments before on the wings of the whiskey he had downed, he now found himself sobering quickly.

When Hawk had not followed him out the door, Monroe waited a few moments, then stepped back inside to see why. Astounded to discover Henry standing frozen, staring at the brawny drifter like a prairie dog trapped by a rattlesnake, Monroe glanced quickly at Hawk. The rangy scout was standing a couple of steps behind Henry, calmly holding the whiskey bottle, watching the confrontation between him and the man who had called him out. When it became obvious that Henry was too frightened to move, Hawk walked over and nudged him with his elbow. "Come on, Henry," he said, and pushed him in the direction of the door. Rafe took a step to the side to block him, but Hawk stepped between them. "Let him be, mister," he said to Rafe. "He ain't out to cause you no trouble. Take your losin' out on somebody else. He don't even wear a gun." He gave Henry a little shove between his shoulder blades to get him started toward the door.

"Maybe I'll take it out on you for stickin' your nose in," Rafe threatened, still in search of satisfaction.

Thinking he had been as patient as he could manage, Hawk said, "Get on back to your cards and quit lookin' for an excuse to shoot somebody." It was enough to ignite the spark of anger Rafe needed to pull his weapon. It wasn't halfway out of his holster when the whiskey bottle in Hawk's right hand flattened his nose, dropping him to the floor in a heap. "Damn," Hawk said, looking in surprise at the unbroken bottle. "That's a pretty stout liquor bottle." He changed hands then, switching his rifle over to his right while he sized up the other men at the table. When there appeared to be no interest on the part of the card players to take up Rafe's cause, he followed Henry to the door, aware of Monroe's pistol out of his holster and ready to use if necessary.

Outside, a nearly sober Henry Denson changed his mind about staying the night in Helena. He decided he'd had enough of the wide-open town and preferred to drive home after dark. "That's a wise decision," Monroe said. "I expect it'll please your wife to see you drove home after dark because you were concerned about your family."

"How you feelin'?" Hawk asked. "You want some help to hitch up your wagon?"

Henry declined the help, suddenly anxious to get started for home, although it was fairly obvious to Hawk that a good deal of the whiskey he had downed might soon make another appearance. "I got a room already paid for," Henry said, and reached in his pocket for the key. "Number three, first room at the top of the stairs. It'll save you from havin' to rent one."

"I appreciate it, Henry," Monroe said, "but I insist on paying you for it." Henry made a weak effort to refuse before graciously accepting the money. "Don't you want to get a little supper before you start back?"

"Thank you just the same," Henry replied, the thought of eating something threatening to trigger an upheaval in his stomach. "But I'd best be gettin' started, else it's gonna be pretty late by the time I get home." He shook hands with both Hawk and Monroe and took his leave.

They waited only a moment to watch him hurry away to the blacksmith shop where his mules were corralled. "He sure sobered up quick when that jasper called him out," Monroe said. "I expect we'd best get along to the dining room before the bastard gets on his feet and comes looking for you."

"I reckon," Hawk agreed.

They turned and headed for the hotel and the dining room next to it. "Seems to me you make a new friend in every town we visit," Monroe remarked as they walked, referring to the belligerent drifter Hawk left behind them on the saloon floor, his nose flattened. "Is that a regular thing with you?"

"Well, it ain't been," Hawk said. "Leastways not till I made your acquaintance. Maybe you've got the sign of bad luck on you. I'm a peaceable man, myself."

Monroe laughed in response to Hawk's japing. "Maybe so," he joked. "But I believe we're gonna have to give Henry the credit for this one. I've never seen a man get that drunk so quick."

"He sobered up just as fast, too," Hawk saw fit to comment.

Hawk, a naturally light sleeper, was disturbed only once during the night when he was awakened by the sounds of a man collecting his saddle from the tack room. He had a friend with him and was noisily explaining to him that he needed his horse even if he had not paid his stable rent. Unaware of the man sleeping two stalls over, he insisted, "Bowen knows I'll pay him next time I'm in town."

"I thought you were gonna stay over till tomorrow," his friend said.

"Hell, so did I," the obviously irate man fumed.

"But I lost every cent I had in that damn poker game, and my credit ain't no good at the hotel. So I ain't got much choice, have I? Besides, I can't hardly breathe through my nose with it flattened all over my face."

"You need to see the doctor," his friend advised. "I bet that hurts like hell."

"Damn right it does, but I'll have the missus fix it up. She's used to patchin' me up."

Lying quietly in the stall, Hawk listened to the conversation between the two men while holding his Colt .44 in his hand, just in case. When he heard them leading the horse out of the stable, he got up and walked to the door behind them. He waited there until the one called Rafe climbed aboard and rode off up the street and his friend walked toward the saloon. He went back to his stall, replaced his Colt in its holster, and settled down to sleep again.

After a peaceful sleep, he awoke early, so he saddled the horses and waited for Monroe to show up at Sophie's Diner, right next to Davis House Hotel. When he had left him the night before, they had agreed to eat breakfast at the diner before riding out to Mullan Pass. This was Monroe's idea, saying that he would like to start out with a good breakfast under his belt. Hawk didn't insist upon starting out before breakfast for two reasons—Mullan Pass was only about a ten-mile ride from Helena, and Monroe seemed no longer in a hurry to find his brother and sister-in-law. Hawk had finally come to the conclusion that Monroe was convinced that Jamie and Rachel were already dead, surely killed by whoever attacked them. That was the reason he was not in a hurry. He simply wanted to find their remains and, if possible, give them a decent burial. When he had first approached Hawk to help him find them, he still had hopes of finding them alive. Hawk couldn't help wondering what had changed his mind. As far as Hawk was concerned, as long as he couldn't find their bodies, there was still hope.

These were the thoughts weighing on Hawk's mind as he sat at a table in Sophie's Diner, drinking coffee. He had arrived before the dining room opened for breakfast, but had persuaded Sophie Hicks to let him wait inside until it was time. Being a gracious lady, Sophie had brought him a cup of coffee, which he truly appreciated. A few minutes before all was ready for the day, she sat down at the table with him and had a cup for herself before she became too busy. Curious, and thinking he didn't strike her as a cowhand, she asked, "What is it you do for a living, Mr. Hawk?"

"Not much of anything," he answered, never having given much thought before as to what he might call an occupation. "This and that, as long as it ain't against the law, I reckon." She shook her head in wonder and smiled. He took it the wrong way. "Oh, don't worry, I can pay for my breakfast."

"I never thought that you couldn't," she quickly replied. "I wouldn't have let you in the door if I had thought that."

" 'Preciate it," he said. "What about yourself? How'd you get set up here, runnin' a dining room? Right next to the hotel, too. You got a husband back there in the kitchen?"

"No," she said, laughing at his innocent brashness. "My sister, Gracie, owns Davis House. Her husband built it. He built this place, too, before he was killed in an accident with a runaway wagon three years ago. Gracie and I took over the two businesses. We're partners in both of them."

"I'll be . . ." he started. "Good for you." He nodded his approval. "So you're Gracie's sister, Sophie Davis."

She laughed again. "No, Davis is Gracie's married name. I'm Sophie Hicks."

"Oh," he responded, feeling a little dumb for his assumption. "I didn't think about that." He shrugged and continued undeterred. "You said you didn't have a husband back there in the kitchen. You got one somewhere else, back workin' a ranch or something?" She shook her head no, obviously amused by his questions. "Well, I don't know what's wrong with the men

141

around here," he said. "You're about the prettiest woman I've ever seen."

"Why, thank you, kind sir," she said sweetly, unable to prevent a blush. His remark was delivered with such innocence that it struck her as sincere. She was tempted to linger awhile longer. "I must say, I've enjoyed visiting with you, but now I've got to go to work." She rose to her feet and went to the front door to turn her OPEN sign around. She smiled at him as she passed back by the table on her way to the kitchen. "Time to feed the hungry, Martha," he heard her say as she disappeared through the doorway. About ten seconds later, Monroe walked in along with a couple of other early risers from the hotel. Reading the sign on the table by the door, he unbuckled his gun belt and deposited it there before joining Hawk.

"Good morning," Monroe greeted him as he pulled a chair back. "How'd you get in here so early? I saw the horses out front, but the dining room didn't open till just now."

"Sophie let me come in and have some coffee while she was gettin' ready to open," Hawk replied.

"I see she didn't insist that you leave your rifle by the door."

"No, she didn't say nothin' about it."

Monroe smiled, remembering the stoic woman named Sadie in the hotel dining room back in

142

Bozeman. She had allowed Hawk to hang on to his rifle there as well. He was beginning to wonder if his scout had a special effect on single women. If that was the case, he was convinced that Hawk wasn't aware of it. That was another side of the man and it seemed to Monroe that the more time he spent with the soft-spoken, easygoing scout, the less he knew about what made him tick. "Did you have a good night?"

"Sure did," Hawk answered. "How 'bout yourself?" Monroe said that he did.

Eggs fried in bacon grease, salt-cured ham, fried potatoes, and strong black coffee, served with two biscuits the size of road apples; Hawk decided it was a breakfast worth the late start on the trail. He and Monroe both did proper justice to the food served and when they were sated and walked out the door, Sophie smiled at Hawk and said, "Come see me when you're back in town." Monroe shook his head in wonder and followed him to the horses.

CHAPTER 7

Guiding on the lofty slopes of the Rocky Mountains standing dark and foreboding before them, Hawk started out to the northwest, figuring to strike the area known as Mullan Pass. The pass was named in honor of the same man, Lieutenant John Mullan, who blazed the road to the west already bearing his name. In order to find safe passage around the feet of the Rockies, the Mullan Road dropped down to within ten miles of Helena before continuing in a westerly direction toward the head of the Bitterroot Valley at Missoula, known as Hell Gate at the time. Hawk had ridden many of the game trails that led into the hidden valleys and canyons that led to the north, sometimes on his own and sometimes with his friend Bloody Hand, a Blackfoot warrior. He had not seen his Blackfoot friend in some time now, since the army had kept him busy scouting in the Yellowstone country. *It's been too long,* he thought to himself. *When I finish this job, maybe I'll try to find Bloody Hand's village and we'll hunt again.* His mind came back to the business at hand then when he saw the flat table rock Grover Bramble had described. On the other side of it, they should come to a stream.

Due to the unusually dry summer so far, the

stream was little more than a trickle, but it was moving, enough so that the horses could drink. By the ruts and slash marks in the dry ground, it was easy to see where the wagon had come to rest after the axle had broken. "There's the rock that broke it," Hawk said, and pointed to a flat spur rising about four feet up from the base of the rock ledge. "They had to be runnin' like hell to be this far off the road. Maybe there was somebody on the road in front of them and that was why they left it. When they hit that rock, it flipped the wagon upside down and right there is where it landed." He pointed to the ruts gouged out of the dirt. "I reckon when the wagon flipped, it stopped the horses, 'cause there wasn't that much damage to it." He continued staring at the flat rock spur and wondered aloud, "Reckon it was thin enough to pass right between the horses."

"Sounds like Indians to me," Monroe said. He looked around him at the impressions left in the dry ground. "Can't tell a helluva lot after all this time."

"Maybe not," Hawk said, trying to create a mental picture of what had happened here. "But you can tell a little." Down on one knee, he traced the faint outlines of several of the prints that stood out a little bolder than the others. "Grover was right, some of these tracks were left by Indians. What I don't know is whether they're the ones that jumped 'em, or they came along

later, 'cause there's shod hoofprints here, too."
He looked up at Monroe. "Trouble is, there was
that cavalry patrol up here, so there's shod prints
mixed in with these unshod prints. A fellow
lookin' at all the tracks would have to think
your folks were jumped by Indians. That's just a
feelin' in my gut. I can't get enough outta these
old tracks to know for sure. There ain't much
more that I can tell you. It'd all be speculation."

Obviously disappointed, Monroe hesitated for
a few moments. He had hoped that Hawk might
find substantial evidence to follow, even though
he had told him that the odds were against that.
Finally, he asked, "If it was your brother, what
would you do?"

"Well, there weren't no bodies here when the
army found the wagon, so we know whoever
jumped 'em either buried their bodies or carried
'em away with 'em. Whether they were white
men or Indians, they weren't likely to wanna
carry the bodies with 'em. So the first thing we
need to do is look around and see if we can find
any graves. If we can't, it's a possibility your
brother and his wife are alive. And I ain't got
no idea where to look for 'em, but I'd start out
by followin' this stream a ways." He pointed
downstream toward a point where it cut through
a narrow ravine in a low ridge directly south of
them. "When that wagon went over, your brother
and his wife most likely jumped, or were thrown

out. Whichever, they were on foot and being chased, and that ravine looks like the closest place to find cover. Let's see if we can find anything in there." He climbed back up into the saddle and headed for the ravine.

Hawk's logic proved to be accurate, for they had not gotten very far into the ravine when they came upon the spot where Jamie had apparently made his stand. Much to Monroe's distress, it was obvious that his brother had been trapped there between the steep sides of the narrow gulch. "I reckon he stood 'em off as long as he could, at least maybe till he ran outta cartridges." He pointed to the empty shells lying about on the ground near a small shoulder of rock. "I expect he had his wife behind that rock." Seeing the heartbreaking effect his speculations were creating in Monroe's eyes, he said, "Maybe that ain't what happened. That's just what it looks like to me."

Monroe quickly reacted. "No, you're probably seeing it like it happened. It sounds like what Jamie would have done. He would have fought until he couldn't anymore. I can't understand why the soldiers didn't say anything about these spent shell casings. Maybe they didn't spend much time looking around." He looked at Hawk as if expecting an explanation. When there was nothing from his scout but a shrug, Monroe continued, "The only hope I have is that we still haven't found any bodies." He motioned around him with a sweep of his arm. "And there's no sign of blood anywhere."

"Well, that's true," Hawk said, hesitating to add that there wasn't likely to be after this amount of time. "But I wouldn't get my hopes up too soon. Let's look a little farther up this stream toward the back of this ravine." They followed the stream to a point where it went into the ground when the ravine ended at the base of a cliff. It was here that they found the evidence Monroe had hoped never to find.

Monroe, a solidly built man, appeared almost to buckle when they came upon the grisly scene. Patches of shredded clothes lay scattered in the narrow confines of the rocky gulch and near the opening in the rocks where the stream went underground, a sun-bleached skeleton's empty sockets stared grimly at the sky above. Unable to speak for a moment, Monroe looked at Hawk, hoping for some chance that it was not his brother. "Ain't much I can tell you," Hawk said. "It looks like a man, from the size of it. Looks like he got boxed in here at the back of this ravine and there wasn't any place left to run. I reckon whoever done this musta carried the woman off. Either that or she somehow climbed up the side of this gulch and got away." He pointed to some loose gravel and dislodged stones in the steep side of the ravine. "It sure looks like somebody, or some animal, tried to climb up over the side.

It'd be a tough climb, specially for a woman."

Stunned, Monroe stood and stared at the gleaming skeleton, still unable to believe it was once his brother. The scraps of clothing that still remained were definitely those of a man. "Nothing but bones," he uttered. "What did they do to him?"

"Most likely it was coyotes or wolves that cleaned up the bones," Hawk answered. "Maybe buzzards, too." He knew that created a horrible picture for Monroe to envision, but he had asked for an explanation.

After a few more moments, Monroe began to regain control of his emotions. "I want to dig a grave and bury what's left of him. We can at least do that."

In spite of the hard ground, they dug a shallow grave in a short amount of time, just deep enough to make sure it was in no danger of being opened by scavenging animals. Hawk stood respectfully by while Monroe stood over the grave and silently offered his regrets for not having been there in time to make a difference. After a few minutes, he turned to Hawk and expressed his intentions. "I want to track down the bastards that did this," he stated in no uncertain terms. "I don't care how long it takes."

"I expect you wanna find the woman," Hawk said, "your sister-in-law."

"Of course I do," Monroe replied at once.

He couldn't help feeling some guilt for having forgotten his brother's new bride in his despair. "I just hope she hasn't been killed, too."

"Most likely not," Hawk said, "being as how she was a young woman. If it was Indians that did this, and it looks like they did, they oftentimes take young women captive. Like I said before, there ain't much chance I can track 'em after this length of time. The best chance I can offer right now is to find Walking Owl's village. He's a Blackfoot chief who usually makes his summer camp near the southern edge of the mountains where his hunters can easily ride down onto the prairie grassland to hunt buffalo."

"You think this business was done by the Blackfeet?" Monroe asked.

"I hope to hell not," Hawk responded, thinking of his friend Bloody Hand, who lived in Walking Owl's village. "But they keep a pretty close eye on everything that's happenin' in this part of the territory."

"And you know where their village is?" Monroe asked.

"Not exactly. I know where a couple of their favorite places are. If they're not there, Rubin Fagan will know if they're anywhere in the area. Rubin runs a tradin' post on the Clark Fork River, a day's ride from here."

"All right," Monroe said. "Let's get started, then."

• • •

Hawk led Monroe up into the mountains, following one game trail after another until Monroe became thoroughly turned around. He began to suspect that the confident scout was, in fact, lost, but they eventually rode out of a thick forest of firs into a wide grassy meadow circling a small lake. This was the spot Hawk had described to him, but there was no Indian camp. Hawk took a little time to look around for sign that might tell him if his Blackfoot friends had been there recently, and there was plenty. The circles in the grass left by the tipis told him that the camp had been moved no more than a week at most. The grass in the meadow had been eaten down significantly, suggesting the reason for moving, and a relatively broad trail down the opposite side of the mountain pointed the way they exited. "The only thing I can't say for sure is whether or not it was Walkin' Owl's village," Hawk said.

"We can follow their tracks and find out," Monroe suggested, looking at the obvious trail down through the trees, created by a whole village of people and horses pulling travois. It was not a large village, having left only twenty-two circles where tipis had stood. And this, Hawk had said, was close to the size of Walking Owl's camp.

"I expect so," Hawk said, in response to

Monroe's suggestion. "But we'd best let these horses rest up a bit right now. We ain't in no hurry. This trail's a week old and most likely they've already got to where they were headed."

It was late in the afternoon when they were back in the saddle and starting out after the Indian camp. When they reached the open prairie at the bottom of the mountain, the trail spread out and headed in a westerly direction. By the time the sun sank below the hills before them, they reached a stream where the village had made their first camp after leaving the mountains. With little daylight left, they made their camp on the same spot. The following morning, they were in the saddle early, following a trail that continued on a westerly course. "You think we're catching up with them?" Monroe asked, thinking that maybe Hawk could tell by examining horse droppings left along the trail.

"No," Hawk reminded him. "Like I said, this trail is about a week old, ain't much I can tell after this time." He knew Monroe was looking for some assurance that they were not riding a wild-goose chase, but he had very little to go on. "If this is Walkin' Owl's bunch, we oughta catch up with 'em by tomorrow night. 'Cause I suspect they're headin' to another one of their favorite spots in another range of mountains," Hawk said, referring to the Garnet Mountains a short distance north of Rubin Fagan's trading post on the Clark Fork River.

The tracks they followed continued to take the route Hawk would have ridden had he been on his way to the often-used campsite where Nevada Creek emptied into the Blackfoot River. It appeared that Walking Owl was secure in his habits of the past several years, and Hawk looked forward to seeing his friend Bloody Hand again. There was a good chance that Blackfoot hunters were responsible for the tracks of the unshod ponies at the site of the attack on the wagon. They might even have seen who did it and what happened to the woman. He hoped by some twist of fate that Rachel Pratt might be with Walking Owl's camp. For the old Blackfoot chief had made peace with the soldiers, and the girl should be safe with his people.

Hawk was mildly surprised when they reached the spot where he expected to find the Blackfoot camp and there was no one there. The tracks they had been following continued on closer to the mountains. Possibly they thought it would be better to camp farther up the creek where there was better cover among the trees. When finally coming to a rise where they could see faint traces of campfires in the trees, Hawk suddenly reined the buckskin to a halt. Something in his brain triggered an alarm. *Instead of riding blissfully into that camp, maybe I'd best be sure it's*

Walking Owl's camp, he thought. When Monroe came up to a halt beside him, he pointed to the mouth of a ravine at the foot of the mountains. "Head for that gulch yonder. We'd best see what's what before we get any closer to that camp."

Sensing Hawk's sudden precaution, Monroe asked, "What's the matter? I thought they were friends of yours."

"Just bein' careful," Hawk answered. "I'm gonna get in a little closer to take a look at the camp to make sure who they are. I'll be able to move in better on foot, so I'll leave my horses with you. If you hear shots fired, mount up and get ready to ride, 'cause I'll most likely be in a powerful hurry." He turned his horse right away and headed for the ravine before Monroe had time to insist on going with him. He preferred to scout the Indian camp alone, knowing he could get in a lot closer without someone else to worry about.

"Damn it, you be careful," Monroe said when they dismounted at the mouth of the ravine and Hawk handed him his reins. "I wanna see you earn that money I promised."

"I plan to," Hawk replied, and was off at a trot.

When within about seventy-five yards of the camp he could see more clearly through the spruce and pines growing along the banks of the creek, although he could still not make out the shapes of the tipis. It occurred to him that the site of the camp looked to have been selected with a thought toward concealment. *Just natural precautions against an enemy raiding party,* he thought with a shrug. *Just Indians being Indians.* Sighting a tangle of berry bushes some twenty-five yards closer to the glow of campfires, he moved silently toward them, seeking the cover they would offer. Making his way through the bushes, he stopped when he came to an opening that gave him a better view of the camp. He could see the warriors moving back and forth among the campfires and realized almost immediately that he had not been following Walking Owl's village. Instead, he found himself peering at a party of Lakota Sioux warriors. There were no women or children. There were no tipis. It struck him that he had happened upon a Sioux raiding party that was tracking the Blackfoot village, just as he was.

Taken totally by surprise, he dropped to one knee while he decided what to do about the unexpected turn of events. He might have known there was a party of warriors following Walking Owl, had not the trail he followed been so old. If he had been able to trail them right when both were fresh, he would have discovered that there were two separate patterns of tracks. His first thoughts were of concern for his Blackfoot friends. *I need to warn them,* he thought, *if I knew where the hell they are.* Longtime enemies of the

Sioux since their overwhelming numbers drove the Blackfeet from the southern plains, Walking Owl had to be warned. But where had he moved his village? Hawk's thoughts were suddenly interrupted by a slight rustling of the branches a few feet from where he knelt. Thinking he had disturbed some small rodent's nest, he reached over and pulled a handful of branches aside. Stunned momentarily, he found himself peering at what appeared to be a child, curled up in a ball. Even in the darkness, he could sense it trembling in fear, too frightened to speak, for which he was thankful. For if the child cried out, he would find himself with a Lakota raiding party after him.

In the confusion of the moment, he didn't remember what he had just realized moments before—there were no other children in the camp. Relying on the little Lakota he knew, he tried to say that he meant no harm, but the child responded by simply crying and trying to draw farther away into the bushes. It was then that he realized it was not a child. It was a woman, a small, fragile woman, and the name leaped immediately to his mind. "Rachel?" She stopped at once, still frightened and confused. "Rachel Pratt?" Hawk asked. Still she did not reply, but nodded her head rapidly. He understood the situation clearly then. "Is somebody after you right now? Are you tryin' to hide from them?" She nodded anxiously again. He looked around him quickly to make sure he was not about to be attacked. "I've come to get you, so let's get the hell outta here." He reached out and she took his hand. "Can you walk?" he asked, not sure if she had been injured or not.

"Yes," she replied, the first word she had spoken.

"I thought you were a child back there under those bushes," he said.

"I thought you were an Indian with that feather stuck in your hat," she said.

He chuckled softly, even in their precarious situation, pleased with the twist of fortune that had brought about this lucky encounter. "Come on," he said, and started back the way he had come. It was not to be that easy, however, and his rescue mission might have ended right there had it not been for the firelight reflected on a knife blade. Reacting with the quickness that had saved his scalp many times before, he brought his rifle up to block the hand holding the knife before it could plunge it into his chest. In the next moment, he shoved Rachel aside and lunged with his shoulder into the midsection of the dark form that had risen up out of the bushes without warning.

The force of Hawk's charge resulted in both parties landing on the ground hard and fighting ferociously to gain advantage. The contest was reduced to which man could take control of the knife still held firmly in the Indian's hand. Hawk locked the Lakota's knife hand with a viselike grip on his wrist. His other hand was captured by the Indian's free hand, neither man willing to risk releasing his grip. While Rachel watched, terrified, the two men strained against each other, rolling over and over on the creek bank. When they finally stopped rolling with Hawk on top, he decided he had to take a chance. He suddenly released the Indian's knife hand and pulled away from him. Already straining with all his might, the warrior's arm came forward in an attempt to stab Hawk. The knife blade came within a hair of Hawk's throat before he grabbed the back of the striking hand, and with all the force he could muster, drove it down and into the warrior's stomach.

Reacting with a deep grunt, the warrior's body stiffened as he arched his back upward. He released Hawk's other hand and began to claw at his face and neck. Hawk responded by driving the knife deeper and deeper. When the Indian suddenly drew a desperate breath, Hawk clamped his hand over the stricken man's mouth, thinking he was about to yell out. Although the warrior wasn't able to make a sound, Hawk held his hand over the warrior's mouth until he finally relaxed in death. "Damn," Hawk gasped, nearly exhausted. He looked over at the wide-eyed terrified woman and asked, "I reckon this is the buck you were tryin' to hide from?" She nodded. "Was anybody else helping him look?"

She shook her head. "I don't think so. He was the only one calling me."

He looked around him hurriedly until he found his rifle in the darkness of the bushes, then took her hand. "Let's get the hell away from here in case somebody else decides to help him look for you."

Monroe Pratt walked a few paces from the mouth of the narrow ravine and peered into the darkness in the direction of the Indian camp. He was beginning to become a little concerned, thinking that the camp wasn't that far. Hawk should have been back by now, or given him a yell to come on in. He took his watch from his pocket and tried to see the time in the dim light but returned it when he found the shadows too dark to see the face. It occurred to him then that he hadn't checked the time when Hawk had left, so it wouldn't have told him how long he had been gone, anyway. Something might have gone wrong. He was in the midst of considering a decision whether or not to go after him when he heard a soft whistle like that of a bird. Not sure, he pulled his .44 handgun and continued to peer into the night. A few moments later he relaxed when he recognized Hawk's voice.

"It's me," Hawk announced. "I brought some-body with me."

"It's a good thing you finally said something," Monroe said. "I was preparing to shoot you if you didn't. Why in hell didn't you just sing out?" He assumed the somebody who was with him was one of his Blackfoot friends from the village, so he was surprised to see the slight figure of a woman behind him. He assumed she was a Blackfoot. It was difficult to make out her features until she moved up close beside Hawk. It was then that he saw the light color of her hair and the tattered cotton dress she wore.

"This, here, is your sister-in-law," Hawk said.

"What?" Monroe blurted, unprepared for the unexpected announcement. "This is Rachel? How in the world . . . ?" He was too stunned to finish.

For her part, Rachel was shaking with the emotions of what had just transpired within a time lapse of no more than an hour. That was when she had been presented with the opportunity to slip away from her Sioux guard when he had a sudden call to evacuate his bowels. She had not given thought at the time as to where she could run to. She just ran, not realizing how hopeless her escape was, but knowing anything would be better than to stay with the savage who had claimed her. The joy she felt for her rescue was all mixed up with the awkward feeling of meeting Jamie's brother under such circumstances. And she still did not know who the man was who actually found her. She did her best to keep from

160

crying, but found it difficult when she finally spoke. "I prayed so hard for someone . . ." she started, but could not finish. She paused in an effort to calm herself before she tried to speak again. "Are you Monroe?" she asked, her voice a little more steady then.

"Yes, I'm Monroe," he answered. "And you're safe now. We're gonna take you home."

"Jamie's dead," she said, then lost control of her emotions again.

"I know," Monroe said, and put his arm around her shoulders. "I'm sorry for what you've had to go through, but you're safe now."

Standing silently watching the dramatic meeting, Hawk felt compelled to remind them both. "I'm thinkin' there's a war party of Sioux warriors back yonder that might start wonderin' what happened to that buck that was lookin' for you. We'd best start back down that valley and put some distance between us and them before they find him." His warning served to immediately bring their attention back to the business at hand and the danger lying about a hundred and fifty yards away.

"You're right," Monroe said, and hurried back to lead the horses out.

Hawk waited until Monroe was up in the saddle before sweeping Rachel up and placing her behind him. "Here," he said, "you can ride behind your brother-in-law. As light as you are, I doubt that roan will notice the extra weight. He'll just think Monroe musta ate an extra biscuit for supper." Talking to Monroe then, he said, "We'll head out that way," pointing toward the south. "We'll stay in close to the east side of these mountains in case we have to ride up in 'em if we get anybody hot on our tails." He hopped up to put one foot in the stirrup, swinging his right leg over to settle in the saddle as the buckskin loped along the base of the hills beside them. If they were lucky, he thought, it would take a while before anybody found the body of the warrior he killed. Chances were good that they wouldn't be able to pick up their trail until morning, when it was light enough to see. By that time, they should be resting their horses at Rubin Fagan's trading post.

They had been in the saddle for the better part of two hours before a three-quarter moon rose high enough over the mountains behind them to lighten the shadows somewhat. It had been Hawk's intention to push the horses on through the night, but he changed his mind when the buckskin began to show signs of tiring. If his horse was tiring, then Monroe's would definitely be also. Hawk allowed that the horses had already been ridden a sizable distance during the day just past, and without adequate rest. It was his estimate that it was still twenty miles to Fagan's and the temporary cavalry fort established there since the increase in hostile attacks during the past year. So when they came to a rapidly flowing stream, he pulled up to allow Monroe to catch up to him. "I reckon if we don't rest these horses pretty soon, we're liable to end up walkin' to the Clark Fork. I'm thinkin' we oughta follow this stream back up the mountain and find a good spot to camp till daylight. I expect we've got enough lead on those Sioux to take a little rest and be gone from here at sunup."

There was no argument from Monroe—he had already begun to wonder if his horse was going to make another twenty miles. They followed the stream for a good one hundred yards to a narrow gulch up through a hillside covered with lodgepole pines. Climbing up the gulch, they reached a point where the stream formed a small pool before continuing down the slope. "This looks as good a place as any," Hawk decided. They pulled the saddles and packs off the horses and let them drink and nibble on what grass they could find around the pond. There was very little, but they would be fed when they reached the river.

"Can we risk a fire?" Monroe asked. "I don't know about Rachel, but you and I haven't eaten anything in quite a while. Even a cup of coffee would be enough to keep me alive." He looked at her. "That would be good right now, wouldn't it, Rachel?"

Still insecure at this point, she had not spoken a word during the long ride down the valley. "Oh, it surely would," she replied. "If you have the coffee and a pot, I would be happy to make it for you." Even though Monroe was her brother-in-law, she felt very much in the company of strangers. It was difficult to dispel a feeling of being lost. She had known her late husband only a few months before finding herself in this dangerous and awkward situation. The Indians that had captured her were a frightening and vicious lot, and the picture of them riding after them still dominated her thoughts. Yet, she could not deny a feeling of confidence in the strange man called Hawk.

"I expect it'll be all right to build a little fire," Hawk said. "It'd be hard to see the smoke come up outta these trees, as dark as it is, even as much smoke as pine makes. And we'll be long gone at daylight. I'll get my coffeepot and you can make us some, long as you make it strong enough," he added with a smile. "Might as well eat something, too; salt pork or deer jerky, we've got both."

Monroe studied his sister-in-law as she went about the business of making the coffee. He had long since resigned himself to the notion that his brother was dead, even before Rachel confirmed the fact that the skeletal remains he and Hawk had buried were Jamie's. There was no question but what the thing to do was to take her home

164

to the family ranch in the Bitterroot Valley. He wondered if that was what she would want, or would she prefer to return to her family in Minnesota? *Hell, I don't even know the woman,* he thought. He realized that he was seeing her at what could hardly be described as her best, but she looked to him to be a little older than Jamie. If he had to guess, he would say she was at least twenty years old, maybe a year or two older, and Jamie had only been eighteen since January.

As if sensing his concentration upon her, Rachel turned to smile at him. "I think the coffee is ready," she said, and filled the two cups he had provided. She waited a moment while Hawk extended his cup to be filled as well. "I guess we should get to know each other," she said, looking back at Monroe. "There's not much I can tell you about myself. I don't know what Jamie might have told you from the letters we exchanged. But when he arrived that day, sitting like a soldier up in the wagon seat, I knew it was the right decision for me. I guess he felt the same because he asked me to marry him. But I don't think it would be fair for your family to make a place for me."

"And do what?" Monroe replied. "Send you packing? Don't you worry, little lady, when Jamie asked you to marry him, that was as good a way as any I know to prove you belong in the family. So I'm planning to take you home." He paused, then said, "Unless you just don't wanna

165

go. Are you aching to go back to Minnesota now that Jamie is gone?"

"No," she quickly said. "I was living with my uncle and his family—six children, all of us in a two-room cabin. They were more than happy when I moved out."

"Well, I guess that settles that," Monroe said. "It'll be real nice to have another woman in the house. I know Ma will be glad to see you. She's gotten too old to do much but sit in her chair and talk. And the only female she's got to talk to is your sister-in-law and the cook, a Salish woman named Lily Bright Bird. So you see, we need you to keep my brother, Thomas, and me from getting too rough around the edges and unfit for company."

An interested spectator to the seemingly cordial inauguration of Rachel into the Pratt family, Hawk sipped his coffee from the one cup he owned. It appeared that Monroe and his new sister-in-law were prepared to do the best they could to carry on after the tragedy of Jamie's death. He saw it as his responsibility to get them safely to Rubin Fagan's trading post. That should remove the threat of an act of vengeance from the Sioux war party because of the soldiers close by. He considered the possibility that his services would no longer be required once they reached the trading post. In that event, he strongly contemplated taking up his hunt for Walking Owl's village. It might be too late to think he had any chance of warning them about the Sioux war party trailing them. It all depended upon what the Sioux did when they found the body of the warrior he had killed and discovered the white woman was gone.

"You are as kind and gracious as Jamie said you were," Rachel said, a trace of moisture forming in her eyes as she spoke. "I thank you for welcoming me as a member of your family and I thank you for saving me from a fate I fear would have been most horrible."

"I reckon we've got Hawk to thank for finding you," Monroe said. "But you oughta know that we would have searched for you till we did find you, no matter how long it took. You're a member of my family, no matter if Jamie is still with us or not." He gave her a warm smile and said, "It's bad enough to see your husband murdered by savage Indians without being captured by them." At once confused by the change in her expression, as her smile suddenly faded to a frown, he was totally astounded by her next statement, as was the ever-stoic Hawk.

"Jamie wasn't killed by the Indians," she said, her expression one of surprise now, having assumed they already knew that.

"What?" Monroe blurted, his confusion complete now. "Whaddaya mean? Who killed him?"

"Why, Jamie was killed by that evil wagon

167

master, that man who lied to everyone on the wagon train, that Roy Nestor!" She looked from one of them to the other, astonished. "I thought you already knew that."

"I sure as hell didn't," Monroe replied, still shaken by this stunning revelation. He was sick with anger when he recalled the meeting he had had with Nestor in Helena when he seemed so sorry to hear that Jamie had not made it to the Bitterroot. From there, his mind went immediately to the encounters he and Hawk had had with the vile murderer and the opportunities to have killed him, only to let him get away. If he had known that day when Hawk had backed Nestor out of the street, he would have shot him down. Devastated with the realization that he had been given several chances to avenge the murder of his brother, but had not known to act upon them, he turned to Hawk as if to ask for help.

Stunned as well, Hawk, however, was not as devastated as Monroe. Accustomed to unexpected twists of fate, he accepted the startling news as a sign of unfinished business that now had to be taken care of. "I'll see to Mr. Nestor," he said.

"I wanna kill him, myself," Monroe uttered through a tightly clenched jaw, his hands trembling with the rage inside him.

"I reckon you do," Hawk said. "But first, you gotta find him and that ain't gonna be easy."

"I don't care," Monroe insisted. "I'll keep

looking for him till I track him down, no matter how long it takes."

"What about Rachel, here?" Hawk asked. "You gonna take her with you while you're trackin' Nestor down?"

His questions caused Monroe to stop and think. Suddenly his speech before about welcoming her into the family lost its sincerity when revenge for his brother took over his mind. Glancing at her now, shivering in fear that she had somehow cast herself in disfavor with an innocent remark, he sought to set her mind at ease. "Hawk's right. The most important thing for me is to see you safely to your new home in the Bitterroot Valley. And that's what we're gonna do. Right, Hawk?"

"If you say so," Hawk replied. He was still interested to hear about the murder of Rachel's husband, however, so he questioned her directly. "How did you end up with that war party if it was Roy Nestor that killed your husband?"

Rachel related the events that led up to her capture, starting with the day she and Jamie loaded the wagon with supplies to replace those consumed on the long trip from Fort Benton. After saying good-bye to some people they had befriended on the journey, they pulled out of Helena late one morning and headed back to intercept the Mullan Road. It was close to sundown when they approached Mullan Pass and met Roy Nestor sitting on his horse in the middle of the road. He called out a friendly greeting, or so it seemed, and rode up to them. He said he had heard that they were pushing on to Missoula and he was concerned for their safety. "Jamie didn't have any use for the man and told him so," she said. "Still he insisted that we would need his protection and said he would take us to Missoula for two hundred dollars. Jamie told him we didn't have two hundred dollars, so he might as well leave us be. It musta made Nestor mad. He pulled his horse back to let us pass, but when we went by him he pulled his pistol and shot Jamie in the back." Her voice rose in pitch as she seemed to be reliving those frightening moments. "Jamie fell over against me. I didn't know what to do. He was hurt so bad, so I grabbed the reins and whipped the horses as hard as I could. I wanted to get away from Nestor, but he jumped off his horse onto the back of the wagon. That's when all those Indians appeared, from nowhere, yelling and screaming and shooting. I couldn't hold the horses. They went crazy and all of a sudden we were flying through the air when the wagon hit something and threw all three of us out."

"So you made it to that gulch, then," Hawk commented. "You and Jamie?"

"Yes, that's right, we were trying to find a place to hide. When we were thrown from the wagon, we didn't have time to get Jamie's rifle or his pistol."

"But somebody had a rifle in that ravine," Hawk said, remembering the spent shell casings he had found.

"Nestor!" she exclaimed. "He came running in the ravine after us. He had a rifle and he tried to hold the Indians off until he ran out of cartridges. When he quit shooting, the Indians crept closer and closer till they were sure he had no more bullets. As soon as he saw what was going to happen, he started crawling up the side of the gulch. Jamie tried to stop him, but he was so weak from his wound he couldn't. That's when Nestor stabbed him with his knife and killed him."

"Well, I'll be . . ." Hawk muttered softly as he put the whole picture together. "So it was Nestor that scrambled up over the side of that ravine. I'm pretty good at readin' sign, but I sure didn't come up with that." He shook his head slowly, thinking about the horrible experience the woman had lived through.

"I couldn't leave Jamie," Rachel said, "even if I could have climbed up the side of that gulch. I thought the Indians would surely kill me but they grabbed me by my hair and dragged me away from him. I begged them to let me bury my husband, but they only laughed."

Hawk pictured the scene. He could pretty well guess why her life was spared. "I expect one of 'em put his rope around your neck and led you

171

like a dog." She nodded, surprised that he knew. "Was that the one you were hidin' from when I ran into you?"

"Yes," she answered meekly, as if ashamed to admit it.

"Ain't no use to hang your head over that," Hawk said. "Wasn't much you could do about it. It's a sorry thing to have to go through, but Monroe and the rest of his family know it ain't no blame on you." He glanced at Monroe, waiting for him to reassure her.

"Why, that surely is the truth," Monroe said, picking up the cue. "You're a part of the Pratt family now, and the first order of business is to get you home to the Triple-P to meet the rest of us. Like Hawk says, we'll go to the trading post in the morning and see if they've got any clothes fit for a woman. We can't expect you to ride all the way to the Bitterroot Valley in that one frock. Then we'll go talk to the soldiers. They'll know if there's any danger in going on to the Bitterroot right away. Just don't you worry your pretty head about it, Hawk and I will take care of you." Hawk nodded, pleased that Monroe had seen fit to comfort her.

CHAPTER 8

The body of Kills Two Bears was discovered by Crooked Leg in the early morning light when the young Lakota warrior decided to search for chokecherries in the thick bushes along the bank. At once alarmed, he cried out to warn the others while looking quickly around him ready to defend himself, but there was no sign of enemy warriors. Looking more closely at Kills Two Bears, he realized that he had been dead for some time by then. He said as much to the other warriors when they came running to see for themselves. The first ones to arrive at the scene agreed with Crooked Leg that Kills Two Bears had been dead for several hours. They all turned to meet Spotted Pony, the dead warrior's brother, when he approached. "It's Kills Two Bears," Crooked Leg said.

"What?" Spotted Pony responded, confused. Then he saw the body of his brother and sank to his knees beside it. His face twisted in agony, he moaned in his grief, lowly at first, but building until he could no longer hold it inside him and he wailed out like a wolf howling. The others spread out at once, searching for sign of an enemy war party, thinking that the Blackfoot village they had

173

been following must have somehow discovered them.

After a short time, they came back to Spotted Pony, who was still kneeling beside his dead brother, moaning in his despair. "It was only one man," Running Bird said. "There is plenty of sign here where they fought. It was not a Blackfoot. This man wore white man's boots. We found his tracks leading that way." He pointed toward the south. "There are other tracks. We think he took the woman, for her tracks follow his."

"I should have known something was wrong," Spotted Pony lamented. "When he complained that his belly was too full and went to relieve himself, he took the woman with him. He didn't come back for a long time. I thought he was with the woman and I went to sleep."

"You could not know," Crooked Leg said. "Someone of her people must have followed our trail and sneaked into our camp to take her. He would not have been able to take the woman if she had not been away from the camp."

Spotted Pony heard the words, but he was not listening, consumed as he was with the growing flame of anger in his veins. He rose to his feet and looked in the direction Running Bird had pointed out. "I must kill this white man," he vowed. "I will tear his heart out with my bare hands." He turned at once to return to his blanket for the rest of his weapons.

"We will help you find him," Crooked Leg said. "Him and the white bitch."

"What about the Blackfoot camp and the horses we were going to steal?" This reminder of the purpose of their war party came from Running Bird. His question brought forth a scowl on Spotted Pony's face. "I am grieved by the loss of your brother, just as every man here," Running Bird went on. "I'm only asking if we should abandon our plans to kill our enemies and capture their horses now that we have come so far into their territory." Seeing that he had caused the others to pause and consider the question, he suggested, "Since it is only one man, maybe only one or two of us need go with Spotted Pony. That is all I am saying."

"Do as you wish," Spotted Pony said. "I don't need any help to kill one white man. I will go alone."

"I will go with you," Crooked Leg volunteered.

"And I, too," Running Bird spoke up.

After wrapping Kills Two Bears's body in his blankets, Spotted Pony fashioned a hasty burial for him in the branches of a large cottonwood. Then the three Lakota warriors were off at once, following the tracks that held close to the slopes of the mountains. The tracks led to the mouth of a ravine and sign that told them the white man had a partner waiting there with their horses.

From there, the trail led toward the southern base of the mountain range and was clearly headed toward the trading post on the river. This caused a feeling of caution in the resolve of Crooked Leg and Running Bird, for this was close to the soldier camp.

As they had suspected, the trail led them to the Clark Fork River, so they continued on to the trading post, moving in close enough to watch the goings and comings to Rubin Fagan's store. The four horses, two of them with saddles, tied up there gave them confidence that they belonged to the men they chased. "We are lucky to have caught up with them this soon," Running Bird said, thinking they must have spent a lot of time visiting with the man, Fagan, to still be there.

Shortly thereafter, they saw the men they chased when they finally came out of Fagan's store. There was no doubt when they saw the woman that Kills Two Bears had captured. Close enough to see clearly, Spotted Pony uttered an oath when he saw the feather in the hatband of one of the men. "It is the man with the feather, the man who led the soldiers down upon us when we were ready to attack the settlers on the river." Suddenly, the magnitude of their hunt took on new importance. This had to be the one called Hawk. He was well-known among the Lakota Sioux. A warrior who killed Hawk would have big medicine and be honored by all his tribe. "I will kill Feather In His Hat, this Hawk," Spotted Pony announced once again.

"We must be very careful," Crooked Leg cautioned. "He has powerful medicine."

"We'll follow him and wait for them to make camp," Spotted Pony said. "Then when it is dark, we'll see how powerful his medicine is. We will kill all three."

"John Hawk!" Rubin Fagan had announced loudly when the three travelers rode up to the front porch of his trading establishment. He grunted with the effort required to lift his considerable bulk out of the rocking chair. "If you ain't a sight for sore eyes. I thought you musta been shot, or scalped, or both."

"How do, Rubin?" Hawk replied. "I was thinkin' the same thing about you. I thought Minnie Red Shirt mighta done the job after wastin' the best years of her life on you."

"Ha!" Fagan snorted in pretended contempt. "Minnie thanks Man Above every night for sendin' her an outstandin' man like myself to travel with her on her life path."

"Looks like she's still feedin' you pretty good," Hawk said. "Either that, or that rockin' chair's startin' to shrink up."

"Huh!" Fagan grunted. "A man's gotta eat if he's gonna do a day's work." Grinning then, he

177

walked out to shake hands with Hawk. "Who's this you brung with you?"

"This is Monroe Pratt and his sister-in-law, Rachel," Hawk replied. "They're fixin' to head out toward Missoula and they might need a few things."

"Well, you folks are welcome to my little store, here, even if you are travelin' in some mighty poor company." He nodded politely to Rachel and shook Monroe's hand. "Come on inside and I'll be glad to help you with anythin' I can. I've got most staples a man could need, and a few things for ladies," he said, taking notice of the tattered dress Rachel wore. He waited then for the explanation.

"Rachel, here, has had enough misfortune to last most folks a lifetime," Hawk said. He went on to tell Fagan about the circumstances that caused him to bring them to his store.

"Lord have mercy," Fagan exclaimed. "That's mighty sorry news, all right," he said to Rachel. "You come on inside and I'll get my missus. She'll fix you up with somethin' to wear. We don't do no business in ladies' dresses, but Minnie can most likely find some deerskin skirts for you to wear."

"That would surely be appreciated," Rachel said. "I would really like to wash this filthy thing I've got on." She glanced at Monroe since she had no money of her own. He nodded his approval.

"Minnie!" Fagan called out as he led them into the store. A few moments later, Minnie Red Shirt appeared at the door to Fagan's residence behind the trading post. Seeing Hawk, she immediately smiled and came to greet him. An ageless Blackfoot woman, Minnie never seemed to have changed in the seven-odd years Hawk had known her and Fagan, while her husband continued to expand on her cooking. Happy to help any friend of Hawk's, she graciously took Rachel by the hand and led her through the door to the house.

With the women gone, Hawk turned to more serious questions. "Do you know Roy Nestor? You seen him around here lately?"

"Roy Nestor," Fagan repeated. "Not for a long while, at least not in the past year. I've seen him a time or two when he was ridin' with an army patrol." He paused to recall the man. "As I recollect, I never had much use for that man. Are you lookin' for him?"

That answered Hawk's question as to whether or not Nestor had come this way when he fled from the ambush on the Missouri River. "Yeah, we're lookin' for Nestor. He's the reason that young woman you just met is a widow."

Fagan looked immediately at Monroe. "Your brother? Well, I'm right sorry to hear that." Hawk went on to tell him about the run-in they had just had with Nestor and the fact that he had managed to escape. And they didn't learn about his killing of Monroe's brother until after Nestor was gone. Hawk next asked about any reported Sioux raiding parties along the Clark Fork and was told that all had been quiet for most of the summer so far. "I expect Lieutenant Conner would be interested to hear about that party you had a run-in with, though," Fagan said.

"Conner," Hawk exclaimed. "Is he in command of that camp?" It would be good to see Lieutenant Conner again.

"Yep," Fagan replied. "He set himself up in a little camp with one company of soldiers."

"Well, I'll let him know he's got a Sioux raidin' party on his hands now. What worries me is they were trailing after Walkin' Owl's village when we found 'em on the eastern edge of the Garnet Mountains. I'd surely like to warn Walkin' Owl if I knew where he was headin'." He glanced over to see that Monroe was looking at something on the counter across the room before lowering his voice. "But I'm bound to take Monroe and Rachel to Missoula."

"Your friend Bloody Hand was in here to trade some pelts a couple of weeks ago," Fagan said. "He told me his village was fixin' to move across to the western slopes of the mountains. I'll send my boy, Robert, to find the village and tell 'em about the Sioux war party."

"That would ease my mind quite a bit," Hawk

said. "But I don't want Robert to take any chances and get himself in trouble."

"You don't have to worry about Robert," Fagan crowed. "He got more of his mother's blood than he did mine. He'll watch his scalp. He knows his mother will whup him good if he loses it."

With their trading all done, Hawk wanted to ride to the small army encampment three quarters of a mile up the river, but Fagan and Minnie insisted on feeding them before they departed. Dressed in a soft doeskin dress, Rachel looked much the Indian maiden as she consented to one quick spin to let them all admire her new clothes. It was not lost on Hawk that it was the first real smile he had seen on her. He couldn't help wondering how long her mourning for Jamie would last, considering the fact that she had known her late husband for only a short time. He hoped it wouldn't be for too long a time, because she was a comely woman and looking to be close to the age when most women start to worry if they're not married. He glanced over at Monroe across the table from him. *Looks about the right age for him,* he thought.

After the meal was finished, Hawk and Monroe shifted the packs around on the horses to provide a little more room for Rachel to ride on Monroe's packhorse. There was not a great deal of adjustment required due to Rachel's diminutive size.

Some of the smaller packs were transferred to Hawk's buckskin and Monroe's roan. To make her ride even more comfortable, Fagan made Monroe a fair price on a child's saddle he had bought for Robert when he was ten years old. It fit Rachel's tiny behind just fine. She was delighted. Although the mood was light when they set out for the soldiers' encampment, Hawk knew there was a heavy cloud of vengeance hanging over Monroe's head. It was something that demanded a reckoning and he knew riding away to leave Roy Nestor running free was hammering on Monroe's conscience. In the short time Hawk had ridden with Monroe Pratt, he had judged him to be a generous and honorable man. So when they made a short stop on their way to the army camp to allow Rachel to seek the privacy of the laurel bushes that lined the bank of the river, Hawk spoke his peace.

"We ain't talked much about our business arrangement, what with all that's happened," Hawk said. "When we started out, you just wanted me to help you find your brother, dead or alive." Monroe nodded and started to speak, but Hawk continued. "Well, we found him, so I reckon that takes care of what we agreed on. We're done with that. Now I figure it's time to decide what we're gonna do next. It's still a good day's ride to Missoula and I don't recall you sayin' how far down the Bitterroot Valley your ranch is from there. I don't know if you want me to ride with you to take Rachel home, or not. But I oughta tell you I'm no longer on your payroll. I'll go with you to Missoula if you want me to, but I won't be expecting any pay for doin' it. Once we get Rachel settled, we can come back and see if we can pick up Roy Nestor's trail, if you wanna do that." He paused a moment while Monroe thought about it. When he continued, he said, "If you don't need me to go to Missoula, I expect I'll go ahead and see if I can pick up Nestor's trail now."

Hawk's offer was not anticipated by Monroe, so he took a moment to digest it. Seeing Rachel emerging from the laurel bushes at that point, he made his decision quickly. "That's damn decent of you to offer to go after that murderer on your own, and I appreciate it. But I've got a bigger stake in this than you have, so it's important to me and my family to punish Nestor by my own hand. That said, I could sure use your help in finding that son of a bitch. Whaddaya say you ride with us to the Bitterroot Valley, then we'll hunt Nestor together?"

"If that's what you want, then hell, fine by me."

Monroe reached over to shake on it. "Good," he said. "I'm a fair man, so I'll see that you get something out of the deal." He walked over to give Rachel a boost up on her horse. "Hawk's gonna keep us company on the way home," he said to her.

"Good," she said, relieved to hear it.

Lieutenant Mathew Conner looked up from his reading when the corporal stuck his head in the tent that served as his headquarters. "Somebody wants to see you, sir. It's somebody you might wanna see and he's got some people with him."

Seeing the generous grin spread across Johnson's face, the lieutenant was puzzled for a moment. "Well, send him in, Corporal . . . No, wait, I'll come outside. It's too damn hot in this tent." He got to his feet and went outside, where he found Hawk with a man and a woman waiting outside the small ring of tents. "Hawk!" Conner exclaimed, grinning while Johnson chuckled. "What are you doing up this way? You must be lost."

"How do, Lieutenant?" Hawk replied, accustomed to Conner's japing. "When I heard it was you the army sent out here in the woods, I figured you musta got in trouble with the major again."

"Not me," Conner pretended to protest. "I'm striving to be the best officer in the regiment." He laughed at the absurdity of his remark. Hawk laughed with him. He was well aware of the lieutenant's penchant for trouble due to his lack of respect for military protocol and his fondness for a practical joke. He was certain it

184

was the reason Conner had been passed over for promotion so many times. "I hope the colonel sent you up here to scout for me. I see you've got someone with you." The sight of Rachel in her doeskin outfit prodded his curiosity.

"This is Monroe Pratt and his sister-in-law, Rachel," Hawk said. "We're on our way to the Bitterroot Valley. They've had a heapin' portion of hard luck and we're tryin' to take the lady home." He quickly told Conner about the murder of Rachel's young husband and her subsequent capture by the war party of Lakota Sioux.

Conner was stunned by the news that Nestor had reappeared. "Are you sure it was him who killed her husband?"

"That's what the lady says," Hawk answered. "Shot him in the back, then finished him off with a knife."

"I always knew Nestor was a worthless piece of trash," Conner said, a deep frown etched across his brow. "But I guess I never suspected how evil he really was. I know he sure had it in for you."

"Reckon so," Hawk said.

Thinking himself remiss in properly greeting his visitors, Conner introduced himself to Monroe and Rachel. "I'm truly sorry for the loss of your husband, ma'am. Can I offer you some water or something to eat? Why don't you have a seat back there under my tent flap?" He turned to the corporal, who was standing by the tent watching. "Johnson, get my camp chair out of the tent for Mrs. Pratt." While Rachel reluctantly followed the corporal down the bank to the tent, Conner returned his attention to Hawk. "If you ain't a sight for sore eyes. Tell me about that Sioux war party. Our scouts haven't turned up any sign of hostile activity north of this river for the entire three months we've been patrolling this area. How many?"

"I don't know for sure," Hawk answered. "I can only guess there aren't many more than twenty or so, just from what I could tell by their tracks." When Conner raised an eyebrow at this, Hawk reminded him that their tracks were mixed up with the tracks left by Walking Owl's village. Then he explained that he didn't have a chance to get in close enough to see because of the sudden discovery of Rachel hiding in the bushes. "It was just luck that I didn't sit down on her when I went into those bushes," he said. "I killed the buck that was lookin' for her. I reckon I coulda asked him how many they were, but he didn't seem to be very talkative at the time."

"Up in the Garnet Range, huh?" Conner asked, ignoring Hawk's attempt to joke. "I'll get a patrol up that way in the morning. We've been concentrating on the Mullan Road, concerned about any attacks on freight trains or traders traveling on it. So now we'd better be watching for a new party of hostiles to show up. Are you sure you've gotta go to Missoula? I could sure use your help in finding that war party."

"You shouldn't have any trouble findin' 'em," Hawk assured him. "Who have you got scoutin' for you?" When told he had two, Ben Mullins and Raymond Red Coyote, a Crow, Hawk commented, "Both of those men are good scouts and I don't reckon anybody knows the mountains north of the river any better than Ben Mullins. You don't need me. I can tell you where to start lookin', though."

After telling Conner what Rubin Fagan had told him, that the Blackfoot village was moving to the western slopes of the Garnet Mountain Range, Hawk decided it was time to get started toward Missoula. The sooner they could see Rachel safely to the Triple-P, the sooner he and Monroe could get started after Nestor. In all honesty, Hawk had doubts about ever tracking Nestor down. He could go in any direction and he was experienced enough to know how to hide his trail. It would be Hawk's guess that Nestor would surely leave the territory, never to leave a trace again. He had expressed these thoughts to Monroe, but Monroe was adamant about his desire to search for Nestor, so Hawk assured him that he would do the best he could to pick up Nestor's trail. So their call on the cavalry camp completed, the three travelers prepared to leave.

Lieutenant Conner stood by as Monroe helped Rachel up into her miniature saddle before climbing aboard his horse. Hawk, already in the saddle, turned the buckskin's head toward the river trail. Before he touched his heels to the willing gelding, Conner said to him, "You shouldn't run into any trouble between here and the Bitterroot River. Our patrols haven't reported any sign of any Indian activity, hostile or friendly, between here and there. And you're not likely to, anyway, with the presence of so many soldiers. Not just my company, two companies of the Seventh Infantry were sent up to Missoula this month to build a permanent fort, so any raiding parties would be damn fools to be anywhere near there. As a matter of fact, I've got a patrol that is probably on their way back from up that way. Maybe you'll run into them."

"Good," Hawk responded while thinking to himself, *It'll still be a healthy idea to keep a sharp eye.* Having just run up on a party of Sioux that he didn't expect to find in Blackfoot, Salish, and Kootenai country, he was not willing to become too careless. He gave Rascal a nudge and the big horse sprang immediately into a trot, leading his packhorse with Rachel, then Monroe following.

"Why don't you come on back to work for me when you're done with that?" Conner called out after him. "They don't need you down at Ellis as bad as I need you here." He received no more than a wave of the hand in acknowledgment. Hawk had committed his services to Monroe for as long as it took to run Roy Nestor to ground. When he left Fort Ellis he had promised Major Brisbin that he would return, so he would keep that promise, even if it would be a longer time than the major expected. Already, they had spent more time at Fagan's and the army camp than he had planned. More likely than not, Conner's small temporary camp would have been called back to Fort Ellis by then, or maybe even sent up to Missoula to reinforce the two companies there.

As best he could remember, it was about fifty miles to Missoula and the easiest way to travel was to use the Mullan Road that the army had built. It followed the Clark Fork all the way. They were getting a late start in the day due to the visit with Lieutenant Conner, but Hawk had planned to make it a day-and-a-half trip, anyway, with the intention of making the trip a little easicr on Rachel. By her own admission, she had never spent much time in a saddle. When looking back from time to time, he thought he saw signs of discomfort on her face and wondered if the small saddle was already causing her grief. She never complained, however, but when they stopped to rest the horses, she appeared unable to stand up straight. He couldn't resist the urge to comment on the matter.

"Are you doin' all right, Rachel?" Hawk asked.

"Oh yes," she replied at once, "I'm doing fine."

"You look kinda like you're walkin' on eggshells," he said. "Maybe that little saddle wasn't a good idea after all. You mighta been more comfortable just ridin' on a blanket."

"Oh no," she insisted. "I'm fine, maybe just a little stiff. That's all." She tried to keep a straight face, but the doubting expressions she saw on both his and Monroe's faces caused her to giggle instead. "My bottom feels sore as a boil," she finally confessed. "And my back might be broken." She shook her head and giggled harder, causing a chuckle from both of them. "I thought my poor bottom was going to have calluses on it after riding on a wagon seat all the way from Minnesota, but this is a different kind of sore."

"I reckon," Hawk said. "I swear, though, I thought you'd be more comfortable on a saddle with your feet in the stirrups."

"So did I," Monroe said. "Maybe it'll help if we put a blanket on the saddle—give you a little cushion. If that doesn't work, you can try it with no saddle at all." They all agreed on that, so when the horses were rested, they continued on along the road, with Rachel sitting high in the saddle atop a folded blanket.

"If that ain't better for you," Hawk suggested,

"we can just let you ride in Monroe's saddlebag, as small as you are."

She responded with a grimace for his attempt at humor. Although she made no more complaints, she was extremely grateful when Hawk declared it was time to make camp while there was still daylight left.

When they came to a small stream that emptied into the river, Hawk entered it, then turned his horse to follow it upstream, cautioning Rachel and Monroe to keep their horses in the water. "I don't think we've got anything to worry about," he explained. "Conner's most likely right about there bein' no Indians in the area, but there's no use in bein' careless." They had advanced no farther than a hundred yards when Hawk abruptly pulled his horse to a stop. He looked back at Monroe and Rachel and motioned for them to be quiet. The faint smoke from a fire had been the reason for his sudden stop, so he dismounted on the bank of the stream and moved forward on foot until reaching a place where he could see what he had almost blundered into. He smiled to himself when he recognized a cavalry patrol in bivouac beside the stream. No doubt it was the patrol Conner had mentioned. He couldn't help wondering if Monroe might question the ability of the scout he had hired if he thought about how close he had come to riding into the camp before he knew it was there.

"I reckon we couldn't find a better place to camp," he told Monroe when he returned to the horses. "We'll camp close to a cavalry patrol tonight." To the surprise of the soldiers, they rode on into the camp and informed them that they'd like to camp a short distance upstream from them if they didn't object. A totally astonished second lieutenant on his way back from a patrol could think of no reason to. In respect to Rachel, he politely introduced himself as Lieutenant Peter Wallace. Aside to Hawk and Monroe, he assured them that his men would confine their individual calls of nature a respectful distance downstream. Hawk thanked him for his consideration, then picked a spot to camp about fifty yards upstream and prepared to spend the night.

Eager to pull her weight on the trip, Rachel was quick to gather wood and soon had a healthy fire burning. Although the blanket on her saddle was easier on her than the bare saddle had been before, she was still stiff and sore from the day's trip. Determined not to show it, she filled the coffeepot and sliced bacon to be fried in the two small frying pans they had with them. She sorely missed her pots and pans, as well as the supplies to cook with, all having been taken from the wagon by the Sioux. She especially regretted the loss of her Dutch oven and expressed as much to her two fellow travelers. "I wish I could bake you some biscuits to go with this salty meat but I don't have anything to bake with."

"You'll have everything you need once we get home to the Triple-P," Monroe said. It was one of the few times he had mentioned the ranch in the Bitterroot Valley, named for the three Pratt brothers. "We'll make it on venison and sowbelly and coffee till we get there. That's about all we've had to eat since Hawk and I teamed up."

"I could make you some slapjack," Hawk volunteered. When his offer was met with two quizzical faces, he explained. "Slapjack," he repeated. "Kinda like biscuits." Their expressions were still blank, so he told them the recipe. When his suggestion was still met with no enthusiasm, he said, "Well, I'll make some up, anyway. I've got some flour and we bought some sugar back at Fagan's. You can try 'em if you wanna." An interested observer, Rachel watched him as he mixed flour with a little sugar and water until he had formed a paste. "They're better with some yeast, but you don't have to have it," he informed her as he patted the paste into little cakes, then dropped them in to fry in the bacon grease. When they were done, he plopped them on a piece of cloth to let them cool.

Making a face like a chipmunk, Rachel bit off a tiny bite after watching Hawk tear into one with apparent gusto. "Well," she allowed, "they're not as bad as I thought they would be." She took another bite, this one a little bigger than the first, but still ladylike. It was enough to give Monroe the incentive to join in. "When we get home," Rachel declared, "I will make us some real biscuits." Her reference to the Triple-P as home didn't escape Monroe's notice. He saw it as a positive sign.

For the better part of the afternoon the three warriors had followed the two white men and the white woman, always staying far enough back to avoid being spotted. All the while, Spotted Pony repeated his medicine words, preparing himself for the attack he planned. When Hawk had left the trading post, there had been no opportunity to plan an ambush because he stopped a short distance later to visit the soldier camp. Afraid to get too close to the encampment of soldiers, the warriors had watched from a distance until Hawk finally led his two companions on the road again. Thinking that at last he would get his chance to avenge his brother, Spotted Pony was eager to ambush them, but his two companions urged him to wait until they were farther away from the soldiers. He reluctantly gave in to their caution and agreed to follow Hawk until he made camp. Then they would surprise them and kill them, even the woman.

"I think we are far enough from the soldiers now," Spotted Pony said, his patience at an end.

"I say we should catch up with them now and kill them."

"Maybe so," Crooked Leg said. "But it is getting late now. They surely will be making camp soon. I think this man has big medicine. It would be wise to attack when he is eating his food and is not alert to danger."

Spotted Pony was not totally satisfied with that plan and insisted on picking up the pace to get closer to the three. His impatience was lessened, however, when they came to a stream where the tracks stopped. Upon closer inspection, they discovered a careless print at the edge of the stream that told them Hawk had turned off the road to find a place to camp. Excited, Spotted Pony was ready to use Crooked Leg's suggestion to attack when Hawk had relaxed his caution by the campfire. The warriors rode a wide arc through the trees, parallel to the course of the stream, seeking to spot the campsite. Spotted Pony stopped suddenly, holding up his hand for silence. "Listen," he whispered. Crooked Leg and Running Bird stopped at once, having heard what he had.

"Voices," Running Bird said. "It sounds like many people talking."

Confused by the unexpected sounds, they tied their ponies in the trees and proceeded to make their way through the heavy forest between them and the stream. When they came to a place where they could see the banks of the stream, they were stunned to discover a party of soldiers camped. There near the center of the camp, they saw Hawk, Monroe, and Rachel talking to the soldiers.

"He came here to join the soldiers," Running Bird whispered.

"It would be foolish to try to kill him now," Crooked Leg said, immediately discouraged. "There are too many soldiers."

"I must avenge my brother," Spotted Pony insisted, almost crushed with his disappointment. "I cannot turn back now."

"There are too many," Crooked Leg repeated. "I won't fight when there is no chance to win. I'm going back to the others."

"Crooked Leg is right," Running Bird said. "It is foolish to try to fight so many. I will go back with him. You must come with us. If it is meant to be, you will have another chance to seek your vengeance. But if you try now, you will only be dead like your brother, by Feather In His Hat's hand, or that of a soldier. Come with us now, live to fight another day."

Spotted Pony did not move for a long moment, staring in the direction of the camp by the stream, but seeing nothing, his eyes glazed by the infuriating frustration that possessed him. His initial reaction to their refusal to support him in his determination to seek his redemption was one of anger. But after a moment, he finally surrendered to the common sense his companions had tried to make him see. He turned and walked with them back to their horses, but with resolve that the day would come when he would face this man and take his vengeance. He felt in his heart that Man Above would not deny him the vengeance he deserved.

CHAPTER 9

With the rising of the sun, the twin camps of soldiers and civilians rekindled the fires of the night before in preparation to cook breakfast before getting under way. Whereas Hawk would normally prefer to start out immediately and stop for breakfast when it was time to rest the horses, he thought it best to alter that today. For one reason, Missoula was now close enough to reach and rest the horses there. A second reason was to allow Rachel time to enjoy some coffee and bacon before having to climb into the saddle again. A brief meeting he and Monroe had with Lieutenant Wallace left him with the notion that there was little danger of encountering a Sioux war party between there and Missoula. And once they reached Missoula, there should be no Indian activity down the Bitterroot Valley, even though there had been reports of isolated encounters with the Salish. So the two camps parted after both had eaten breakfast. Had there been anyone watching, they would have seen that they went in opposite directions. But the three Sioux warriors were no longer there to see that the two white men and the white woman were left to defend themselves in the event of an ambush.

After a ride of approximately twenty miles,

the three travelers came upon the site of the new permanent fort under construction that Lieutenant Conner had told them about. Since the fort, aptly named Fort Missoula, was to be an open fort, there were no walls being built, consequently they could see that the buildings, though under way, were not in the final stages of construction. Both Hawk and Monroe were surprised to see only a few soldiers on the site, instead of the expected crew of workers, two full companies of men, according to Conner. Thinking it a good place to rest and water the horses, they selected a shady spot not far from what Hawk guessed to be a barracks.

"How far do you reckon your ranch is from here?" Hawk asked Monroe.

"From right here, I'd say about twenty, maybe twenty-five miles," Monroe replied. He glanced at Rachel, who was busy filling the coffeepot. Obviously hearing Hawk's question, she paused to hear his answer. It was easy to imagine that she might be getting nervous about meeting the rest of her family now that the time was rapidly approaching. "If you'd rather have something a little more substantial to eat than bacon or jerky," he said to her, "there's a nice little diner in town."

"Oh no . . ." she replied, pausing. "Whatever you men want to do is all right with me." She suspended the half-filled coffeepot over the water, waiting for a decision.

"Maybe we'll eat in town," Monroe decided. "But a cup of coffee would go well while we're waiting for the horses to rest up."

"Might as well make it a full pot," Hawk advised, nodding toward a soldier who was approaching from the unfinished barracks building.

"How you folks doin'?" Corporal Moss greeted them. "Ma'am," he added in deference to the lady.

They returned the corporal's greetings, then Monroe commented, "Doesn't look like much building going on. Must not be in much of a hurry to finish the fort."

Moss looked surprised. "I reckon you folks ain't heard the news." He could see by their expressions that they had not. "Captain Rawn, he's the company commander, took every man but my squad to chase after a bunch of Nez Perce Injuns."

"Nez Perce?" Monroe replied. "I thought they were going to the reservation."

"Not all of 'em," Moss said. "Chief Joseph and Chief Lookin' Glass said they ain't goin' to no reservation. Said they're goin' to Canada. They came down the mountains and Captain Rawn tried to stop 'em on Lolo Pass, but the Injuns just went around him. Now our boys are chasin' after 'em down the Bitterroot Valley."

This immediately captured Monroe's attention.

"Down the Bitterroot!" He exclaimed, at once concerned for the safety of his mother and brother. He looked at Hawk. "We've got to get down to the Triple-P right away! We don't have time for coffee or eating!"

"How long ago did the Nez Perce start down the valley?" Hawk asked the corporal. When Moss said that was two days ago, Hawk turned to Monroe. "Two days ago—that means they've already passed your ranch, if it ain't but twenty-five miles from here. I expect they were movin' pretty fast, too, if the soldiers were after 'em." He could see that that didn't ease Monroe's concern, so he said, "We'll go right on down there, but we'll get there quicker if we give the horses a chance to rest first."

Even as anxious as he was, Monroe couldn't argue with that, and he resigned himself to the probability that the Nez Perce were already past the Triple-P and there was nothing he could do to prevent any harm that may have been done. "You're right," he conceded. "What's done is done. We'll wait till the horses are ready to go." He gave Rachel an apologetic look, glanced over at the questioning expression on Corporal Moss's face, then looked back at Rachel and said, "Go ahead and make the coffee. Maybe the corporal would like a cup."

"Yes, sir, I surely would," Moss responded. "That's mighty nice of you folks."

• • •

Leaving the small settlement of Missoula, with Monroe leading now, they followed the Bitterroot River down a valley framed by the rugged peaks of the Bitterroots on their west and the Sapphire Mountains to the east. The valley, a pristine example of nature's more beautiful creations, seemed unspoiled by the passage of a whole village of Indians. This, even though they could readily see the trail cut by the large number of Indian men, women, and children as well as that left by two companies of soldiers and civilian volunteers. Although anxiously looking for signs of destruction as they passed a series of small farms, there were none to be seen. When within three miles of the ranch, they came upon a man and his small son about to cross the river. They pulled up to ask about the Nez Perce exodus.

"You're Pratt, ain'tcha?" the man asked before Monroe could inquire.

"One of 'em," Monroe replied.

"I thought so. I've seen you a couple of times at Skinner's," the man said, referring to a small trading post a mile above the northern boundary of the Triple-P. "The name's Wooten," he went on, "Lonnie Wooten. I've got a farm on the other side of the river."

"Monroe Pratt," Monroe said, impatient with the introductions. "I've been away for a spell and I just heard about the Nez Perce uprising. Was there much damage?"

"No, there weren't no damage," Wooten replied. "There weren't no uprisin', neither. They was just peacefully passin' through, tryin' to get to Canada. Matter of fact, I did some tradin' with a group of 'em, peaceful as you please. You wouldn'ta thought so, though, when the soldiers came chasin' after 'em."

"They did no damage, then?" Monroe asked.

"None I heard of. The soldiers shoulda just let 'em go on up to Canada. Those folks weren't lookin' for a fight. They just wanted to go someplace where they could live free."

Monroe was still confused. "But they went down the valley. If they were trying to go to Canada, they should have been going north."

"Would seem that way, wouldn't it?" Wooten replied. "I reckon the soldiers kept 'em from headin' north, so they musta figured on circlin' around 'em."

"But there were no attacks on the people in the valley?" Monroe asked. Wooten assured him there were none.

Hawk thought he could almost see the flood of relief on Monroe's face, but his urge to hurry home was no less. They bade Lonnie Wooten a good day and were quickly on their way. Although the concern for his family's safety was lessened, Monroe was still burdened with the tragic news of the cruel death of his brother Jamie and the introduction of Jamie's widow. He was not alone in his anxiety, however, for Rachel was facing the uncertainty of her reception by her mother-in-law and brother-in-law. And according to Monroe, they were now no more than half an hour from the house. To Hawk, long a loner, it might prove to be an uncomfortable reunion for him, caught up in a family's problems. He was tempted to ride up into the mountains to hunt while Monroe and his family dealt with the trauma of the youngest brother's death.

Eight-year-old Tommy Pratt was the first to spot the three riders approaching from the north. He propped his single-shot .22 against the front steps of the house and walked toward the edge of the yard in an effort to see the riders more clearly. In a few minutes' time, he recognized the formidable figure of his uncle and the red roan he rode. About to burst with excitement, he waited a moment to identify the other two riders. One was a woman, but the man sitting tall in the saddle on a big buckskin did not favor his uncle Jamie. "Ma!" He let out a yell, picked up his rifle, and ran into the house. "Ma!" he let out again as he ran into the kitchen.

"Good grief, Tommy, what are you yelling about?" Dora Pratt responded. "You'll wake your grandma. She's trying to take a nap."

"It's Uncle Monroe!" Tommy announced, even more excited.

This was enough to cause his mother to immediately respond, as well as catching the attention of the stoic Salish woman working over the stove. "Where?" Dora asked.

"Coming down the path from the river," Tommy replied. "There's a man and a woman with him, but the man doesn't look like Uncle Jamie."

A man and a woman, Dora thought, *but not Jamie. That can't be good.* Then she said, "Go find your father." Nervously wiping her hands on her apron, she hurried to the front door. Lily Bright Bird quickly pulled a pot to the edge of the stove to keep it from boiling over and followed her. Out on the front porch, Dora murmured to herself, "Who in the world . . . ?" The tall man with a feather in his hatband and the woman with him were strangers to her. She looked at Lily, but Lily shook her head. In a few minutes, her husband and Tommy came running from the barn.

"It's Monroe, all right," Thomas Pratt said. "But who's that with him? It's sure as hell not Jamie." He looked at his wife as if she might know.

"I guess we'll find out if we just wait a few minutes," Dora replied.

They stood there on the front steps until the three riders walked their horses up to the house.

Monroe wasted no time in giving them the grievous news. "I come bearing sad news," he blurted, almost before he dismounted, anxious to get it out. "Jamie is dead, murdered by the evil devil who was supposed to lead the wagon train to Washington Territory." He waited a few moments to let them get past the initial shock of his announcement before gesturing toward Rachel. "This is his widow, your sister-in-law, who escaped her death only because she was captured by a band of Sioux."

His staggering announcement hit them with the blunt force of a gunshot, leaving them all stunned for a long moment. Thomas was speechless. His wife would most likely have fainted had she not been possessed of the strong sinew most frontier wives developed in order to survive. She recovered quickly and turned to face the trembling woman who climbed down from her horse with an assist from Monroe. "So I reckon you're Rachel," she said, and held her arms out to her. Rachel came at once to receive Dora's embrace. "You're such a tiny thing," Dora said. "I feel like we already know you, Jamie talked about you so much just from the letters you sent."

Still staggered by the news of his brother's death, Thomas stood there for a long minute just slowly shaking his head back and forth in disbelief. When he had recovered somewhat from the shock of learning that Jamie was gone, he glanced up at the tall, somber man still seated in the saddle. "You haven't said who this fellow is that you brought with you."

"This is John Hawk," Monroe said. "He's the man who helped me find Jamie and the man who actually brought Rachel back from that band of Sioux."

Hawk stepped down from the saddle, shook hands with Thomas, and nodded to Dora. "Ma'am."

Back to Monroe, Thomas asked, "So you know who killed Jamie?" There was obviously a great deal more to the story of how Rachel came to be captured by Indians. But Jamie's death was the most important thing at the moment.

"Yeah, I know," Monroe answered. "A man named Roy Nestor. Poor Rachel saw him do it."

"Oh, you poor dear," Dora cooed, and put her arm around Rachel again. "Why don't we go in the house, instead of standing out here in the hot sun?" She turned the still-trembling young woman toward the front door. "Come on, Lily," she said to the Indian woman beside her. "We'd best hurry up that supper. They're probably hungry."

After the women had gone inside, Thomas asked Monroe, "What about this Nestor fellow? Is he dead?" Monroe shook his head. "Did you try to find him?"

"Sure, I thought about it," Monroe replied, "but he isn't that easy to find when you're running like hell to keep from being caught by a Sioux war party, especially after Hawk, here, killed the one who was chasing after Rachel."

Thomas, who was suspicious by nature, cast a wary eye at the formidable figure with a hawk feather stuck in his hat, whose somber expression seemed to convey indifference to their plight. "So, did Mr. Hawk help you out of the kindness of his heart, or are you paying him?" He had been struck hard with the news of Jamie's death, and he was in no disposition to tolerate a saddle tramp looking to gain from their tragedy.

Well familiar with his brother's sense of skepticism, Monroe was quick to straighten him out. "Hawk is with me because I rode up the Boulder River to find him when the army had quit looking for Jamie. By recommendation from the commanding officer at Fort Ellis, I might add. And yes, I paid him to help me, but he has refused to take anything more for accompanying me to bring Rachel home, and insists that he will try to track Nestor down, also free of charge. Does that answer all your questions?"

Thomas visibly flinched at his brother's obvious irritation with his line of questioning. He looked at Hawk as if to apologize for his mistrust, only to receive a casual smile and a nod. "I meant no offense, Hawk. I reckon I was still irritated by a little trouble we've had here of late."

"None taken," Hawk replied with a shrug.

"What kind of trouble?" Monroe wanted to know.

"Indian, maybe, or maybe rustlers," Thomas replied. "We've been missing some cattle, and with those bands of Nez Perce that just passed down the valley, I was afraid we'd been feeding some of 'em. But the Nez Perce have already passed through. When we got word Chief Joseph was bringing a bunch of people through here, we drove most of the cattle over toward the Sapphire Mountains. The Indians have been gone a few days now, but we're still missing some cows. Bob and Pete are up that way today to see if they can find out what's happening to 'em."

"Damn," Monroe muttered, "if it ain't one thing, it's another." He hadn't counted on coming home to a problem with the cattle. His main focus was on tracking down the man who had killed Jamie and he had planned to turn around right away and go back with Hawk. Time was their enemy—the longer they waited, the less likely they were to find any trace of Roy Nestor. "How many cows are we talking about?" he asked Thomas.

"Don't know for sure," Thomas answered. "It looks like whoever's stealing 'em are cutting out a dozen or more at a time. We just started noticing the shortage right after you left for Helena. Like I said, I thought it mighta been Indians too lazy to hunt 'cause there weren't that many cows missing. There's a couple of bands of Salish that are still raiding in the valley. And there's still talk about driving them out to the reservation, but the army hasn't done anything about it. But now, it looks like we're just getting rustled by somebody. I doubt that it's any of our neighbors. They might be getting cattle stolen, too. If it were Indians, seems like they would just take what they need for food. We're losing too many for that."

"Have you found any bones or remains of carcasses?" Hawk asked, since Monroe hadn't.

"Not so far," Thomas said. "Maybe Bob and Pete found something today. They'll be back tonight. I'm damn sorry about Jamie, but I'm awful glad to see you back. We need to find out what's happening to our cattle."

"We will," Monroe assured him. "We'll decide what to do tonight when the boys get back. Right now, we need to take care of these horses and maybe get ready to eat a little supper." He made an effort to seem casual about the cattle problem, but it was already weighing heavily on his mind. He had sworn to avenge Jamie, but it appeared that Thomas needed his help here. So Monroe was afraid he was going to be forced to choose between punishing Jamie's killer and hanging on to their livestock.

Other than his one question, Hawk remained a silent observer of the meeting between the brothers. It was unfortunate that the trouble with their cattle hit at a time when the family was grieving the loss of one of the brothers. As for his part, he felt more comfortable going after Roy Nestor alone and letting Monroe handle the problem with the cattle rustlers.

The conversation about missing cattle continued at the supper table in spite of Dora's occasional complaining that too much serious discussion resulted in letting the food get cold. "Lily and I hustled our behinds to cook you men a hot meal. If you're determined to let it get cold, we won't cook yours next time. We'll just cook for the boys down at the bunkhouse." She was primarily scolding Monroe and Thomas. The somewhat mysterious scout that Monroe brought home with him, along with Tommy, seemed not to be distracted by the talk of Indians and rustlers. Had she known the man called Hawk better, she would have appreciated the fact that a real sit-down supper was a rare treat. The closest he came to it was an occasional meal he might buy in a diner, so he gave it his full attention. As for Tommy, nothing was more important to him than eating.

"Dora, damn it," Thomas finally exclaimed. "We're eating the damn food, but we've got some important decisions to make here." He looked at Lily and asked, "Did you take the food to the bunkhouse?" Lily nodded. "Were Pete and Bob back yet?"

Lily nodded again. "They come back, say they come see you after they eat. They want to eat while food still hot."

"See?" Dora blurted. "Your hired hands have enough sense to eat their supper while it's still hot."

"For God's sake, let it be, Dora," Thomas reacted.

Finished eating, Hawk pushed his chair back a little from the table while he drank the rest of his coffee and took the moment to study the Pratt family. The matriarch of the Pratt family, Mrs. Emily Thompson Pratt, was not present at the table, so her supper was taken to her bedroom by Lily. Hawk assumed the mother was bedridden. It was obvious that Monroe was head of the family. While interesting to watch, Hawk found the scene not to his liking. He preferred his solitary existence. Perhaps it came natural to him, since he had been orphaned at the age of six, after having been abandoned by his aunt and uncle at a campsite on the North Platte River. At the time, he thought his aunt was under the impression that he was in the back of the wagon with her two youngest children. When they didn't come back looking for him, he figured that with a total of four children, she and his uncle decided they couldn't take on one more. He couldn't remember having been afraid—it was more a feeling of a new chapter in his young life. He wasn't alone for long before he was found by a cavalry patrol returning to Fort Laramie.

The soldiers dropped him off with a missionary who was intent upon converting the Crow Indians to Christianity. The boy stayed for four years until the missionary died, leaving the youngster with an easy choice, to join a band of Crows, whom he had come to know better than whites. It was not until he reached his nineteenth year that he left the village to see the mountains to the northwest and ultimately become a scout for the army out of Fort Ellis. It had never bothered him that the Indian tribe he ultimately became close to was a village of Blackfeet, traditional enemies of the Crow.

Drawn from his revelry when Rachel got up to remove his plate, he let his attention drift back to the talk between Thomas and Monroe. A moment later, there was a knock at the kitchen door and they were joined by Pete Little and Bob Boston. They both expressed their sympathy for the death of Jamie before making their report to Thomas. "I swear, Boss, we still can't tell for sure what's happenin' to our cows, but ain't nobody killin' 'em to eat. They're drivin' 'em off somewhere. We've been tryin' to keep an eye on about sixty head that have been bunched up in a canyon near Lost Creek. Near as I can guess, it looks like there's about eight or ten of 'em missin' since two days ago."

His interest tweaked again in their cattle problems, Hawk asked an obvious question. "How well do you know your neighbors?"

"Pretty well," Thomas answered. "We all participate in roundup every year, and none of the ranches near us have ever failed to deliver cows with our brand back to our range. I don't suspect any of our neighbors of rustling our cattle."

"What does your brand look like?" Hawk asked.

"Triple-P," Monroe answered him. "It's a simple brand, PPP." He drew an imaginary brand on the tablecloth with his finger."

"None of your neighbors have a brand close to yours?" Hawk asked. He was told there was no brand close to PPP. "If it was me," Hawk went on, "I'd be lookin' for somebody who could change my brand to look like theirs."

"Ain't none of the ranches that share our boundaries the kind of folks that would alter brands," Thomas said.

"But what about that Barfield crowd that set up a homestead on the eastern side of the Sapphires?" Pete asked. "Randolph Barfield, I ran into him last month at Skinner's—bought me a drink—had his daughter with him. He said him and his two sons were buildin' a herd over in that valley on the other side of the mountains, said his brand was a lot like the Triple-P's. Only difference is his brand is just his initials, RPB."

Hawk waited for one of them to see the obvious, but it didn't occur, so he said, "That would sure as hell tickle my curiosity. I believe I'd wanna take a look at this Barfield fellow's cows to check their brands. Wouldn't take much to change your brand to RPB, one bar and a curlicue burnt over PPP and you've got Barfield's brand. He mighta figured he's landed in a gold mine."

"Why in the hell didn't I think of that?" Thomas complained. "He must take us for a bunch of fools. That son of a bitch."

"Hawk's right," Monroe cautioned. "But just because it would be easy to do doesn't mean that's what he did. We need to get a look at some of his brands. If that's what's happening, it ought to be easy to spot, depending on how good the man with the iron is."

As was usually the case, Hawk felt no urgency in regards to his time or plans, but he had to wonder what Monroe's priorities were. After all, he had agreed to accompany Monroe to deliver Rachel to the ranch with the idea that they would return immediately to search for Roy Nestor. As the discussion between him and his ranch hands progressed, it was beginning to sound like Monroe was intent upon replacing Nestor's day of reckoning as his top priority. Hawk could understand that. Monroe could not ignore the poaching of his livestock. The only thing left to decide, as far as Hawk was concerned, was whether or not Monroe wanted him to return to search for Nestor on his own. His answer came in a short time.

"We'll take a little ride up over the mountains in the morning," Monroe said to Bob and Pete. "We'll leave Marvin to watch after things here till we get back." He sent them on their way, then turned to Hawk. "I know I hired you as a tracker, but I've got to hold up on running Roy Nestor to ground till we straighten out this business with our cattle."

"Stands to reason," Hawk said. "That's what I would do if I was in your boots." He shrugged indifferently. "I said I'd help you find Roy Nestor, so I reckon I can go on back and see if I can find some trace of him. I'm not in any hurry to get back to Fort Ellis." This was said in spite of the fact he had already been away from Fort Ellis longer than he told Lieutenant Meade he would be. He couldn't help feeling caught between his obligation to Meade and his promise to help Monroe.

"I appreciate that," Monroe said. "But I'd rather have you with me tomorrow when we cross over the mountains. I don't know if we'll run into any trouble or not, but I've seen you shoot. So whaddaya say?" When Hawk shrugged again, Monroe continued. "Good. I'm putting you back on the payroll."

"Whatever you say," Hawk said. "You're the boss." At least he was drawing steady pay for doing very little work.

CHAPTER 10

In contrast to the taller Bitterroot Mountains to the west, with their steep, heavily forested faces and deep canyons, the mountains of the Sapphire Range on the eastern side of the valley were more rounded with less tree coverage. The Triple-P took advantage of the open grassy slopes from time to time, as in the case when they utilized them to move their cattle out of the valley when the Nez Perce moved through. It was not unusual for some of their cattle to wander onto the lower slopes of the Sapphires, requiring the Pratts and their men to drive them back to the main herd. Consequently, they were well familiar with the easiest trails to follow when searching for strays. It was on one of these trails that Hawk rode with Monroe, Thomas, and the two hands that had reported the cows recently missing. With Bob Boston leading, they rode up a wide canyon to an open grassy area where a stream crossed through the lower corner. There were about a dozen cows grazing near the stream.

"See there," Bob said. "We drove about twice that many outta this little pocket yesterday." Ordinarily, this would cause little concern, but that was before they began to have cattle missing.

They rode in among the cows to check the

218

brands. They were all wearing the Triple-P. "Well," Pete said, "if they are changin' brands, I reckon they ain't had time to get around to these yet."

"Bob, you and Pete round these cows up and drive 'em back down in the valley." All five men helped the roundup and got the cows started down the trail they had just come up. Once they were on their way, Hawk and the two Pratt brothers turned back and started up the mountain. Picking the easiest route possible to climb the slopes, they rode up a wide ravine until reaching the top, where they paused to look over the downward slope and the valley beyond.

"Just where is this ranch house they're supposed to be living in?" Monroe asked.

"Damned if I know," Thomas answered. "I've never had a reason to look for it before. That fellow Barfield doesn't seem to be the friendly type. At least, none of the other men I've talked to have ever seen much of him and his two boys. Pete is the only one of our crew that's talked to him."

"Sounds to me like nobody knows what size herd this fellow has," Monroe suggested, "or if he came here with any cows at all."

Scanning the valley back and forth while the brothers talked, Hawk's sharp eye picked up some movement in a stand of fir trees near the bottom of the slope. He watched it closely for a few minutes before interrupting the conversation. "There's a bunch of cows in those trees down there." He pointed to the spot.

Both brothers stared at the stand of trees for a few moments before they were able to see what had caught his eye. "You're right," Thomas said. "There's something moving in those trees. Let's go take a look."

After moving down closer, they could actually see a small gathering of about thirty-five cows that had most likely sought the shade of the trees to settle in for the night. Now, with the sun climbing in the morning sky, they had begun to make their way toward a stream on the other side of the firs. The three riders rode into the trees and began to inspect the brands. All were branded with the same RPB, save one. That one wore the brand, but it was different from the others because of the broken leg on the *R* and the ragged bottom on the *B*. "Well, I'll be damned," Monroe muttered while staring at the obviously altered brand. He glanced up at Hawk. "Looks like you were right. A six-year-old could have done a better job than this. I guess it's time we paid a little visit to our new neighbor."

Since no one of the three knew where Randolph Barfield's ranch headquarters was, it seemed the logical step would be to follow the stream. So that's what they did, and after a ride of about a quarter of an hour, they passed through a lower band of firs to emerge onto a wide-open plain where they saw a couple hundred cows grazing. Sitting close by the stream was one log cabin with a small barn built beside it. "I reckon we've found the RPB ranch," was Monroe's droll announcement.

"Appears that way," Thomas responded, equally as cynical. "It's not much of a base, is it?"

Hawk refrained from adding to the sarcastic remarks, thinking instead that the simple cabin and barn looked like some outlaw camp more so than the initial stages of a cattle ranch. Maybe the occupants of the cabin had set out to start in the cattle business. But based on the altered brand they had just seen, they intended to build their herd at the expense of the Triple-P and the other ranches in the Bitterroot Valley. *They ain't gonna like it,* he said to himself, thinking of the visit he and the Pratts were about to make. He unconsciously reached down and loosened the Winchester in his saddle sling.

"Somebody's comin'," Lorena Barfield announced. She turned away from the window to address the three men seated at the table. "Three men, ridin' this way," she said, and stepped aside when her father got up and came to the window.

"Ain't nobody I've ever seen before," Randolph Barfield said after studying the three riders approaching the cabin. "Most likely some of our fine neighbors come to look us over," he decided.

"Ain't that nice," Clint snarled. "They coulda waited till after breakfast, though." He got up from the table and went to get his holster from a peg on the wall by the front door. After strapping it on, he took a second gun belt off another hook and tossed it toward the table. "Come on, Jake, get your tail offa that bench." The thrown weapon landed in the middle of the table, knocking his coffee cup off and causing his brother to jump backward to keep from getting a lap full of hot coffee.

"Damn you, Clint!" Jake blurted as he tried to keep from stumbling over the bench he had knocked over when he jumped back. "I oughta knock some sense into your head."

"You oughta try," Clint responded. "Put that gun on, you might need it."

"You damn fool," Lorena cursed. "I reckon you expect me to clean that up off the floor. Well, I ain't gonna do it. Me and Ma ain't got no intention of cleanin' up after you two hogs."

Clint chuckled. "Hell, it ain't gonna hurt them rough boards. It don't need to be cleaned up. Ain't that right, Ma?"

"I wish you wouldn't always be goin' after each other," Pearl Barfield complained. It was an oft-repeated lament from the tired-out, sad-eyed woman, only one month past her forty-third birthday, but looking as if approaching sixty.

"Shut up, all of you!" Randolph commanded, still peering out the window at the approaching riders. "Let's see who this is nosin' around." He was especially interested in the broad-shouldered one with a feather in his hat. He was joined at the window by his two sons, both armed now.

"We could pick 'em off right out the window," Jake suggested, halfway serious. "Then I could finish my breakfast."

"That would be really smart," Lorena chided. "You ain't got the brains God promised a tick."

"Shut up, I told you," her father scolded. "Come on, boys, let's go see what they want." He went to the door. His two sons trailed outside after him, and Lorena and her mother moved to the window to watch as their visitors pulled up before the cabin.

"Morning," Monroe said, and started to dismount.

"I ain't invited you to step down," Barfield replied, ignoring Monroe's attempt to start things on a polite note. "What is your business here?" He glared at Monroe while frequently shifting his gaze to the man with the feather in his hat, having already sized him up as the most dangerous of the three.

When Clint Barfield moved a few yards to the right of his father, Hawk reined his horse over to the side to continue facing him. Following his lead, Thomas pulled his horse over when Jake put some space between him and his father, resulting in a three-on-three face-off. There followed a brief silence before Monroe recovered from the surprise of the rude greeting. He had expected at least a show of neighborliness. "I guess you'd be Randolph Barfield," Monroe finally went on.

"I be," Barfield replied. "And this is my land. I asked you what business you have here."

"Well, seeing as how your attitude is so damn neighborly, I'll get straight to the point," Monroe said. "It seems like some of my cattle have wound up over here in this valley. My place is on the other side of this mountain range, so it's mighty unusual for my cows to wander all the way over the mountains to this valley."

"If I see any of your cows on my range, I'll head 'em back over the mountains," Barfield said. "So I reckon that takes care of any business we have to talk about. Now, you and your friends can ride on back to where you came from."

Another silent void followed, this one with a deadly cloud of apprehension hanging over it. The six men stood, eyeballing one another, ready to act at the first sign. When Monroe seemed hesitant to push the stand-off further, Hawk decided that it was necessary to call the old man's bluff. " 'Preciate your cooperation, neighbor. Now we'll take a look at those cows back near the foot of the hills on our way out— just in case you and your boys ain't had time to notice some of our strays mighta mixed in with 'em." He said it with a polite smile on his face, but his gaze was focused on the younger son facing Thomas. "Your son seems mighty fidgety with his hand brushin' back and forth over that gun he's wearin'. I've seen men accidentally shoot themselves gettin' careless with a handgun. That's why I've always been partial to a rifle." He drew the Winchester from his saddle sling so smoothly that no one had time to realize he was going to, and there was no time to react. He held it up for them to see. "You have to cock it before it's ready to shoot," he said as he cranked a cartridge into the cylinder. "Now, when I shoot it, it won't be on accident." He lowered his rifle casually toward Barfield.

"Hold still, Jake," Barfield barked, lest one of his sons make a move. "Both of you," he cautioned, totally aware that Hawk's rifle was aimed at him. Realizing that he had just been bamboozled, but still defiant, he said, "I don't know nothin' about your cattle. If there's any on my land, then they strayed here on their own. I'd advise you to keep 'em on your own range and I'd advise you and your hired gunman to stay the hell off my range."

"Good advice for both of us," Monroe spoke again. "I don't expect to lose any more cattle and that's a fact." Following Hawk's example then, he and Thomas backed their horses away slowly, keeping a steady eye on the three men of the Barfield family. Once he thought it a safe distance, Hawk turned the buckskin and loped toward the hills, leaving the perplexed Barfield men to stand and gawk.

"Damned if that son of a bitch didn't buffalo us good," Clint complained. "I can't believe we just stood here and let him get away with it."

"There weren't nothin' we could do about it without gettin' shot," his father said. "We mighta got him, but if he had pulled that trigger, I'd be a dead man. He's mighty slick to get one over on me like that. More'n likely he's some gunman the Pratt bunch brought in here to stop the rustlin'. And I figure that's who they are, the Triple-P." He thought about it for a moment, then said, "Saddle the horses. Maybe we can catch up with 'em while they're lookin' over our cattle. We can sure as hell shoot 'em for tryin' to rustle our cattle." Both sons ran to do his bidding, in hopes of getting a shot at the three riders.

Up ahead, about a quarter of a mile from the cabin, Hawk and the two Pratt brothers rode up a grassy draw to come out near the upper part of the stream where they had first seen the cows. There were about thirty cows still grazing close to the water. "Whaddaya think we oughta do?" Thomas asked Monroe. "It'll take a little time to look at all the brands. I don't know if we can risk doing that." He was thinking about the possibility of being chased.

"I hate to leave here without taking what belongs to us," Monroe said.

"You and Thomas drive the whole bunch back up toward the top of that mountain," Hawk said, pointing toward the lower slope in the range. "I'm gonna ride back a ways and keep them from catchin' up. I expect it didn't set too well with ol' Barfield, lettin' us get away clean like that."

"We don't know how many of those cattle are ours till we get a chance to look at the brands," Monroe said.

"That's up to you what you wanna do," Hawk said, getting impatient now. "You can drive the whole bunch up that mountain, look 'em over, and drive Barfield's cows back down. Or keep 'em all. Hell, he probably owes you more'n what's in this pocket. Just get goin'." With time running short, he wheeled the buckskin and galloped back toward the cabin.

One thing Hawk felt certain about, Barfield was not about to sit tight and let three people get the word out that he was building a herd at his neighbors' expense. The only choice he had was to kill the three of them before they spread the word to the other ranches in the Bitterroot Valley. And if he could catch them while they were on his range, he could probably get away with accusing them of rustling his cattle. Hawk's thinking was right on the money, for Barfield and his sons were already saddling their horses. They knew for a fact that there was a loosely formed association of the cattlemen in the valley and Barfield could not afford to have all the owners stirred up against him. He had hoped to continue to get away with rustling cattle randomly from each of three ranches within twenty miles of his place. But now, with that plan endangered, he would not hesitate to commit murder to keep from losing the operation he had started.

Hawk could still hear the bawling of the cows Thomas and Monroe were pushing up the slope behind him when he tied Rascal to a stunted pine tree in a band bordering a wide trench. He took his rifle and dropped down into the trench to await the arrival of his pursuers. It would be better if Barfield thought they were still inspecting all the brands, cutting out only those that had been altered. He turned to look up toward the top of the slope behind him, hoping to see the two brothers drive the cattle over the crest. There was no sign of them yet, so it looked as if he was going to have to hold the Barfields longer than he had anticipated. He looked down toward the cabin before taking another look up toward the mountaintop. This time, he spotted the herd of cattle crossing over the treeless grassy top. *Good,* he thought. *Now, if I can slow these boys up, Monroe might have enough lead to get those cows to the Triple-P.* He rested the barrel of the Winchester on the edge of the gully and waited.

Within a few short minutes, he heard the pounding of horses' hooves approaching the stand of pines between him and the cabin. A couple of seconds later, the first rider could be seen coming through the trees, the other two in single file behind him. Even at that distance, Hawk recognized the leading rider as the son who had squared off in front of Thomas and had shown signs that he was thinking about going for his handgun. For a brief moment, Hawk hesitated, thinking how young the boy was, sixteen or seventeen, he estimated, a pup bred from a no-good sire, but a pup nonetheless. *Damn,* he cursed himself for his reluctance. *He'll kill you if he gets a chance and most likely think nothing of it.* The riders thundered toward him, almost out of the trees now. *Hell,* he cursed again, shifted the front sight of his rifle away from the center of the young man's chest, and squeezed the trigger.

Jolted by the sudden impact of the .44 slug in his shoulder, Jake Barfield was knocked from his horse, almost before the sound of the Winchester's harsh report rang out. It was followed by three more quick shots that sent Clint and his father scurrying back into the trees to find cover. Hawk drew the rifle back from the edge of the gully to keep them from pinpointing his position and waited. He watched the wounded boy as he got up on his hands and knees and crawled back toward the trees. It would have been an easy shot to finish Jake off, but Hawk felt no temptation to do so. He was hoping that wounding the boy would discourage the father from pursuing the issue, but it was sure to force Barfield to take some action. He was either going to have to choose to fight, or choose to run. Hawk hoped that Barfield would decide it best to run before the rest of the ranchers in the valley rose up to come after him. It took the wounded boy several minutes to reach the edge of the pines. Hawk saw no sign of the other two until he spotted an arm motioning from behind a tree, encouraging Jake to continue. Once he disappeared into the stand of pines, Hawk withdrew from the gully and crawled back into the trees. Moving back through the firs, he untied Rascal's reins and led the buckskin carefully up the slope to take up a position higher up.

Closer to the top of the mountain now, he found another gully that afforded him concealment and protection while providing an overall view of a good bit of the mountainside below him and the gully from which he had ambushed the three of them a few short minutes before. If Barfield was set on coming after him, Hawk figured he'd choose to circle around the gully, using the trees to hide his movements. The only question was, in which direction? Right or left? So with his horse tied out of sight at the edge of an open pasture above him, he concentrated his gaze on the slope below him.

He was almost of the opinion that Barfield had decided against coming after him when he caught a glimpse of a white shirtsleeve as one of his stalkers passed by a small opening in the trees just below the left side of the gully he had just vacated. He had to search his memory to recall who was wearing a white shirt, the father or the son, then told himself it didn't matter. He shifted his gaze to the other end of the gully, but saw no movement there until finally he saw Barfield suddenly spring out of the trees to charge the gully. As if on signal, Clint sprang up from the other side, his rifle ready. Hawk fired three shots in rapid succession that kicked up dirt between the father and son and caused them to dive into the gully. To make sure they kept their heads down, Hawk fired a couple more rounds to kick up more dirt from the rim of the trench. Then he waited and watched, knowing they weren't likely to get out of their trap without his seeing them. A quarter of an hour passed, then another with no sign of any attempt to escape.

Lying as flat as he possibly could, Clint Barfield spit the last of a mouthful of dust he had gulped when he dived into the shallow gully. "You reckon that jasper is fixin' to set up there all day, waitin' for us to come out?"

"I don't know," his father replied. "Maybe." He grunted in pain as he reached under his belly in an effort to move a sizable rock he had dived on, being careful not to raise his body above the rim of the gully.

"It's been a long time," Clint complained. "Maybe he's gone."

"I don't know. I think he just wants to keep us pinned down long enough for his partners to get those damn cows back over the hill." They waited for another lengthy period spent hugging the ground that was heating up with the sun now high overhead.

"Reckon Jake's all right?" Clint asked. "He said he could make it back to the cabin all right, but he might notta made it."

"He oughta have. He got hit in the shoulder. Ought not be nothin' wrong with his legs." The awkwardness of their situation began to irritate Barfield's nerves. "I ain't fixin' to lie in this dust all day," he finally declared. "I bet he's done snuck off and left us layin' here in the dirt like a couple of lizards." Still not completely convinced he was right, he decided to find out cautiously. He pulled his hat off and placed it over the muzzle of his rifle. Then he raised the rifle barrel very slowly, about an inch at a time, until only a couple of inches of the crown rose above the rim of the gully. It was immediately knocked off the barrel with the snap of a rifle slug splitting the air over his head. Barfield dropped his rifle and clawed the ground frantically. "The son of a bitch is still there," he blurted.

"He ain't goin' away!" Clint agonized. "He's gonna wait us out till he gets a clean shot. We jumped right in his trap. He's got us pinned down till dark, and it's a long time till dark. Reckon what Mama and Lorena are thinkin'? Maybe if they get Jake fixed up, he'll be back to help us."

"I ain't countin' on it," Barfield said. He tried to think what he would do if the roles were reversed. "Hell, he ain't gonna set up there on that hill all day long. We'll wait him out a little longer, then see if he don't hightail it for the other side of the mountains. He's just set on givin' them time to move them cows over the mountains." With little choice, they resigned themselves to wait, even if they had to wait until nightfall to slip out. After approximately thirty additional minutes passed, Barfield asked, "What did you say?"

"I said, 'Give me the slightest reason and I'll send you straight to hell, both of you.'" Both father and son froze, stunned by the voice that seemed to come from right over them. They both looked up to see Hawk standing at the end of the gully, his rifle pointed at them. Clint started to raise his rifle, but stopped abruptly when Hawk warned, "Don't even think about it." Motioning with his Winchester, he said, "Pick those rifles up by the barrel and toss 'em up outta that gully."

"We do that and you'll shoot us down," Barfield complained.

"I'll shoot you down if you don't," Hawk answered him. "Now, do like I told you and you won't get shot." Barfield reluctantly did as he was told, grasping his rifle by the barrel and tossing it up over the rim of the trench. Thinking Hawk was distracted while watching his father surrender his weapon, Clint suddenly raised his rifle to his shoulder. The slug from Hawk's Winchester caught him in the left shoulder before he had time to aim. The force of the bullet's impact spun him around, causing him to sit down hard on the ground. Hawk cranked a new cartridge in the chamber. "Pick his rifle up by the barrel and toss it outta that gully," Hawk instructed calmly. Barfield acted quickly to follow his order.

"You gonna just shoot us down in cold blood?" Barfield complained.

"If I was plannin' to do that," Hawk calmly answered, "you'd both be dead already." He motioned for them to climb up out of the gully. "I told you you wouldn't get hurt if you did like I told you. Your boys are kinda hardheaded, though, ain't they?" He moved quickly over to pick up the rifle. "Now you've got both sons each with a bullet in his shoulder. I advise you to forget about killin' anybody, go home, and tend to your wounds. But one thing you need to understand, your days of raidin' Triple-P cattle are over. If we have any more cattle missin', we ain't gonna bother tryin' to find out who's rustlin' 'em. We'll figure it's you and we won't come thinkin' about shoulder wounds. Whether you clear out of here or stay, makes no difference to the Triple-P. You won't be bothered by us unless we start missin' stock again." He walked over and picked up their rifles. "I'll leave these up the hill a ways. They won't be too hard to find after I'm gone. Right now, I expect you'd best walk back to your cabin and take care of that boy's shoulder."

Barfield was confused. Clint lay in the bottom of the gully holding his shoulder, moaning in pain, looking to his father for help. No longer certain Hawk was going to kill them, the old man asked a question. "You tellin' me you ain't comin' back here with some of them other ranchers to run us out of our home?"

"The Triple-P's not interested in startin' a range war. Like I said, if you stay on your side of the mountains and we don't lose any more cows, then we'll let you be. But if you don't think you can stay here and work an honest ranch, you'd best leave, 'cause if we have to come back here lookin' for our cows, we'll clean this rat's nest out for good."

"That might not be as easy as you make it out," Barfield said, feeling some sense of his defiance return.

Hawk brought his rifle up to bear on him. "Maybe I'd best just go ahead and take care of this now," he threatened.

"No!" Barfield exclaimed. "Hold on, you win! I'm goin'! We won't bother your cows no more. Just let me take care of my boy before he bleeds to death." He reached down to help Clint get on his feet.

Hawk watched them carefully as they climbed out of the gully and started walking back down toward the cabin. *We'll see about that,* he thought, knowing there was little chance this brief encounter was enough to put Barfield on the straight and narrow path to honesty. But it was something to hope for, maybe for a while, anyway. However it turned out, it would be left to Monroe and Thomas and their men to handle it in the future. He didn't anticipate being here this long to begin with. That brought thoughts of Roy Nestor to mind as he walked back up the slope. After this amount of time, Nestor could be a hell of a long way from that ambush on the river, in any direction. As he agreed to do, however, he would nose around on the chance he could find some trace of him. But that would have to wait until he returned to Helena. "Needle in a haystack," he mumbled, then whistled. In a few moments, Rascal appeared at the edge of the pines across the clearing and trotted toward him.

"Well, if this ain't a fine sight," Lorena Barfield announced sarcastically as she looked out the window to see her father leading his and Clint's horse with her brother sitting in the saddle. When her mother moved up beside her, Lorena continued, "Look at that, Clint got shot, too!" She promptly went to the door to find out what happened. Her mother remained at the window a few moments more before releasing a tired sigh and turning to look at her younger son, sitting on a pallet leaning back against the wall. She could hear her daughter outside, greeting the returning men.

"Look at you," Lorena said to Clint. "I just got done pickin' a slug outta Jake's shoulder." She looked back at her father. "I reckon them three that came ridin' in here like they was gonna run us out are dead." She waited for his answer.

"I reckon not," Barfield replied. He tied the horses at the corner of the porch next to Jake's horse. "They've gone." He was in no mood to explain his failure to anyone, especially his daughter, who was always quick to criticize. It was bad enough that he had led his sons into a trap, getting them both shot. But there was no way to silence her, beyond putting a bullet in her skull.

Not at all satisfied with the non-report, Lorena pressed. "You ran 'em off, right—without any of our cows?"

"No, damn it!" Barfield barked. "They got away with thirty head or more. There weren't no way we could stop 'em. They ambushed us. We never stood a chance." He turned away from her to help Clint climb down from the saddle.

"It wasn't but one of 'em," Clint muttered, "that spooky-lookin' jasper with the feather in his hat. He pinned us down where we couldn't do nothin'."

With a deep frown of disgust, Lorena said, "I shoulda gone with you, I swear. One of you coulda stayed here and helped Ma with the cookin'." She shook her head in a stern sign of her disapproval. "One man, I swear."

"That's about enough outta you," Barfield scolded. "I'm tired of you runnin' off at the mouth. I thought about throwin' you in the creek when your mama squeezed out a damn girl. I shoulda done it."

Long indifferent to her father's threats and insults, Lorena smirked and said, "I'da come back to haunt you every day of your life." Since a small child, she had demonstrated a defiant nature and a competitive attitude with her two younger brothers. The only soft spot in her armor were her feelings for her mother. Since Pearl Barfield never showed the backbone to stand up to her husband, her daughter felt it her responsibility to do it for her. It often led to heated face-offs, just short of physical violence. "Come on, Clint," she said, abruptly breaking off the argument with her father. "Set yourself down at the table and I'll dig that bullet outta your shoulder." Knowing it useless to protest, Clint sat down and prepared to withstand his sister's none-too-gentle surgical manner.

During the removal of Hawk's bullet, Clint related the happenings of the past couple of hours that caused him, Jake, and her father to have been completely helpless against one lone man with a rifle. "Yeah, but it was still just one man against three of you," Lorena protested.

Clint insisted that this one man was different from any man he had ever run into. "I ain't ever seen anybody handle a rifle like he did. He was as handy with that Winchester as most men would be with a handgun."

"He must notta been as good as you say he was," she said, still skeptical, "or you and Jake would both be dead. Hell, he missed both of you with a wound in your shoulder. If he was so good with it, he'da nailed you dead center in your chest."

"I don't know 'bout that," Clint insisted. "I think he wasn't goin' for a kill shot." He told her then what the man with the feather had said about letting them alone as long as the cattle rustling stopped on the Triple-P. "He had me and Pa where there weren't nothin' we could do, standin' over us with his rifle and us with no guns. It he had wanted to kill us, there wasn't nothin' stoppin' him."

She looked up at her father, who was watching her doctoring. "You believe what he said about just lettin' us be as long as we don't mess with his cattle? That don't make sense to me."

"No," Barfield said. "I've been thinkin' about that and it strikes me now that he's just wantin' to make us sit tight while they round up some of the other ranchers. Then one fine day they'll all ride in here, kill every one of us, and divide up our cattle. That's what I think."

Lorena paused to give that some thought. "Well, that's one way of lookin' at it, I reckon. Whatever they've got in mind sure as hell ain't gonna be to our likin'. The question now is, what are we gonna do about it? We can't sit around here waitin' for a gang of men to come ridin' in and shoot the place up."

CHAPTER 11

When Hawk got back to the Triple-P ranch, he found Monroe and Thomas still examining the brands on the cattle they had driven back. Eager to hear Hawk's report, they walked to meet him as he pulled the buckskin to a stop. "We heard the shooting," Monroe said. "Wondered if you were in any trouble."

Hawk gave an accounting of everything that happened after they left, including the part where he told Barfield they would be left alone if they ceased their poaching of Triple-P cattle. When Monroe asked if he really thought Barfield would stay on, Hawk responded, "I doubt if a man like Barfield has any notion about tryin' to make an honest livin'. He's gonna start up again, or move on. I figured I'd give him a chance to pack up and go someplace else to try his game. I put a bullet in the shoulder of both his boys, so he might have to wait awhile before he can think about tryin' to get even." He shrugged and explained, "I didn't go to put a bullet in that second boy's shoulder, but he made a move to take a shot at me."

They went on to discuss the best plan to protect themselves from any possible raids in retaliation for the damage Barfield suffered. There wasn't much they could do except to keep a wary eye out when going about the business of running the ranch, that and a night guard every night. It was unnecessary to explain, but Monroe told Hawk he was going to have to stay on the ranch until this thing with the Barfields was settled one way or another. "How 'bout if I keep you on the payroll, same as Bob and Pete and the other men?"

"That would be fine with me," Hawk replied. "But I oughta warn you, I don't know much about raising cattle and I ain't ever had any burnin' desire to learn."

His statement brought a laugh from Monroe. "I didn't think you did. It's that rifle of yours I'd be hirin'."

"I ain't ever been hired out as a gunman, either, but I'll try to help you keep an eye on the place." He shook his head in wonder, thinking about how involved things had become since the simple proposition of finding out what had happened to Monroe's brother Jamie. With that settled, he asked about the cattle they had driven back from Barfield's.

"Three were our brand obviously altered," Thomas piped up. "The rest were RPB, so I reckon that officially makes us cattle rustlers, too."

"Maybe just traders," Hawk suggested, "swappin' out some of their cows for the ones of yours still on their side of the mountains."

"That sounds fair to me," Monroe said. "Let's

go to the house and get something to eat. Rustling cattle makes me hungry and Lily said she was gonna be ringing the dinner bell as soon as the biscuits were done."

"I reckon I'd best take care of my horse first," Hawk said, and turned toward the barn.

Before he had taken two steps, Monroe reminded him, "When you get through with your horse, you know we expect you to come to the house for supper, right?" He knew it was necessary to tell him, otherwise, he would more than likely go to the bunkhouse to eat with the hired hands.

"Why do you wear that feather in your hat?" Eight-year-old Tommy Pratt asked when Hawk came in and removed his hat before seating himself at the table. "Are you an Indian like Lily?"

"Nope," Hawk replied. "I reckon I've spent enough time with 'em to think like one sometimes."

"Tommy," Dora scolded, "let Mr. Hawk eat his supper in peace. Don't bother him with your questions."

Hawk smiled at her. "It's no trouble, ma'am. I don't mind tellin' the boy why I wear the feather in my hat." He turned back to Tommy and said, "It was one powerful cold day up in the Beartooth Mountains . . ." To Tommy's rapt attention, he

243

went on to tell him of a time when he was trying to make his way back to his camp when he was stopped by an avalanche of snow. It was so deep that it blocked his way through the one pass he was familiar with. In the process of trying to find a way around it, he became hopelessly lost. Pushing on, he began to fear he might freeze to death when a red-tailed hawk suddenly appeared to circle over a rocky ledge a short distance off to his right. There didn't seem to be a trail up over the ledge, but somehow he felt the hawk was trying to tell him to follow him. Since he was totally lost and getting colder by the minute, he decided to trust the hawk. "That hawk led me for miles. I'd lose track of him every once in a while, then when I thought I'd just been a fool, he'd pop up again. I followed that hawk all the way around that mountain before he disappeared for good. Well, I kept goin' the way he had been leadin' me till I came to a fork in the trail—one went left, one went right. But there was no hawk to lead me down one or the other. I figured I was lost for good then, but I looked up ahead and saw something lyin' on the snow on the trail to the right. It was one hawk feather, the one I wear in my hat. He was tellin' me which fork to take."

Totally fascinated by then, Tommy asked, "Did it take you back to your camp?"

"Sure did," Hawk said, and glanced up to discover he had captured the attention of the adults as well, especially the women. Lily, who nodded her head solemnly as the tale unwound, was well attuned to dreams and the Salish belief in the closeness between man and the animals. "I reckon we'd best get after this fine supper the ladies have fixed before it gets cold," Hawk concluded.

After supper was finished, Monroe and Thomas wrote a "duty roster" to give to their men, to establish a nightly guard detail. Counting Hawk, who volunteered to take the first night, they had enough men so that each man would be on duty every eight days. "That's not too much to ask," Monroe said, "night-hawking every eight days."

"I reckon, since I've got the first night's watch, I'd best saddle up one of your horses. I think Rascal might need a rest." He got up from the table, picked up his hat, and walked through the kitchen, where the women already had a good start on cleaning up the supper dishes. "That was a really fine supper, ma'am," he said to Dora.

"Well, I'm glad you enjoyed it," Dora replied. "I have to give Rachel and Lily a great deal of the credit, though." He started to leave, then hesitated. She took the opportunity to comment, "That was quite an interesting story about that feather in your hat. It sure kept Tommy quiet for a long time."

Suddenly embarrassed, Hawk replied. "Yes, ma'am." Still lingering, he glanced at Rachel, who smiled at him. Then lowering his voice, he turned back to Dora. "I reckon I owe you an apology," he said, bringing a puzzled expression to her face. "I made up that story as I went along. I figured a youngster Tommy's age would rather hear a little magic about that feather than the fact that I just found it beside a game trail one time when I was huntin'. I thought it was pretty, I reckon. And my name's Hawk, so I stuck it in my hatband and I just never bothered to pull it out."

Dora shook her head slowly, then laughed delightedly. "Mr. Hawk," she chortled. "You surprise me. Do you have children of your own?"

"Oh no, ma'am, I ain't ever been married," he quickly replied.

"Well, you don't look that old to me. You've still got time to find the right girl."

He chuckled at the thought. "I reckon she'd have to love to hunt and fish. Anyway, I thought I oughta tell you I made that story up."

"Don't worry about it," she said. "And don't tell Tommy. You're right, you gave him something special to keep." She watched him until he was out the back door, then turned to Rachel. "He's an interesting man."

"You don't know the half of it," Rachel replied, thinking of that dark night near the Blackfoot River when she first met the man called Hawk and the fight to the death he had with Kills Two Bears.

Hawk threw his saddle on a dark sorrel he selected from the horse herd after a silent apology to Rascal. *Your hide's too light for night-hawkin', anyway,* he thought. As he had told Monroe, he planned to concentrate his time between the two most commonly used paths the cattle had created to the grassy slopes of the Sapphire Mountains. He figured if Barfield had any trouble in mind, he would most likely come down that way. It would be a night when his vigilance was unnecessary, however, for things were not going well at Barfield's cabin.

"What did you do to it?" Lorena demanded. "You musta got some dirt or something in it for it to get so red and swollen."

"I didn't do nothin' to it," Jake rasped painfully. "You're the one done all the diggin' around in it."

"I dug the bullet outta Clint's shoulder, too," Lorena insisted, "and his wound don't look like yours. You musta rubbed something in it."

"What are you two bellyachin' about?" Barfield asked.

"Ah, it's ol' crybaby here," Lorena answered. "He's gone and got that bullet hole infected." She reached over and felt Jake's forehead. "He's got a fever, too. He's burnin' up. We're gonna have to get him to a doctor."

"A doctor?" Barfield responded. "There ain't no doctor around here. He's just gonna have to hold on till the fever leaves him." It was bad enough that both sons were hampered with shoulder wounds, enough to discourage him from retaliation against the Triple-P right away. And now this. He bent over Jake and examined him closely. Lorena was right, her brother was not looking good.

Lorena took another look at the inflamed wound. "He's gonna have to die to get better," she opined callously. "I bet there's a doctor in Stevensville. They oughta be gettin' big enough to have a doctor."

"Hell, that's on the other side of the mountains in the Bitterroot Valley," Barfield complained. He took another look at Jake. "I ain't sure he could stay on a horse that long."

"I ain't sure I can even get on a horse right now," Jake muttered, his voice weaker still. "Just let me lie here awhile."

Almost a spectator until then, Pearl Barfield knelt down beside her son. She held a basin, filled with water from the stream, which she set on the floor beside him. Then she took a cloth from the basin, wrung the water out of it, and placed it across Jake's forehead. "This'll help you cool down some," she said.

"We'll see if his fever breaks in the mornin'," her husband decided. "If it don't, then maybe we'll see about haulin' him over to find a doctor."

The decision upset Pearl. Never one to question

her husband before, she felt she was compelled to plead for her youngest. "Randolph," she implored, "he's in a bad way. What if he gets worse tonight? We need to take him right away."

"You talk like a crazy woman," Barfield replied. "Hell, it ain't long before dark now. We'd play hell tryin' to find our way through those mountains in the dark. Nah, you heard what I said, he'll be better in the mornin'. He ain't got nothin' but a shoulder wound. Most men walk around with a shoulder wound like it never happened. Hell, look at Clint. Jake'll be all right after he gives it a little time."

"You hear that, Jake?" Lorena taunted. "We're gonna decide what to do with you in the mornin'. Either you're gonna get better, or we're gonna dig a hole in the ground and bury you. Or we could take you to that little gully on the south end of the mountains. They probably got room for one more. So I reckon you'd best start gettin' better." She thumped him on the head, causing him to groan. She seemed to find humor in his reaction.

Her japing wasn't appreciated by her father and he was quick to let her know. "Damn it, Lorena," he cursed, "I've told you to keep your mouth shut about that gully. Next time, I'm gonna slam you in the mouth with the butt of this rifle." She responded with a taunting cackle. The gully he referred to held the tattered remains of five innocent souls who had had the misfortune of having a cabin in a remote valley right at the time Barfield needed one to start up his ranch. His only regret was how small the herd of cattle was the man had acquired. *Henson,* he tried to recall, *I think his name was Henson.*

Two nights had passed since the confrontation with Randolph Barfield with no sign of any attempt to retaliate against the family or the ranch hands of the Triple-P. There were also no cows missing. It was too soon to assume it was the end of the trouble with Barfield, so the nightly posting of a guard continued. It was natural to think that Barfield couldn't risk any kind of attack against the Triple-P, however, for the simple reason he had no one to back him but two sons, and both of them were wounded. For Hawk, it was a slow time, even though he tried to make himself useful. He had just finished splitting some firewood for Lily's stove when Monroe came out of the barn looking for him. "You ever been to Stevensville?" Monroe asked.

"Nope, can't say as I have," Hawk answered. "Where is it?"

"About four miles south of here. Thought you might want to see it."

"I reckon I wouldn't mind," Hawk allowed, since he had no serious responsibilities at the ranch that would prevent him from going.

"Good," Monroe said. "Pete's taking Dora into town to pick up some supplies. Rachel wants to go with her. Pete's a good man, but I'd feel better if you went with them."

"Well, all right." Hawk shrugged. "I reckon I could handle that," he said, although he was beginning to get the feeling that Monroe was starting to use him as a hired gunman. He didn't see himself in that role and he wondered if it had been a mistake to come to the Triple-P. He was a scout, a tracker, and a hunter. He had no desire to be anything else. He could not in good conscience run out on the Pratts until this conflict with Randolph Barfield was put to rest, however. He was in it too deep, considering he was the one who shot the two sons. *At least I'm drawing pay for hanging around,* he thought.

Further speculation along those lines was interrupted when Pete came from behind the barn, driving the wagon. "Boss said you're goin' with me," Pete said as he pulled the wagon up to a stop.

"Looks that way," Hawk replied.

"You ridin' with me in the wagon, or on a horse?" Pete asked.

"On a horse. Rascal's gettin' lazy just standin' around doin' nothin'. He might get to expectin' it all the time."

"All right, then, I'll drive on up to the house to fetch the ladies while you saddle your horse." He gave the horses a gentle slap across their croups with his reins and headed for the front porch.

By the time Hawk saddled Rascal and rode up from the barn, Pete was already helping the two women into the wagon. Dora seated herself on the wagon seat and brought a pillow to fashion a seat for Rachel behind her in the wagon bed. "I was wondering if we were going to have to help you get ready to go," Dora teased when Hawk rode up. "It's usually the women who are the slowpokes about that."

After this short time, Hawk was already aware of Dora's fondness for japing, so he responded in kind. "It took a little time to persuade Rascal to go. He thinks women are bad luck."

Dora threw her head back and laughed, delighted that a man who looked so rugged and somber could still have a sense of humor. Sometimes she wished that Monroe or Thomas could waver slightly from their humorless poses. Then she had to remind herself that these were not humorous times, what with Jamie's death and cattle trouble with the Barfields. The thought of Jamie caused her to glance at Rachel. Such a delicate little woman, Dora wondered if she would ever recover from seeing her husband murdered right before her eyes. She knew it would be a while yet, for she had heard her crying in her room at night. A woman like Rachel should be thinking about marrying again. She was still young enough if she didn't wait too much longer. *There's precious little chance she'll meet another man as long as she's on this ranch,* she told herself. She thought then about Monroe, considered that as a possibility, then decided he might be closer to a father than a beau. There was not that much difference as far as actual number of years. But responsibility had aged Monroe since he had been obliged to take over as the head of the family with the death of his father. Having a wife might be what he needed to take some of the stiffness out of his personality. He was always so serious. It wouldn't hurt him to smile once in a while. *It isn't my concern,* she finally told herself, and dismissed it from her thoughts.

Stevensville was a town still in the early stages of growth and didn't distinguish itself from a hundred other little developments Hawk had seen. There was a general store, a post office, a stable, a barbershop, a saloon, and several other small enterprises that included a rooming house and a doctor. Pete's eyes wandered quite naturally toward the saloon as he drove the wagon past, causing Dora to comment, "Just keep your eyes on the general store, Pete. And if we get finished with our list of supplies in good time, maybe we'll take a few minutes for you two to have one drink."

"Yes, ma'am," Pete replied obediently.

Dora looked over at Hawk, riding right beside her. "I know that's what Pete has been thinking about all the way from the ranch. I expect you're no different."

Hawk responded with a patient smile. "I enjoy a little drink once in a while. I hadn't thought much about it today, though." His response jogged her memory and she recalled then that Monroe had made a comment that Hawk was not much of a drinker. *That's probably one reason he wanted Hawk to accompany us to town,* she told herself.

Dora went about the buying of supplies in a businesslike manner, calling off her list and directing Pete and Hawk in carrying her purchases to the wagon. She took time to help Rachel pick out some dress material, however, since the young widow sorely needed clothes. All finished, she told Pete to have that drink he desired while she and Rachel looked at some ladies' shoes that Louise, the store owner's wife, wanted to show them. As the men started out, Dora pulled Hawk aside and whispered, "Make sure he doesn't have more than two drinks, or we might end up hauling him home in the back of the wagon." He nodded and followed Pete out the door. He didn't bother to tell her that Monroe had told him the same thing just as they were leaving the ranch.

"Why on earth did you wait so long to bring him in?" Dr. Garland Smollet scolded. "That whole arm is infected—looks like gangrene is already setting in. I swear, I can't understand why it hasn't spread to his heart. It's just a matter of time. If you'd have brought him in sooner, I could have stopped it. Maybe we can still stop it, but I'm gonna have to take his arm off to do it." Smollet knew what he was talking about, having amputated more limbs than he could remember during the war. He was a young surgeon then, and it had been many years ago, but he still recognized the deadly signs when he saw them.

"Hah," Lorena snorted, "Jake ain't gonna like that too much. I coulda brought him in sooner, but we thought he'd get better. His brother got shot, too—in the shoulder, just like Jake. And he's walkin' around just fine. We thought Jake would, too." She shrugged indifferently. "I reckon you've gotta do what you've gotta do. How long will it take you to cut his arm off? I'd like to get back to the house before dark."

Amazed by the woman's callous attitude regarding the amputation of her brother's arm, Dr. Smollet could only stare, speechless for a moment before explaining. "This is a lengthy operation to remove his arm—hours, at least. You're going to have to leave him here for a while after the operation, too, so I can watch the progress of his recovery."

This was unwelcome news to Lorena. It meant she would likely have to make another trip to town to pick Jake up. It also meant Jake's treatment was going to cost more than her father expected. He might want to take his chances that Jake would recover on his own and keep his arm, too. "What the hell . . ." She shrugged. "Do what you think best."

"All right," Smollet said, "but you might as well not come back until day after tomorrow. He's gonna take a little time to recover." He knew it was going to take Jake longer than that to recover, but he figured he could be moved day after tomorrow without too much risk. "My fee for amputating an arm is usually one hundred and twenty-five dollars." He paused when she cocked her head back at that. "But seeing as how it's your brother, I'll do the job for seventy-five."

She didn't reply right away, instead gracing him with a knowing smile. "Seventy-five, huh? I'll see if we can scrape up that much. We might have to let you hold him for a while till we raise the money." She walked over to the examining table to take a look at Jake before leaving him in the doctor's care. He looked in a bad way, lying there with his eyes closed and his arm all blue and bloated. She poked him in the side, causing him to grunt painfully, just to make sure he was still alive. If he wasn't, she didn't want the doctor to tell her Jake died after a day or more of doctoring and wanted to charge her for it.

Well, I reckon I can go on back home, she thought when she left the doctor's office and walked back down the walk to the hitching rail. She hesitated a moment while she decided whether or not she desired a drink of whiskey. It was a treat she never got at home, because her father thought drinking was a man's right and not a woman's. Anytime she felt she wanted a drink at home, she had to sneak it out of the cupboard and pour a little water back in the bottle. After climbing up into the saddle, she took a look at the saloon and decided. "What the hell?" Leading the horse that Jake had somehow managed to stay on, she headed for the saloon only to stop before she got there, all thoughts of a drink forgotten. *It's him!*

The man with the feather! The man she had seen from the window of the cabin was walking with another man. They were coming from the general store. Frozen stone-still in the middle of the street, she stared, hardly believing her eyes. Taking no notice of the woman on a horse, standing motionless in the street, the man with the feather and his friend walked into the saloon. As soon as Hawk disappeared through the saloon door, Lorena recovered from the shock of seeing the man responsible for wounding her brothers.

"That son of a bitch," she muttered, and nudged her horse forward. A whirlpool of confusion spun around in her brain as she tried to decide what to do. Her initial inclination was simply to walk into the saloon and shoot him down, but she had to consider the potential consequences of such a move. Stevensville had a sheriff, also there was another man with Hawk, who might be a problem. Lorena, by nature, was not one to sacrifice her life to avenge an attack on her brothers. But also by nature, she was not willing to let a man's attack against her family go unpunished. Still undecided, she continued on to the saloon and tied her horses to the rail while she thought about it. One thing she was certain of was that she was going to take a good look at this man with the rifle and the feather. She was strangely drawn to see him up close and it occurred to her that she could approach him without fear. She had seen him that morning at the cabin, but he had not seen her and likely did not know of her existence. That thought brought a devious smile to her face, for she realized the advantage it gave her.

Taking a quick moment to untie the cord holding her hair back from her face, she let it drop around her shoulders. With no comb or brush, the best she could do was to run her fingers through it and pinch her cheeks for a little color in her face. *Hell,* she thought, *too bad I ain't wearing a dress.* She dismissed the thought as quickly as it occurred. *I ain't no beauty, but I ain't hog's-ass ugly, either.* Ready to go then, she hesitated to decide whether or not to pull the rifle out of Jake's saddle sling. Whatever surprise she might have for the man with the feather would surely be compromised if she walked in carrying a rifle. She thought of the .44 Colt in Jake's saddlebag and decided that was her best bet. But it would be better if she could hide it some way. So she took the small canvas bag hooked over her saddle horn and dropped the weapon in it. Satisfied that she had options, she walked into the saloon, confident that she would know what to do if an opportunity presented itself. She couldn't help thinking of the satisfaction she would enjoy if she was the one who put the Pratts' hired gunman in the ground. *That would be hard for Pa and the boys to swallow,* she thought.

Hawk and Pete stood at the bar, talking to Ed Wiggins, the bartender, while he poured them another shot of whiskey. Pete picked up his glass and downed it while Hawk let his sit for a while. As was his custom, he planned to drink no more than two shots, and if Pete decided to have a third, he intended to cut him off there because he didn't want to have to drive the wagon back to the ranch. While Pete became engrossed in a conversation with Ed about the recent passage through the valley by the Nez Perce, Hawk turned to gaze over the half-filled barroom. At that moment, several heads were turned toward the door when a young woman walked in. She created a natural curiosity since she was not dressed like one of the usual "painted ladies" who usually worked in saloons. She was wearing pants. Hawk gave her a few moments' scrutiny, the same as he would for a deer or a man, then shifted his gaze to watch reactions of the men seated at the tables before returning his attention back to his glass.

Lorena paused in the doorway to look the room over. It didn't take much searching to spot the man she sought. Standing at the bar, he stood as tall as a pine. She would have recognized him even without the buckskin shirt and the feather. Walking as casually as she could affect, she strolled over to the end of the bar close to Hawk, who only glanced in her direction. Ed interrupted his conversation with Pete and walked down the bar to serve her. "Can I help you, miss?"

"I think I'd like a drink of whatever this gentleman is drinkin'," she replied, giving Hawk a smiling nod.

"Ma'am, that's straight corn whiskey he's got there," Ed said. "Are you sure that's what you want?"

"Unless you got something stronger," she came back brashly, and thought it would be an ironic occurrence to have a drink with a man she was about to kill, for she had already discarded the precautions she had concerned herself with before. It was too great an opportunity to let pass, one she could crow about to the boys. "Make it a double," she said, intent upon remembering every move leading up to the assassination she had in mind. The more time she hesitated, the more details she would be able to tell her family.

"Yes, ma'am," Ed replied politely, and produced a glass from under the bar.

"Give my friend, here, another shot, too," she said, smiling up at Hawk, realizing at that point how much she had to crane her neck to address him.

Getting Hawk's full attention then, she looked him boldly in the eye when he turned toward her. "That's mighty nice of you, miss, but I'll just settle for this one Ed already poured. I'll be glad to drink with you, though." He picked up his glass, waiting for her to shift her canvas bag over to her left hand.

Pete tossed his third drink back, then turned to see who Hawk had engaged in conversation. Busy talking to the bartender before, it was the first real notice he had taken of the woman since she had come in. Like the other customers, his curiosity was aroused when he saw her, dressed as she was, as out of place as could be, yet there was something familiar about her. Then it struck him. "You're Randolph Barfield's daughter!" he blurted, remembering that he had seen her with her father at Skinner's Trading Post.

The seductive smile turned immediately to an angry grimace as Lorena thrust her hand into her bag to grasp the Colt she carried there. Hawk's reactions were swift. He clamped his hand around the bag, trapping her hand inside before she could cock the pistol. Frantic in her anger, she struck out at his face with her free hand, but he caught her wrist before she could land the blow. "Damn you!" she screamed, and tried to free herself, but she was helpless against his strength.

In spite of her kicking and cursing, he easily dragged her over to a table by the door and sat her down in a chair. "You got any rope back there?" Hawk called out to Ed. Ed responded that he sure did and hurried to the back room to fetch it. All the while, Hawk endured a steady stream of insults, threats, and curses, to which he made no response. "That'll do just fine," he said when Ed returned with a coil of rope. "Pete, take a couple of quick loops around Miss Barfield's ankles and tie 'em to the chair." Once Pete had done that, Hawk said, "Now, hold on to this arm while I get a hold on that gun she's got in that bag." With both hands free, he was able to wrest the pistol from her hand. He held it up briefly to inspect it before shoving it in his belt. Then he pulled her arms back and held them while Pete tied them to the back of the chair. Once she was secured to the chair, Hawk was inspired to say, "Well, it surely is nice to meet you, Miss Barfield. I must say you're every bit as nice as the menfolk in your family."

"You go to hell," she spat back at him.

"In due time," he replied. "I'd love to stay and get to know you better," Hawk went on, "but I've got to get on back to the Triple-P. Ain't that right, Pete?" He looked at Ed, who was an amused spectator during the confrontation. "Is that sheriff in his office, you reckon?"

"Hell, he ain't never no place else," Ed answered. "Want me to send somebody over there to get him?" When Hawk said he would appreciate it, Ed got one of his regular customers to go for Sheriff Barney Mack.

When the sheriff arrived, he was not quite sure what his proper course of action should be until Hawk explained what had just happened. "Sheriff, Pete and I are from the Triple-P, just came to town to get some supplies. I expect the two ladies with us are most likely waitin' for us in the wagon right now. Now, any of these folks here can tell you what happened. The fact of the matter is this young woman decided she'd come in the saloon, here, and shoot me. I ain't blamin' her for it, she wouldn't be the first to try it. So I ain't interested in makin' any charges against her. All I'm askin' is for you to hold her in your jail for a few hours to give us a head start, so we can get the ladies back to the ranch without worryin' about this one takin' a shot at us. Fair enough?"

Sheriff Mack was at a loss. He wasn't sure if a crime had been committed or not, and if it had, who committed it and what he should do about it. He was still thinking of his reply when Ed commented, "It was like he said, Barney. He didn't do nothin' but try to have a drink in peace."

"There, you see," Hawk said. "So if you'll just accommodate the lady for a while, I'd be much obliged. Come on, Pete." Before he herded Pete out the door, he bent close to Lorena and whispered, "The next time you come after me, I'll shoot you down like the ornery bitch you are." Too angry to form the words to describe her hatred for the way she had been trussed up so easily, she was struck mute until he had gone through the door. Then she hurled insults and threats after him that left the men still sitting there feeling inadequate in their knowledge of foul language.

Outside, Hawk and Pete walked down the street toward the general store just in time to see Dora and Rachel coming out the door. They both carried packages of some kind. "Looks like they found some shoes they like," Pete commented. "Wait'll I tell 'em about that Barfield woman."

"Maybe it wouldn't be a good idea to tell 'em what happened back there," Hawk said, "at least till we get 'em back home safely. They might get upset if they think there's a chance that wildcat will be comin' after us. I don't know if we can trust that sheriff or not. He looked to me like he didn't know what to do."

They were soon under way, with Pete calling for the horses to pull hard. He was anxious to get back before supper, eager to tell the rest of the crew they had met Lorena Barfield. When they arrived at the Triple-P, Pete drove the wagon to the kitchen door. He jumped down and assisted Dora down and then Rachel. Hardly had Rachel's foot struck the ground when Pete blurted, "We run into the Barfield girl in the saloon and she tried to shoot Hawk. We tied her to a chair in the saloon." His statement left both women astonished. He then excitedly re-created the entire scene for the benefit of the ladies, including Lily, who came outside to help unload the supplies. Before he finished, Thomas walked up from the barn and Pete gladly told the story once more. Since Pete was occupied, Hawk volunteered to unhitch the wagon and take the horses to water. When he returned they had moved to the porch and Pete was still talking about the incident at the saloon. Hawk was surprised to see another person who had joined Pete's audience. He knew at once who she was, even though it was the first time he had seen the old lady. In fact, he had just about come to believe that Miss Emily didn't exist, that she was actually a legend everyone referred to, but was never seen outside her room.

"Hawk," Dora said, "come up on the porch and meet Tommy's grandma."

He went up the steps and walked over near the front door, where the old woman was sitting in a wheelchair. Gray and fragile, she was bundled in a blanket even though the afternoon sun was still shining hot on the porch. Moving slowly, seemingly with great effort, she held out her hand to him. He was at once gentle when he took it, as if holding a tiny animal, being careful not to crush it. "How do, ma'am?" he asked respectfully.

She continued to hold his hand, meeting his gaze with eyes milky and gray. "Mr. Hawk, is it?" Her voice, though weak, was steady.

"Yes, ma'am," he replied.

Still she held his hand. "You have no parents." It was not a question.

Astonished, he responded, "No, ma'am. How'd you know that?"

She didn't answer his question. "Hawk is a good name for you," she said. "You have seen many evil things, but you are a good man. Thank you for helping my family." She withdrew her hand then and looked at Lily, who was standing beside her chair, and nodded. Needing no verbal instructions, Lily immediately stepped behind the wheelchair and wheeled the old lady back inside the house.

Totally at a loss, Hawk stood there staring after her. When he turned away from the door, he was to find Dora watching him, an impish grin plastered upon her face. "Well," she said, "now you've met Miss Emily and looks like you've met with her approval."

"I reckon," Hawk said. "I'm mighty glad I did." The meeting with the old lady was very much like meeting with a Blackfoot or Crow medicine man.

While Pete had made it his business to tell everybody at the Triple-P about the incident in town, four miles away Sheriff Barney Mack returned to the saloon to check on his prisoner. Having had no desire to untie Lorena from the chair that held her secure, he had opted to leave her in the saloon until he deemed it time enough to release her. It was certainly an easier choice than transporting her to the jail. The fierce expression in her eyes had convinced the sheriff that she may have been too much to handle if set free of the chair. Ed Wiggins had voiced no complaints about leaving Lorena in his saloon for an hour or more. In fact, he welcomed it. She provided an attraction that brought more customers in and sold more whiskey to those already drinking.

As for the now-silent woman sitting with hands and feet bound, while a grinning gaggle of men stared at her, Lorena stewed in the humiliation she now endured. Hawk was the name his friend had called him and it was now a name burned deeply into her brain. Thoughts of her brother Jake, his arm awaiting the surgeon's saw, had long since left her mind. The foul jokes at her expense, loudly passed among the saloon customers, had no bearing, either. The only thing there was room for was the vow to take her revenge on the man responsible for her predicament. If she never accomplished another vow in her life, she swore to bring this hawk to earth. She was only partially distracted from these thoughts when Sheriff Mack approached her.

"I reckon I'm gonna let you go now," he said. "That is, if you'll behave yourself," he added. "'Cause, if you don't, I'll lock you up in the jail. I've got cause to do that, anyway, seein' as how you was goin' after this gun you were totin' in your sack." He held the Colt .44 up for her to see. "Since that feller said he wasn't makin' no charges against you, I'm gonna return your gun and let you go. I took the bullets out of it, just in case you took any crazy notions. You understand?"

Her steady, unblinking gaze locked on Mack's eyes while he spoke, and in response to his question, she only nodded slowly. She sat still while he untied her ankles and gave no indication of hearing him when he warned her again to behave before untying her wrists. As soon as she was free, she moved very deliberately, taking her pistol from him and dropping it in her canvas bag. The barroom, loud and noisy moments before, was now deadly silent as she took her time straightening out her blouse and tucking her shirttail in. The noisy din of the saloon returned as soon as she walked out the door. "Damned if that ain't the scariest woman I've ever seen," Mack said to Ed. "Pour me a drink of that whiskey."

Outside, Lorena went to the end of the hitching rail where she had left her horse, her heart filled with a hatred she had never before experienced and her mind set on killing the man called Hawk. There were half a dozen other horses tied up at the rail, and in a small act of retaliation, she untied them all and shooed them away. When they refused to scatter, she pulled the rifle from Jake's saddle and fired it into the air. Satisfied to see them bolt in several directions, she gave her horse her heels and was already at the end of the street when the sheriff and Ed's customers poured out of the saloon.

CHAPTER 12

During the next few days, Hawk's job for the Triple-P was exclusively that of a scout, since that was what he was good at. After Monroe and Thomas talked it over, they decided that it might be a good idea to let Barfield know they were keeping an eye on his activities. So Hawk agreed to let himself be seen at the top of the mountain overlooking the cabin once or twice a day and that's what he did. Never at the same time of day, and always just out of reasonable rifle range. It was hoped that the constant surveillance would prompt Barfield to move away from the valley. Hawk began a more intense scout of the valley Barfield had claimed as his range to find out approximately how many head of cattle he was actually grazing. What herd he had was scattered in small- and medium-sized bunches, left to wander at will. It was obvious that Barfield had no hands to work even a small outfit. Hawk estimated a herd of close to two hundred cattle. He couldn't imagine what the man had in mind to do. His guess was that he would eventually abandon the cattle and move on. *Till he does,* Hawk thought, *I'll keep an eye on him. Then maybe I can leave this valley and say good-bye to working cattle.*

• • •

"Look at him up there by that lonesome pine," Clint Barfield spat when he walked inside the cabin, "actin' like he owns that damn mountain."

"He's tryin' to draw us outta here, get us to come up there after him," his father said. "Most likely has a dozen men waitin' to pick us off like crows on a fence."

"What are we gonna do about it?" Lorena demanded. "Set here like a bunch of rats in a hole? I say, if he's tryin' to draw us out, then let's do what he's askin' for and go up there and kill the son of a bitch."

Her mother gazed at her, worried. Something had happened to her daughter ever since she took Jake in to see the doctor. She had always had a cynical streak in her, but it had usually been laced with a generous portion of sass and sarcasm. Now she seemed to have fallen into a cold, vengeful mood that constantly pushed for retaliation against the Pratts and their hired hands. This in spite of the advantage Pratt had in numbers as well as the obvious disadvantage of having both her brothers hampered by wounds. Randolph had taken the wagon in to Stevensville that very morning to bring Jake home, without his arm, and still so sick he could barely sit up. She could not understand how her daughter could keep pushing her father to go up against such odds. Lorena's agitated state seemed to have arisen after that trip

271

to town. Thinking that had something to do with her sullen mood, Pearl walked over to the table and placed her hand on her daughter's shoulder. Lorena flinched as if she had been touched with a poker.

"Goodness sakes, honey," Pearl exclaimed. "You're jumpy as a frog on a hot skillet. What's the matter with you?"

"What's the matter with me?" Lorena repeated sarcastically. "The same thing that oughta be the matter with you . . . and Pa . . . and Clint. That son of a bitch settin' up on that mountain laughin' at us. That's what's the matter with me."

Pearl recoiled slightly. Lorena never used that tone of voice on her as a rule, on her brothers often, but not on her. Again, her mother connected Lorena's hostile disposition to the trip into Stevensville. "Something happened to you in town," she said, "something you ain't told us about."

"Ha!" Lorena cried out defiantly. "Nothing happens to me unless I want it to!" She couldn't bear the thought of their finding out how badly she had been humiliated. There was no concern that the men in her family might endanger themselves in an attempt to avenge her. The only way she could feel satisfaction would be to put a bullet into the heart of the arrogant gunman with the stupid feather in his hat—the man called Hawk.

Pearl was about to try to comfort her daughter again when Randolph Barfield interrupted, having heard enough of his daughter's harping on the lack of aggression on the part of the men in the family. "Shut the hell up, Lorena! I'm tired of hearin' your bellyachin' about goin' after that feller Hawk. Damn you, you don't care if the rest of us gets killed, do ya? He ain't out there all by himself. He's just wantin' us to think he is, so we'll do some damn fool thing like you're talkin' about. Then I reckon they'd finish off what they started. Hell, Clint can't use both arms yet, and one look at Jake layin' on the floor in there and you can tell he might not make it till mornin'. So that just leaves me, and I ain't that damn dumb." He looked at his wife. "Mama, I reckon I know when we ain't got no chance a-tall. We're leavin' this valley, tomorrow, if Jake ain't too sick to travel. We can't fight that gang ridin' for Pratt."

There was a long silence after he made his announcement with his daughter the only one not relieved to hear his decision. He looked back at Lorena and said, "I know what's eatin' at your gizzard. That bartender in the saloon told me you had a little run-in with the one they call Hawk. He was right polite about it. Told me he hoped you got home all right after being tied to a chair in the saloon for a couple of hours. I ain't never been so ashamed in my life . . ." He paused and shook his head. "I wasn't gonna tell

273

nobody about it, but you can't shut your mouth about what we oughta be doin'." An even longer silence followed that, until Lorena stormed out of the cabin without a word.

It was her brother Clint who first broke the silence. "Damn," he exclaimed with a chuckle of amusement. "Ol' Lorena, she sure stuck her foot in her mouth that time." He laughed again. "I gotta go tell Jake about this."

"I meant what I said about leavin' this place," Randolph said to him. "Tell him he needs to be gettin' fit enough to ride."

Outside, Lorena stormed over to the corner of the corral that offered the best place to see the tall pine that stood apart from the rest of the trees at the top of the mountain. Whenever they spotted Hawk, it was usually by this tree. She peered up at the tree and, as happened on days before, he was there, watching. Even in the fading light of sunset, she could see him and the sight of him caused her to clench her fists tightly. Having heard her father's announcement of his decision to leave, she wanted to cry out in anguish. Instead, she made a decision of her own, one she felt might rally her retreating family to stand up against the Pratts, instead of running away. This, she told herself, was the main reason she was going to do what she had decided to, when in fact it was strictly personal. The man called Hawk was the first person she had ever truly, genuinely hated. Before her encounter with him, she had no use for any man—was contemptuous of most of them, including the men in her own family, but never let any of them get into her head the way this smug man with the feather had. He seemed to be the ultimate warrior, undefeatable, and she could not know peace until she stood over his bloody body. She could still see him, waiting in the fading light as she continued to peer up at the mountaintop. "Wait for me," she whispered, then turned away.

Deciding it best not to tell anyone in the cabin, she quickly saddled Jake's horse, checking to see if his rifle was still in the saddle scabbard. It was, giving her another opportunity to be critical of her brother's careless ways. *If somebody rides in here tonight to run us out, you'd be a helluva lotta good with your rifle out here,* she thought, forgetting his near-death condition. Thinking of all three men of her family, she told herself, *When I'm through tonight, you'll have to fight.* She led the horse around the cabin, where she wouldn't be seen from above, before climbing up into the saddle and riding away.

Without regard for sparing her horse, she rode a wide arc around the foot of the mountain, so she could climb up behind the lone pine at the top. With still enough light to see, she made her way up a narrow ravine that would take her to the mountaintop a comfortable distance from the spot where her target lingered. To make sure she was not spotted before she was in position to take the shot, she dismounted before reaching the top and climbed the rest of the way on foot. With her rifle cocked and ready, she came up out of the ravine no more than fifty yards from the solitary pine only to find Hawk no longer there. *Damn!* She cursed under her breath and looked quickly around her in case he had somehow detected her approaching behind him, but there was no sign of man or horse. He was gone. It could have been no more than a few minutes, she told herself. He had no doubt given up his vigil for the day and was heading back to the Triple-P. Another thought struck her then and she would be sure to tell her father there was no gang of Triple-P men set to ambush her.

With no thoughts of giving up on her plan, she hurried back to her horse to give chase. There was more than one trail down the western slope of the mountain, but betting that he was on his way back to the ranch, she picked the most direct one and hoped to catch up with him before he reached home. With that in mind, she guided her horse down the slope as darkness began to descend upon the trail, being careful not to become reckless in her effort to catch up with Hawk. It might be disastrous if he became aware of being followed and she rode into an ambush. As the darkness became deeper, she was forced to slow her pace for fear she would overtake him unexpectedly and consequently alert him to defend himself. This would not do, for she wanted him to have no warning.

She began to feel moments of panic when at last she reached the floor of the Bitterroot Valley with still no sign of the man she followed. He couldn't be that far ahead of her, she thought. Maybe he had taken another trail. She nudged her horse to pick up her pace as she began to encounter small groups of cattle and knew she was on Triple-P range now, but she was not concerned under the cover of darkness. She had never been to the Pratt ranch before, but she knew she could not be very far away at this point. Suddenly she saw him! A dark figure of a man on a horse, it could only be the man she followed. But she was not yet close enough to be sure of her shot. She kicked her horse into a lope and immediately began to reduce the distance between them, but reined the horse back to a full stop when the man she followed suddenly stopped and turned to face her. "Is that you, Pete?" he called out.

Knowing this was likely her only chance, she drew her rifle and brought it to her shoulder, trying to steady it while her horse settled down. As soon as the horse became still, she squeezed the trigger, feeling an instant elation when her target sagged to one side before sliding to the ground. A moment later, she was knocked from the saddle when a .44 slug slammed into her back, leaving her senseless as she lay stunned on the ground. The bawling of the frightened cattle dulled rapidly in her ears until all sound went away completely. She closed her eyes, barely feeling the hand on her shoulder.

"You!" Hawk exclaimed when he rolled her over, hardly able to believe it was Barfield's daughter. Her eyes fluttered open briefly, only long enough to see who had killed her. With one painful moan of frustration, she released her final breath. "Damn it," he complained. "I told you this would happen if you came after me again." He truly had no idea who had been following him. He assumed it was Barfield, himself, or one of the sons. And while he didn't like the idea of killing a woman, he told himself it was no different from killing a female rattlesnake if one comes after you. He got up then and went to check on Marvin Tatum, who had been unfortunate to have been riding nighthawk. Luckily, he had escaped with a wound in his side and the bullet had gone straight through.

"Damn, Hawk," Marvin gasped painfully when he recognized him, "what'd you shoot me for?"

"I didn't shoot you," Hawk answered. "I shot the one who did, though." He couldn't help feeling responsible for Marvin's wound, however. He had become aware of someone on a horse coming on behind him when he was still only halfway down the mountain. He was thinking now that he should have set up a trap for the rider instead of pulling off the trail to let him pass. But he had wanted to see how far the rider would go and what he would do when he got to the ranch. It still bothered him a little that he had killed a woman, even though he had no choice. He couldn't have afforded the shooter time to put another round into poor Marvin. When he had warned Lorena that he would shoot her next time, he really only meant it to scare her. The question now was, what was going to happen when Barfield found out he shot his daughter? *Have to deal with that later,* he thought. "Right now, we'd best get you back to take a look at that hole in your side," he said to Marvin. "Think you can ride?"

"Yeah, I can ride," Marvin said. "I only slid off my horse so they wouldn't shoot again. It's painin' me right smart, but I can stay on my horse." He stopped to think then. "Who did shoot me?" When told who the shooter was and the circumstances that led up to it, he was amazed. "The daughter, I swear . . ."

After helping Marvin up into the saddle, Hawk went back to make sure Lorena was dead. Then he picked up her body and laid it across her saddle, intending to take it on in to the ranch to decide how to handle the business of notifying Randolph Barfield.

Since the scene of the shooting was only three quarters of a mile from the ranch house, the shots fired were clearly heard by the folks there. Consequently, Monroe and a couple of the men were in the process of saddling up, intent upon investigating when Hawk and Marvin Tatum arrived. At once concerned, when he saw the body lying across the saddle of the horse Hawk led, Monroe immediately asked, "Who is that?"

"The Barfield girl," Hawk replied. "We'd best take care of Marvin. He's got a hole in his side." Bob Boston and Pete Little, who were standing with Monroe, moved quickly to help Marvin off his horse. They hesitated for a few moments, however, eager to hear the circumstances that caused the wound, as well as being curious about the presence of Lorena's body. "She followed me down the mountain, but in the dark she thought Marvin was me, I reckon, and she shot him. So I shot her. Now, you'd best take Marvin into the bunkhouse before he bleeds to death." Thomas Pratt came from the house to join them in time to hear Hawk's explanation.

Even in the dark, he could see the frown of concern deepen on Monroe's face, so Hawk could well guess what was going through his mind. What would be the results of this when Barfield found out that his daughter had been killed? "I don't know," Hawk said before Monroe asked the question. "She was tailin' me ever since I came down the mountain, so I pulled off into some pines to let her pass on by—just thought I'd see what she was up to. It was poor luck for Marvin, though. She came up on him and I reckon she thought she'd caught up with me 'cause she didn't hesitate a second, just raised her rifle and shot him. I couldn't let her throw another shot at him, so I shot her. I didn't know it was a woman till I rolled her over."

Monroe nodded thoughtfully. "Well, I can't fault you for what you did. I don't see as how you had any choice. I'm wondering how we'd best handle it now."

"Well, I was thinkin' that over on the way in and I figured the best thing we could do is to get the sheriff involved in it," Hawk suggested. "It's a little late to do it tonight, but we could take the girl's body into town to the sheriff in the mornin'. Tell him what happened and let him decide what to do about it. We'd take Marvin in to see the doctor, so the sheriff could see that he got shot. Maybe he'll see it his duty to tell Barfield about his daughter."

Monroe considered that for a few moments, looked at his brother, and when Thomas shrugged, said, "I can't think of any better way—makes it look like we were trying to handle it with the law in mind. I don't see as how it's up to us to notify Barfield about it, but we do need to take her body into the sheriff's office and let him handle it. And we're still gonna have to be alert to find out what Barfield will do in retaliation for killing his daughter. Marvin might not be the only one who gets shot." Thomas nodded his agreement.

"Well, I thought about that, too," Hawk said. "I'm thinkin' there's gonna be a damn good chance that Barfield and his sons are gonna be lookin' to take their revenge. And maybe if I take Marvin and the girl into town and tell the sheriff I shot her, then Barfield might just come after me to settle up. That would sure be better than havin' him and his boys hidin' out on your range takin' potshots at your hands every chance they got."

"They'd still be coming on our range looking for you," Thomas said.

"Not if I move on into town," Hawk replied, "and let the sheriff know I ain't out here any-more."

The Pratt brothers looked at each other, obviously preferring that the chance of snipers be removed from their home range. "That's asking you to take all the responsibility for what Barfield might do," Monroe said nonetheless.

"I can't see it as anybody else's responsibility," Hawk said. "I'm the one that shot her." When they hesitated still, he explained his reasoning further. "Look, I'm the one they want. I've already shot both of his sons, so I'm the one he'll come after, and I like my chances better in town than I do out in this open range. Besides, maybe I'll have the sheriff to help me." His logic was sound and they appreciated the fact that he preferred to take any chance of danger away from the Triple-P, so they didn't argue.

"Where's Lorena?" Pearl Barfield asked. It had been some time since her daughter stomped out of the cabin and it was getting along toward bedtime.

Clint laughed. "She was pretty hot. I'll bet she's settin' down there in the barn poutin' 'cause Pa found out about her little business with that Hawk feller. I'll go see about her."

"Tell her I said to get her hind end in here and help your mama clean up them supper dishes still on the table," Randolph said. "She gets her ass up on her shoulders every now and then and don't wanna do a woman's chores."

In a matter of minutes, Clint returned to tell them, "Lorena's gone. She ain't at the barn."

"Musta had to go to the bushes," Randolph said.

"That ain't all," Clint said. "Jake's horse and saddle are gone, too."

At once alarmed, Pearl said, "Clint, you go look for your sister. She ain't been actin' right ever since she went to Stevensville."

"Where, Ma?" Clint replied. "I ain't got no

idea where she mighta run off to, crazy as she is. I could be wanderin' around up in the mountains all night long lookin' for her."

"Clint's right," Randolph said. "She'll come back when she's good and ready. Do her some good to get it outta her system. Then maybe she'll be fit to live with." He got up from the table and headed for the door to get rid of some of the coffee he had consumed at supper before retiring for the night. When Clint followed him outside to perform the same function, Randolph said, "Take a look at Jake before you turn in."

"Yes, sir," Clint responded obediently. They stood side by side at the edge of the cabin's tiny porch while they emptied their bladders. "Reckon how long Lorena's gonna be gone?"

"Hard to say," his father replied. "Till she gets over her little fit, I reckon. She's always had too much of that Beecher blood in her," he said, referring to his wife's father, Leonard Beecher. "That whole family's crazy as hell." When they went back inside, they were met by Pearl, tears streaming down her cheeks. "Now what's the matter?" Randolph asked.

"Jake," she wailed. "He's gone, Jake's gone!"

"Whaddaya mean, gone?" Barfield demanded. "You mean dead?"

"He's dead," she sobbed. "I went in to ask him if he was all right and he didn't answer me."

"Maybe he's asleep," her husband said, and

went by her to see for himself. Clint followed behind him into the bedroom. They found Jake lying cold and still, his eyes staring up at the rafters. "Damn, he's dead all right," Barfield pronounced after laying his ear on Jake's chest to listen for a heartbeat. "And I spent seventy-five dollars for that damn doctor to saw his arm off. I oughta saddle up my horse and go get that doctor outta bed right now—get my seventy-five dollars back."

Pearl stared at her husband, shocked by the callous reaction to her son's death. "Randolph," she gasped, "your son is lyin' dead and you're just interested in the money you spent tryin' to save him? Shame on you, Randolph Barfield."

"Dead is dead," her husband replied. "And there ain't nothin' you can do about that now. You ought not be mad at me. That feller Hawk, that's the one to get mad at. He's the one who shot Jake."

"What are we gonna do, Pa?" Clint wanted to know. "Are we goin' after him?"

Barfield didn't answer at once while he tried to decide just what he could do. "Yeah," he finally said. "We're goin' after him. I ain't about to let anybody get away with killin' my son." It was the reaction he felt he should have, and he would dearly love to have an opportunity to shoot Hawk. But he was sane enough to be aware of the possibility that any attempt on Hawk's life would surely reap dangerous consequences for himself. "There's too many of 'em for us to take on," he said. "We've got to wait till we can catch the son of a bitch by himself. We'll wait till Lorena gets home. She always thinks she's as good as any man. We'll give her a chance to prove it." He turned toward Pearl. "For now, you'd best get Jake ready for buryin' and we'll put him in the ground in the mornin'." She nodded in response, her tears starting anew, tears for the passing of her youngest, but also tears of anger for the casualness of her husband's response to Jake's death. Shifting her gaze to Clint, she also despaired that he reflected the same indifference.

The night passed, but with the first light of morning there was still no sign of Lorena. Her worried mother dragged herself into the kitchen to put a pot of coffee on the stove. Her husband and her son would expect it to be ready for them when they woke up. As for her, she had not slept during the entire night, keeping vigil over her dead son, while his brother snored lustily on a pallet a few feet away. On the other side of the quilt that served as a wall she could hear the rumbling, guttural noises her husband made in his sleep. Combined with Clint's snoring, it reminded her of a bunch of frogs in a pond, singing a chorus of indifference, and she suddenly brought to mind a thought she had often had before. *I curse the day I ever decided to run off with Randolph Barfield.* As before, she shook her head in despair, knowing there was no one to blame but herself. After poking the ashes in the stove around to bring the fire back to life, she went out on the porch to fetch some wood to feed it. Before going back inside, she took a long pause to peer toward the barn and corral, but there was still no sign of Lorena.

Another hour passed before Barfield roused himself from sleep, and as usual, he roused Clint up as well, thinking that if he was out of bed, everyone else should be, too. He took a short look at Jake and muttered, "Still dead, I reckon," before going to the kitchen for his coffee. "Where's Lorena?" he asked Pearl.

"She still ain't come back," his wife answered, never pausing to face him. She cast a glance at Clint as he walked out the door to answer nature's morning call. "I expect you'd best go lookin' for her after you eat your breakfast," she called after him. He returned an unenthusiastic "yes'm" in response.

"After you see 'bout the cattle," his father said.

"We got a grave to dig," Clint reminded him.

"After that, then," Barfield said, even though Clint was already out the door. With no experience in raising cattle, his idea of tending them was merely to see if they were still there. His plan had been to steal enough to accumulate a

287

herd big enough to drive to market, thinking him and his two sons could manage a sizable herd.

Barfield and his son had just finished digging a grave when Clint spotted a rider approaching, leading a horse with what appeared to be a body draped across the saddle. "Who the hell . . . ?" Barfield blurted when Clint pointed toward the mountain path. Both men scrambled out of the hole they had just dug and ran to the barn, where they had left their rifles. Back outside, they waited, weapons ready while the rider continued to ride toward them. "It's that sheriff over in Stevensville," he replied, recognizing the slumped shoulders of Barney Mack. Pearl came out of the barn when she heard that to wait with them for the sheriff to arrive.

When Sheriff Mack reached the edge of the yard, Clint said, "That looks like Jake's sorrel he's leadin'." A few steps closer and they realized what the long bundle lying awkwardly across the saddle had to be. "It is Jake's horse. It's Lorena!"

Pearl's knees started to buckle and she would have collapsed had not Clint been close enough to grab her and lead her over to a stump where he helped her sit down. She immediately began to sway back and forth, moaning in her grief. The impact of seeing her daughter's body across the saddle was too big a burden to bear so shortly after her son's death. His eyes still on the sheriff,

Barfield strode forward to confront him. "Is that my daughter?" Barfield demanded.

"I'm sorry to say it is," the sheriff replied. "She's been shot and I took it on myself to bring her home and tell you folks what happened."

"Who shot her? Was it you?" Barfield demanded, thinking that Lorena must have gone into town to seek revenge for her treatment in the saloon.

"No, sir, I did not," Mack immediately replied. "I just thought I'd do you folks the courtesy of bringin' your daughter home, so you could bury her proper."

"Who shot her?" Barfield repeated. "You ain't said yet who shot her."

"Well, she was brought into town by that feller Hawk this mornin'." As soon as he said the name, he could see the reaction in the eyes of both father and son, so he hurried to explain. "A couple of the Triple-P hands were with him and one of them had been shot, too. They took him to the doctor to treat the bullet wound. It seems your daughter rode over there last night and shot that feller and Hawk shot her to keep her from shootin' again." It was apparent that his explanation did little to quell the anger smoldering in Barfield's eyes. "They said it was so dark there weren't no way to tell that it was a woman doin' the shootin'." That, too, failed to appease the father and son. To make matters worse, at that moment the distraught woman sitting on the stump began wailing mournfully. At a loss for what else he could say, Mack offered one last condolence. "The women at the Triple-P wrapped your daughter up in that sheet, so nobody could gawk at her in town." Pearl wailed louder upon hearing that. "Like I said, I didn't have nothin' to do with the shootin'. I'm just bringin' her home for you." He remembered something else then. "That feller, Hawk, that shot her, he don't work for the Triple-P no more. I think they let him go."

This sparked immediate interest from Barfield. "He ain't at the Triple-P no more? Where is he?"

"I don't know where he's gonna go," Mack said. "He was in town when I left this mornin', but he didn't say where he was thinkin' about goin'." He handed the reins for Jake's horse to Clint and stepped up into the saddle again. "Well, I'd best get back to town to make sure ever'thin's peaceful there. That's my job. I just wanted to take time to bring your daughter home."

"Much obliged," Barfield grumbled reluctantly as the sheriff turned his horse and rode away at a spirited lope. Barfield turned to look at Clint standing there holding the reins. "I reckon we've got another grave to dig. Then I reckon we need to take a little ride to town."

CHAPTER 13

"Whaddaya say, Doc, is he gonna be all right?" Hawk asked when Marvin walked out on the porch with Pete Little and Dr. Smollet right behind him.

"I don't see why not," Smollet said, "as long as he keeps it clean. There wasn't much for me to do. Whoever cleaned him up did a pretty nice job."

"We have to give Lily all the credit for that," Pete said. "She's the doctor when we can't get to you." He took the money Thomas Pratt had given him to pay the doctor's bill and counted out the exact amount. With that taken care of, he asked Hawk, "You sure you don't wanna go on back to the ranch with us?"

"Yeah, I'm sure," Hawk replied. "I'm gonna go see that fellow that owns the stable—what's his name?"

"Clell Blanton," Marvin supplied.

"Right, Blanton," Hawk repeated. "I'm gonna see about puttin' my horse up there for a couple of days and see how much he'll charge me for sleepin' in the stall with him. We'll see what happens when Barfield finds out about his daughter. The sheriff oughta be back this afternoon, then maybe he'll know whether we can look for trouble or not."

"He might tell you to take your trouble outta town," Pete said.

"There's that possibility, I reckon," Hawk allowed. "We'll wait and see. Anyway, you and Marvin keep a sharp eye on your way back to the Triple-P, just in case."

"You can count on that," Pete said. He reached in his pocket and took out a roll of bills. "Doc didn't charge as much as Boss gave me. There's a little left over, enough for a couple of drinks of Ed Wiggins's rotgut—make the ride back a little easier."

Hawk laughed. "One wouldn't hurt, I reckon, but I don't know if Marvin oughta take a drink or not, him being wounded and all."

"I'm willin' to take a chance," Marvin said. "If it starts runnin' out those holes in my side, I'll ease up a bit."

Ed Wiggins greeted the three men cheerfully when they walked into the Valley House Saloon, a fancy name for a common saloon, as Pete had commented. Ed was ready with the bottle and glasses, but was disappointed to learn that they planned for no more than a quick drink before departing. "Sheriff Mack told me a man could get a decent supper here," Hawk said to Ed.

"Sure can," Ed replied. "The sheriff takes supper here most every night. We've got a dandy cook, Ruthie. She used to be a cook in Bozeman before some woman came along and opened a diner in the hotel."

Hawk nodded, thinking that would be Sadie's Diner. "I think I've ate there before. I'll most likely be back later to give Ruthie a try."

After one more drink at Monroe Pratt's expense, they decided it time to head back to the ranch, so Pete and Marvin wished Hawk good luck and headed out the north end of town. Hawk untied his horse from the rail and led him down the short street to the stables to find Clell Blanton. He found him in the process of cleaning out a couple of stalls in the rear of the stable. "Mr. Hawk," Clell sang out when he saw the rangy man walk in. "Barney Mack said you'd probably be wantin' to board your horse here. I'm cleanin' 'em out right now. You can take your pick."

"Mr. Blanton," Hawk returned, and walked back to look the stalls over, taking special note of the solid walls at the back of them and the convenience to the rear door of the stable. "That one will do," he said, nodding toward the one closest to the door. After negotiating the price for him and his horse, they shook hands and Hawk pulled the saddle off Rascal and stowed it in the corner of the stall. It was still a little early for supper, so he decided to kill some time and look the little town over. He drew the Winchester from his saddle sling and walked out into the street.

He was in front of the general store when Sheriff Mack came riding back from transporting Lorena Barfield's body home. When the sheriff spotted him, he guided his horse toward him. Hawk stepped off the short boardwalk to meet him. "Just the man I wanna see," Mack blurted right away. "I ain't so sure it's a good idea for you to be hangin' around town, now that I've thought it over. It's my job to keep the peace in this town and that might be hard to do with you in town."

"That so?" Hawk replied. "I take it Barfield wasn't too happy to see his daughter dead. Did you tell him I've left the Triple-P?"

"Yeah, I told him and he didn't seem too happy about that, either. I'm thinkin' he might figure you're in town and come lookin' for you here and I don't want no shoot-out in my town."

"I can understand that," Hawk said. "But I'm not gonna start anything. You have my word on that and I'll do my best to avoid any trouble Barfield might start. Did you tell him that his daughter shot Marvin Tatum and that's the reason she got shot?"

"From the look in his eye, it seemed like that didn't keep him from wantin' to settle the score." He shook his head, concerned. "I'll tell you something else that don't make it too healthy for you. That son of his, the one they brought to the doctor, well, he died. And if I ain't mistaken, I believe you're the one who shot him. I swear, I can't understand why you'd wanna hang around here after what you've done to Barfield. Looks like you'd wanna be headin' for the high country just as fast as a horse could carry you."

"Yeah, I reckon that would make sense, wouldn't it? Seems to me like everything's got turned around, though. I haven't broken any laws, haven't done anything but protect myself when I had to. Barfield and his crowd have been stealin' cattle and changing brands, the daughter trespassed on Triple-P range, intending to murder me. Seems to me you oughta arrest Barfield if he shows up here lookin' for revenge." Another thought crossed his mind. Thomas Pratt had said that the Triple-P started losing cattle not long after the first of summer. "How long has Barfield been over in that valley?"

Mack had to think a minute. "I don't know. I don't think I remember seein' him in town before the first of the summer." He pushed his hat back and scratched his head, trying to recall. "He ain't been here long."

"You just came from his place. Did that house and barn look like they were just built at the first of the summer?" When Mack failed to answer, Hawk continued, "I've seen those buildin's and they looked pretty damn weathered to me, like they've been there as long as these stores here. Maybe somebody else built that place before Barfield came along."

Suddenly a light came on behind Mack's eyes. "Hell, I expect that was Matt Henson's place. I never went over there, but Matt and his wife and their young'uns built a place in that valley."

"That so?" Hawk replied. "Reckon where he is? When's the last time you saw any of his family?"

"It's been a while," Mack said, straining to recall, "not since before summer, I reckon." He was beginning to see the picture Hawk was helping him create and he didn't like the look of it. "You ain't thinkin' . . ." he started. "Hell, folks here just figured they decided to move on."

"Maybe they did." Hawk shrugged. "And maybe their bones are bleachin' out in one of those cuts and gullies around the foot of those mountains. It's enough to make you wonder, ain't it?" He could see that Mack was beginning to wonder as well. The concept was pure speculation on his part, but he thought it a strong possibility. Barfield was clearly not a builder, he was prone to take what others had built, just as he had proven with his method of building a herd—take what others have worked to create. It's easier to steal it from them than do the work yourself. The more he thought about it, the more certain he became of the possibility there were bodies hidden in those hills. "I don't reckon anybody ever rode over to that valley lookin' for this fellow, Henson, did they?"

"If they did, they didn't say anything to anybody else about it," Mack said. "And if you're askin' if I ever went to check on 'em, I ain't had any reason to. Folks settle on some land, give up on it, and move on—happens all the time. It ain't none of my concern. My business is keepin' the peace in the town. And what I'm tellin' you is, I don't want no shoot-outs in Stevensville."

"Your message is pretty clear on that," Hawk said. "And like I said, you don't have to worry about me startin' any trouble."

Mack glared at him for a few moments, trying to decide whether or not to take it further by ordering Hawk to get out of town. He was reluctant to issue ultimatums to a man who was obviously indifferent to them. Like so many of the townfolk, the sheriff assumed that Hawk was a hired gun the Pratts had brought in to clean up their cattle rustling problems. Finally deciding it better not to force a confrontation with him, one in which he might come out on the short end, Mack said, "I 'preciate your cooperation." He turned his horse and continued on to his office. Hawk decided it was not too early for supper, so he headed back to the saloon.

It was nearly dark by the time Barfield and his son had finished digging a second grave beside the one already dug for Jake. They carried his body out of the cabin and dropped it into the grave without the dignity of lowering it gently with the use of ropes. When his sobbing mother complained, Barfield told her it was too much trouble with no one to help him and Clint. "He ain't gonna know the difference, anyway," he said. "He's already halfway to hell by now."

"Randolph," she cried, "he's your son, our youngest boy. Don't talk that way about him." Her tears began to flow in earnest again. "Please be more gentle with Lorena." She looked from her husband to her surviving son for sympathy. There was none apparent in either face. It was enough to break her heart to realize there was no love for one another in her family, not even the decency anyone accords the deceased. She thought to say a prayer for Jake before they shoveled the dirt back over him, but realized that she had not called upon the Lord in all these many years. How would He hear her prayer now, after so long a time? With all the stealing and rustling her family had done, especially the taking of lives, the murders her men had committed, maybe it was God's hand that took Jake's life. She decided she was not worthy of asking for forgiveness, so she went back where Lorena's body was lying on the ground and sat down beside it while the men filled in Jake's grave.

"All right," Barfield grunted, already tired from burying Jake. "Let's get Lorena in the ground, so we can be done with it."

"Why don't we wait till after supper?" Clint

asked, also tired from the work of digging graves. "She ain't goin' nowhere," he said, motioning toward his sister's body.

"Yeah, but I am," Barfield growled. "And so are you, so let's get her in the ground." He walked over beside the body. "Come on, take hold of her feet," he ordered when Clint was not quick enough to suit him.

They carried the body over to the hole in the ground with Pearl walking along beside, her arms under Lorena's back, trying to support her, even though her body was as stiff as a pine log. "Be gentle," she pleaded. "Please be gentle. Don't drop her into that hole like you did with Jake."

"If you don't get the hell outta the way, I'm gonna drop you in there with her," Randolph threatened.

"Maybe we can try to lower her down if we get on our knees," Clint suggested. He looked at his mother, who had dropped to her knees and begun to pray aloud, asking for forgiveness and begging God to accept her daughter, the only one of her family who had ever stood up for her.

With no compassion for his suffering wife, Barfield pretended to give in. "All right, we'll put her in gentle-like. Put her feet down at the end of the grave." Clint did as he was told and lowered his end of the bundle to the ground at the edge of the grave. Still holding her shoulders up, Barfield said, "Slide her feet over the edge." When Clint did so, his father let her slide down until her feet reached the bottom of the grave. She looked as if she was standing with only her head and the top of her shoulders aboveground. He gave her a shove then and the body keeled over to land flat on her stomach. "There," he said with a satisfied grin, "that oughta be gentle enough to suit you. Cover her up, Clint." Pearl remained on her knees, rocking back and forth, praying as hard as she could until Barfield ordered her to get up and go in the house to fix him something to eat. "Me and Clint have gotta ride tonight," he told her. "There's killin' to be done and I don't aim to do it on an empty belly."

She voiced no objection, but got to her feet and obediently went to the house to cook something for them. Barfield paused to watch her for a few moments, thinking he might have to keep an eye on her after this. She had been acting strange ever since they had come to this place east of the Sapphire Mountains. The first fuss she had made was when she had pleaded for him to spare the family that was living in the cabin, no matter how he tried to explain that it had to be done if they were to have a place to live. And he had no intention of building one when this one was just what they needed. *She'll straighten out,* he thought and dismissed it.

Inside the cabin, Pearl sliced some salt pork to fry and put some coffee on the stove. She would fix him something to eat, but it would be for the last time. For she had made up her mind while praying beside Lorena's grave that she was not going to be there when they returned from town. It had been in her mind to leave for some time and the loss of two of her children was the spark that had given her the will to do it.

"What if he ain't there?" Clint asked as they sat at the table eating.

"Then we'll hunt him down till we find him," Barfield said. "But I expect he'll be there. That's where he was this afternoon, accordin' to what the sheriff said. If we hurry up, we can get over to town before it's too late."

There was no conversation between the vengeance-seeking men and the sallow-eyed woman until they had finished eating. Then there was no more until Barfield said, "I expect we'll be back pretty late."

"You be careful," Pearl whispered to her son as he and his father passed out the door. He nodded and grinned in return. She stood by the kitchen door, watching until she saw them ride out of the barn and take the trail toward town. With a tired sigh, she turned and went to the bedroom to bundle her few belongings up in a bedroll she could tie on her horse. She chose Jake's horse because it was a better one than Lorena's and considerably better than the old roan she had ridden into this cursed valley. And when she had saddled up, she paused only a moment to offer a final apology to the two fresh graves behind the barn before setting out on the trail they had followed in. If Randolph had followed through with his vow the night before about leaving this place, she would have stayed with him. But he chose to expose their only surviving son to more killing and she had had all she could stand. She would not be here when he returned to tell her that Clint had been killed—or he did not come back himself. With a little luck, maybe she could find her way back to Butte. If she couldn't, it really didn't matter to her at this point.

"You want some more coffee?" Ruth Wiggins asked. "Or are you thinking about switching over to something stronger?"

"No," Hawk answered. "I reckon I've had enough and I expect Ed is gonna charge me rent on this table if I don't get outta here."

The short, plump woman with the graying hair smiled warmly at him. Ruthie, as she was called by the patrons of the Valley House Saloon, was in fact Ed Wiggins's sister-in-law. Her husband, Ed's brother, Dale, was crushed to death by a giant fir tree while cutting timber to be used to build the saloon. Ruthie had volunteered this information during the short conversation she had had with Hawk. He wondered why she seemed so friendly, as if she had known him for a long time.

He had to figure that it was because he made it a point to compliment her cooking, when, in fact, he had eaten much better food in any number of saloons. It was his guess that she had not likely received many compliments on her cooking, so he thought she could use the encouragement. Whatever, she had certainly given him plenty of attention and never let his coffee cup get empty. "You set as long as you want," she said in response to his comment. "I'll take care of Ed if he gets snippety. There's plenty of empty tables, anyway."

There was no certainty that Randolph Barfield would show up in town looking for him, but Hawk had to conduct himself as if he would. *I reckon I should be thankful he left me in peace while I had my supper,* he thought, but he was tired of sitting at the table. So he got to his feet. "Well, I thank you again for the fine supper," he said to Ruthie. "I'd best go see about my horse. Then I'll maybe come back later for a little drink before I turn in for the night."

"I won't be here much later," she said. "But if I'm not here when you come back, I'll wish you a good night. Come back to eat with us. I'll bake fresh biscuits in the morning."

"I might at that," he said, and walked by the bar to settle up with Ed. After that, he went to the door and paused there for a few moments, looking up and down the short street before walking outside. There was very little activity on the street, except for the patrons of the saloon. Glancing across the street at the sheriff's office, he noticed the lamp inside was out and he recalled that Ed had told him that the sheriff often ate supper at his place. *But not tonight, evidently,* he told himself. *Wonder if his little visit with Randolph Barfield had anything to do with that?* He didn't count on Barney Mack for much support, anyway. Being naturally cautious, he walked down to the stable, staying close to the storefronts in case he suddenly had to find cover, his rifle held ready to fire any moment.

Reaching the stable, he paused when he heard the rumble of thunder overhead. He looked up and studied the dark mass of clouds that had threatened ever since he went into the saloon for supper. They were now moving rapidly over the town, pushed by the wind slipping over the mountaintops to the west. In a few minutes, the first drops fell, big, heavy drops that landed on the dry street, raising tiny clouds of dust. He knew it wouldn't be long, so he hurried through the stable door where he found Rascal munching away contentedly from a feed bag filled with a portion of oats. The big buckskin whinnied a greeting when Hawk walked in. A moment later, a rustle of hay behind him caused him to spin around instantly, his rifle ready to fire, only to find Clell Blanton staring wide-eyed and openmouthed in shock. Hawk immediately dropped the Winchester down by his side. "Sorry, Clell. I reckon I'm a little bit jumpy tonight for some reason. Musta been too much of Ruthie's coffee."

"I didn't mean to sneak up on you like that," Clell said. "I reckon I thought you saw me in that front stall when you walked in."

"I guess I wasn't payin' much attention," Hawk said. "I'm sorry I drew down on you—don't know what I was thinkin'." *I'm damn lucky that wasn't one of the Barfields,* he berated himself.

"You fixin' to turn in for the night?" Blanton asked.

"Reckon not, at least not for a while yet. I just thought I'd see how Rascal was gettin' along. Then I think I'll go back and have a drink before I turn in."

"I'll see you in the mornin', then," Blanton said. "I'm fixin' to go to the house, soon as your horse empties that feed bag. I'll lock the front door, but I'll not put the lock on the back door, so you can come and go as you please."

"Much obliged," Hawk said.

He spent a little time in the stable with Rascal. Seeing a brush hanging on a hook, he decided to use it to give his horse a little grooming, something Rascal wasn't accustomed to. While he was at it, he checked the buckskin's hooves, something else that was overdue. He knew he was just killing time with no idea if Barfield was coming and if he was, how long it would take him to make the trip into town. But he figured if he did come, the saloon was most likely the first place he would look. Giving Rascal a final pat on the neck, he walked to the back door and stood there awhile watching the rain fall. *Beautiful night for a killing,* he thought. Then another thought struck him. *What in hell am I doing here?* And he suddenly realized that the role that had been cast upon him was one completely foreign to him. This job he had volunteered to take on was that of a lawman, or a gunman, and it was not in his nature. He was an army scout and a good one and yet here he was, waiting for a showdown with a man and his son, a man whose family he had already torn apart with two killings. That seemed enough punishment for any family, the loss of a son and a daughter. Maybe he should saddle Rascal and ride away and let the rain cover his tracks behind him. "Damn it to hell," he cursed, knowing he had no choice. If Barfield wasn't stopped here, he would take his vengeance to the Triple-P. He pulled his hat brim low on his forehead and stepped out into the rain.

The rain had driven the few men standing around in front of the saloon inside, leaving two horses standing at the hitching rail. There was no light from any of the other businesses on the street, giving the town a cold, dead appearance that seemed fitting for the occasion. Because there were two horses out front, he paused just inside the door of the saloon and quickly scanned the room. Satisfied that the horses didn't belong to Barfield and his son, he walked over to the bar. "Come back for that drink?" Ed Wiggins asked when he walked up.

"I reckon," Hawk replied. "Looks like the kinda night when you need a little fire in your belly. Pour me a double shot." He watched Ed pour the whiskey. "I think I'll take it over to a table," he said when he paid, "sit down, and drink it real slow." He picked up the glass and walked to a table in the back corner where he could watch the entire room. He propped his rifle against the wall beside his chair, pulled the .44 Colt from his holster, and placed it in his lap. Then he sat and waited, sipping occasionally from his glass, as he watched every man who came in the front door.

He had long since finished his double shot of whiskey when Ed walked over to the table. "You've been settin' at this table for about two hours. You sure you ain't ready for another drink?"

"Reckon not," Hawk said. "Two shots are usually my limit."

"It's a good thing all of my customers don't think that way. I wouldn't be able to make a livin'."

Hawk smiled. "I guess you're right. I was thinkin' a fellow I know mighta showed up, but it looks like he ain't gonna make it. Tell you the truth, I didn't realize I'd been here that long. I guess I'll go turn in for the night. Maybe I'll see that fellow tomorrow sometime." Suddenly feeling very tired, he slipped his .44 back in its holster and pushed his chair back. For whatever reason, Barfield must have decided against retaliation. Maybe he had suffered enough loss of family to risk his one remaining offspring. No matter the reason, Hawk was glad the old man had made the choice to live and he hoped he was already on his way to find a new place somewhere far away from the Bitterroot Valley. When he thought about it, he had no reason to want to kill Barfield. It was enough to just be done with him. "I expect I'll see you in the mornin'," he said to Ed on his way out. "Ruthie said she was gonna bake biscuits in the mornin'."

"She usually does," Ed replied.

Outside, the rain had slackened to a light drizzle as the sudden thunderstorm moved down the valley. Hawk stood in the doorway for a few moments, breathing in the fresh air to rid his lungs of the heavy atmosphere inside the saloon. Feeling his head was clear then, he stepped off the board stoop. His foot had no sooner touched the muddy street when he was suddenly jolted sideways by a blow to his shoulder. He knew at once that he had been shot, even though he didn't remember hearing the report of the weapon. Although he was only staggered, he instinctively dropped to the ground as another shot snapped through the air above him. He thought about trying to crawl back to the door of the saloon, but knew he wouldn't make it without catching another bullet. So he lay still, hoping his assailant would think him dead, or dying, and come forward to finish the job at close range. It was a hell of a gamble, but he couldn't see that he had any other hope. There was little doubt who had shot him, so he knew he had two to deal with, if he had a chance at all. He was still clutching his rifle, but there was no cartridge in the chamber and the odds of his cranking one in, firing, then cocking it again, were not at all good. At this point, he was determined to take at least one of them with him, no matter what.

A heavy sense of silence seemed to descend upon the muddy street after the shock of the two shots. Even the incessant murmuring of voices pressed close against the windows of the saloon seemed distant. After what felt like a long time, he heard the sound of boots in the mud behind him. If he managed to get off a shot, it was going to be even more difficult with his assailant standing behind him. With these thoughts pounding in his brain, he gave very little thought to the bullet in his shoulder. He could feel the man standing over him more than the slug. When should he make his move? He realized then that it was impossible to escape with his life. The best he could hope for was to get a shot off before he was snuffed out.

"Now, by God, Mr. Hawk, it's time for you to settle up for killin' my son and my daughter. I hope you can hear what I'm sayin', 'cause I want you to know who's sendin' your murderin' ass to hell."

What the hell, he thought when he heard the metallic clicking of a hammer cocking, his signal to go for broke. He hadn't turned halfway over when he heard the shot that slammed Barfield in the chest. In the space of an instant, he rolled all the way over to see Clint aiming his pistol, but not at him. He reacted immediately, cutting Barfield's son down before he could pull the trigger. Amazed to still be alive, he looked quickly from one body to the other to be sure they were no longer threats. Then he looked toward the corner of the saloon and saw Sheriff Barney Mack approaching, reloading a double-barrel shotgun.

"How bad are you hurt?" Mack asked when Hawk got up.

"Not as bad as I woulda been if you hadn't showed up when you did," Hawk answered. "I reckon I don't have to tell you how happy I was to see you, 'cause I was in a bad way there. Tell you the truth, I didn't think you were around."

"I just didn't think it was a good idea to let people know I was, so I could see what they were up to. I knew there was gonna be trouble." The fact of the matter was that Mack had decided to be out of town until morning. But his conscience had begun to work on him until he shamed himself for being cowardly. After the way it turned out, he was especially glad that he had returned. It would surely give the citizens of Stevensville confidence in the man they had hired for sheriff.

"Well, Sheriff, you sure saved my bacon," Hawk said. "And I thank you."

"Just doin' my job," Mack replied modestly. "But I owe you some thanks, too. If you hadn't rolled over and fired, the young one woulda got me for sure. When I shot his daddy, I musta got my fingers tangled up, 'cause I pulled both triggers—fired both barrels at the same time—damn near knocked me down. I wouldn't have had time to reload."

They stood there, looking at the bodies lying in the muddy street for a while until the saloon emptied out and the spectators gathered around. Jim Mosley made his way through the small crowd to take a look. "Reckon you'da been sendin' for me," he said to Sheriff Mack.

"Reckon so. Nothin' fancy, just a plain box," Mack said, with cost in mind. Finished with the undertaker, he turned back to Hawk. "Reckon it's up to me to see about his widow. Far as I know, the old lady is the only one of the family left and I guess I'll have to be the one to tell her."

"Reckon so," Hawk said. "I'd offer to go for you, but I don't think she'd think too kindly of that. I'll be gettin' outta town come mornin'."

"Good," Mack said. "Don't be in too big a hurry to come back to see us." He fashioned a wide grin to make sure Hawk knew he was joking. "I don't know if the town can handle another visit from you."

CHAPTER 14

Well able to walk without help, Hawk went to
Dr. Smollet's house to get his wound taken care
of, leaving the business of taking care of the
bodies to the sheriff. The good doctor was not at
all happy to see him so far past the supper hour.
But after Hawk knocked continuously, Smollet
finally came to the door. "Sorry to interrupt your
evenin'," Hawk said, "but I'd sure appreciate it if
you could take a look at my shoulder."

"I should have known when I heard the
shooting that somebody would come knocking
on my door. I was hoping they'd be calling Jim
Mosley out instead of me," Smollet complained,
referring to the undertaker.

"Sheriff Mack has already talked to him,"
Hawk said.

Smollet held his lantern up to get a better look
at his visitor. "Oh, it's you again. Hawk, is it?"
Hawk nodded. "You look all right to me. What's
wrong with your shoulder?"

"It's got a bullet in it," Hawk replied, and
pointed to the hole in the left shoulder of his
buckskin shirt.

"No wonder I couldn't see it," Smollet said,
still irritated. "You're covered with mud. What
have you been doing, rolling in the street? Oh,

well, come on inside so I can get a look at it. Take your boots off and leave them on the porch."

Hawk followed the doctor into the house, stepping carefully as he tiptoed across the parlor carpet in his stocking feet. Near the door to the examining room, the doctor's wife stood watching him silently, her arms folded in front of her chest. "Sorry to intrude on you this late, ma'am," Hawk said as he passed. She said nothing in reply, instead asking her husband if he was going to want some water boiled. He nodded and she spun on her heel to go to the kitchen.

"Can you get out of that shirt, or am I gonna have to cut it off of you?" Smollet asked. Hawk quickly replied that he could get out of it, pain or no pain. It was the best shirt he owned and he didn't want to part with it. Smollet watched, amused, while Hawk pulled it over his head, grimacing with the movement of his left arm. "What was all the shooting about?" Smollet asked, and Hawk told him of the attempted ambush in front of the saloon. "So Barfield's dead, is he—and the son, too?"

"That's a fact," Hawk answered as Smollet examined his wound.

"What am I going to do for patients?" he joked. "I was making a good living off the Barfields." He waited for his wife to pour hot water in a basin on the table beside him, then he cleaned the area around the wound before starting to probe for the bullet. "I don't suppose the other son was with them, the one I had to amputate an arm."

"Nope," Hawk replied. "He's dead."

Smollet paused to give him a look. "I'm not surprised. They waited way too long to get that infection treated." He shrugged, obviously not overly concerned. "You got off lucky," he said after a few minutes of probing. "You'd probably have gotten by if you'd just left it in there, but there it is if you want it for a souvenir."

"Reckon not," Hawk said. "How much I owe you?"

He took his time before starting back to the Triple-P the following morning, a good deal of it trying to clean up his shirt and trousers after his roll in the mud the night before. When they were as good as he could get them, he headed for the saloon, planning to treat himself to breakfast before leaving town. His shoulder, although stiff and sore, didn't hamper his use of his other arm to attack a plate of eggs, ham, and potatoes, tamped down with three of Ruthie's biscuits. Ed Wiggins sat with him for most of the time, getting up occasionally to pour whiskey for some of his early-morning drinkers. The conversation naturally had to do with the shooting of the night before. "So ol' Barney Mack was right there with his shotgun," Ed marveled. Somehow he hadn't

315

figured Mack to be inclined to get involved with any altercation as threatening as this one. "I reckon Barney's got a little more starch in him than a lot of us figured. There's been some talk about maybe lookin' for a new sheriff. Lotta folks thinkin' Barney might not have the backbone to stand up to a tough situation. The only reason he got the job is because we couldn't get anybody else to take it."

"Well, all I can say is he was sure as hell there when I needed him. From the way you're talkin', I reckon that's the first tight spot he's had to face since he got the job. And he was there when it counted. You might have yourself a good man for the job." Hawk was not sure if he was doing Barney Mack a favor or not. His initial opinion of the man was that he would run at the first sign of real trouble, which he did, but he summoned the courage to come back to face it. To Hawk, that was reason enough to give him a chance if that's what he wanted.

When Hawk had finished the last of his coffee, he paid Ed and stuck his head inside the kitchen door to compliment Ruthie on his breakfast, even though he figured anybody could fry eggs and ham. He had to admit the biscuits were better than passable. She was obviously pleased by his comments, which was his objective. As far as he knew, his business in Stevensville was finished and he didn't expect to visit the town again. But it never hurt to make yourself welcome in the event you did return one day.

The morning felt fresh and clean after the thunderstorm of the night before as he turned Rascal toward the Triple-P. It would be interesting to find out if Monroe still had his mind set on returning to Helena to try to pick up Roy Nestor's trail. Maybe that desire for vengeance had faded somewhat after this length of time and the trouble with Barfield. As far as Hawk was concerned, he'd just as soon Monroe would decide what was done was done and get on with the business of running a ranch. He had spent very little of the money Monroe had paid him so far and he had more coming, so he felt he was in good shape with the end of the summer coming on. The job Monroe had originally hired him to do had turned into one that was totally unexpected, but one that had to be done by someone, he allowed. Lieutenant Meade was probably wondering where the hell he was by now. And he had some hunting to do and work to be done at his cabin on the Boulder River. He felt like it was time to move on.

He was spotted by young Tommy Pratt when he was still a hundred yards from the house. Tommy ran to the barn to tell his father and by the time Hawk reined Rascal to a halt in the barnyard, both Thomas and Monroe were waiting for him, anxious to hear what happened in town. "Looks

317

like your rustlin' problems are over," Hawk said, "at least till the next rustler moves in that cabin." When pressed to explain what had happened, Hawk gave them the details.

"So all the men in the family are dead?" Thomas asked.

"The girl, too," Hawk reminded him.

They were joined right away by Dora and Rachel when they hurried from the house. Overhearing the exchange between Hawk and Thomas, Rachel asked, "What about the mother? Is she dead, too?"

"I don't reckon," Hawk said. "At least, she wasn't part of what went on in town last night. Sheriff Mack said he would ride over there today to tell her about the shootin'—said maybe he might offer to help her if he could."

"What in the world can he do for her?" Dora asked. "All her family gone, the poor woman, I can't help feeling sorry for her. It's not her fault that all her men were outlaws. And now she's all by herself on the other side of those mountains. I hope the sheriff at least brings her back to town with him." She turned to her husband. "Thomas, something should be done for that poor woman, outlaw's wife or not."

"All right," Thomas said. "I'll send some of the boys over that way tomorrow. There's a few cattle over there that need to be rounded up and driven back to our range. I'll have Pete and Bob check on the woman to see if she's still there. I'll tell them to make sure she's got food and firewood. If she's smart, she'll let the sheriff take her back to town with him—better than her staying out there by herself."

While that discussion was going on, Rachel couldn't help noticing the shape of Hawk's clothes. They seemed unusually dirty and stained and as she continued to stare, she realized there was a hole in the left shoulder. "What happened to your shirt?" she finally asked. "Is that a hole?" She pointed to his shoulder.

"Yes, ma'am," he replied. "I got shot."

Astonished, she gasped, "You've been shot? Why didn't you say something? We're all standing around worrying about that poor woman and you're standing here wounded." Her observation brought the others to turn their attention to him. "We need to get you inside where you can sit down. Do you need some water or something?"

He couldn't help laughing. "No, ma'am, thank you just the same. It's just a shoulder wound. Dr. Smollet dug the bullet out and bandaged it up. It'll heal just fine. I wish I could say the same about my shirt. It's my best shirt."

"If you have a spare shirt, you can give me that one and I'll try to clean it up for you," Rachel said. "I'm not sure what's the best way to clean a buckskin shirt, but I'm sure I can improve it a little."

"Thank you just the same, ma'am, but as soon as I take care of my horse, I'm goin' into the river with a cake of lye soap and a scrub brush. That's the best way to clean the mud offa this buckskin. I tried to clean it best I could at the stable, but I just got the biggest part of it off."

"Do you need a blanket or something to wrap around you while you're washing your clothes?" Rachel asked.

"Oh no, ma'am. I ain't comin' outta my clothes. It's a lot easier to clean 'em while they're still on you, especially buckskin." He glanced up at the sun. "I've got plenty of time for the sun to dry 'em."

"Oh," Rachel responded, and looked quickly at Dora, who met her gaze of amusement with one of her own, then shook her head. "Well, whatever's best." She had thought to do something for the evidently indestructible man who had done so much for everybody else. But it appeared he was totally self-sufficient. "Do you want something to eat before you jump in the river?"

"No, ma'am, I ate a pretty good-sized breakfast. I reckon that oughta hold me till suppertime."

"All right, then," she said, and paused to think about it before she complained. "And stop calling me ma'am. You make me feel like I'm a hundred years old."

"Sorry, ma'am," he replied before catching himself. "I mean, sorry, Rachel." He gave her a big grin and added, "You look a couple of years younger than a hundred." He looked at Monroe then and said, "Maybe we can talk a little after supper."

Monroe, having been entertained by Rachel's attempt to be hospitable to the untamed army scout, became serious then, knowing what Hawk wanted to talk about. "I expect we need to," was all he said, however, giving Hawk the impression that he might have been giving it a lot of thought already.

It was getting along toward suppertime and Hawk's clothes had failed to dry out in the sun as quickly as he had planned. He had succeeded in cleaning most of the mud from his shirt and pants, but his underdrawers were still uncomfortably damp. So he was forced to change into his spare set. When he came from his room in the ranch house, he found Rachel waiting outside his door. "Rachel," he acknowledged.

"Did your clothes have time to really get dry, or are you gonna sit around and suffer in your wet ones?" Rachel teased.

Puzzled by her apparent concern, he replied, "They're pretty near dry. A little longer wouldn't hurt, though."

"What about the bandage on your shoulder? Did you take it off before you jumped in the river?"

"No," he answered. "Tell you the truth, I didn't

think about it till after I was already in the water." He shrugged. "It most likely needed washin', too."

Exasperated, as if talking to a child, she shook her head slowly. He gave her a big grin and started toward the back door, but she stopped him with a hand on his arm. "Supper's almost ready. Don't wander off." He nodded and started to speak, but she interrupted. "I wanted to catch you before supper. I wanted to talk to you in private. I know you're probably going to be leaving soon and there's something I wanted you to know."

"Oh?" It was all he could think to say, confused as he was by her strange behavior. It suddenly struck him that she had never approached him in such a manner before.

"Yes," she continued. "I think it is way past the time when I should have told you how grateful I am for having you come along in my life. Just when I so desperately needed someone, you were there. You will always be very special to me." She paused when he appeared to be dumbfounded. "I just wanted you to know that." She gave him a great big smile. "Now, I've got to get back to help Dora and Lily get supper on the table. Don't go wandering off," she repeated, then spun on her heel and hurried away, leaving Hawk to stand confounded by the confrontation. He was pleased to think that Rachel thought it important to let him know how he had impacted her life. He couldn't help thinking that she wanted him to know that she had found peace on the Triple-P, and he was glad for that. Further thoughts on the matter were interrupted when Lily rang the bell for supper.

As usual, the Pratt women set a fine table with plenty of food. The conversation was light, a pleasant respite from the talk about fighting and rustling that had dominated mealtime discussions before. When everyone was finished and Lily had poured coffee again to wash it all down, Monroe announced that there was something he wanted to say. "Several of you have already noticed it and even suggested something should be done about it." He paused to grin sheepishly before diving in. "Rachel and I have decided it would be a good thing if we got married." He paused again while all eyes turned toward a blushing Rachel. "We talked it over and decided that Jamie would approve and I hope the rest of you do as well."

Although taken by surprise, the reaction of the family was unanimous, a welcome one, for they all wanted Rachel to be a permanent member. Hawk smiled, thinking of the private conversation he had with her just before supper. *No wonder she seemed so happy,* he thought. *I reckon there ain't any need to have that talk with Monroe now. He ain't going anywhere.*

Not surprisingly, the family sat around the supper table a great deal longer than usual with talk of plans to be made for the wedding. After wishing the couple well, Hawk took his last cup of coffee out to the front porch to escape the noisy conversation. In a short while, he was joined by Monroe and Thomas. "I suppose we can have that talk now," Monroe said. "Thomas and I have talked it over and decided that it's best if I forget about trying to track Roy Nestor down. I hate to go back on my vow to make him pay for killing Jamie, but Thomas needs me here, and there would be no telling how long and how far I would end up looking for Nestor. I don't think there's any doubt that he's left this part of the country and it doesn't make sense to sacrifice a big part of my life looking for him. We agree that Jamie would approve." He looked at his brother, and Thomas responded with a nod of affirmation, so Monroe went on. "I know I dragged you out here on the premise that you would be hired to guide me on my hunt for Nestor. But to tell you the truth, I'm not sure what we would have done without your help with Barfield. So in addition to what I promised and your wages since you've been here, we're giving you a hundred-dollar bonus. Does that sound fair to you?"

"More than fair," Hawk said. They were right in thinking the likelihood of tracking Roy Nestor down was extremely slim because there would be no sense for him to stay in the territory. "I'll pack up my possibles and ride outta here in the mornin', if that's all right."

"Of course that's all right," Monroe was quick to reply, "if that's what you want to do. But there's no hurry for you to leave. Why don't you stay around for the wedding?"

" 'Preciate it," Hawk said. "But I expect I'd best get on back to my place and to Fort Ellis. I've been gone so long already that I'll be lucky if I've still got a job."

Both Monroe and Thomas stepped forward to offer their hands, both thanked him again for his help. He had to admit that he had begun to feel like part of the family, so in a way, it made him feel a little sad to leave the Triple-P. On the other hand, he suspected that he would no doubt soon be feeling fenced in. Anyway, he knew he still didn't care much for punching cows. "Well, the wedding planning is still going on inside, so I guess I'd better get back in there to make sure they don't get outta hand with it," Monroe finally announced.

"Reckon you'd better," Hawk said. "I think I'll go down to the barn to look my pack rig over. I think I might have to repair one of those straps." He started to go back inside, but Thomas offered to take his cup back for him. "Right," Hawk said. " 'Preciate it."

While checking over his packs, most of the cowhands came in to say "so long" and to wish him well. Marvin Tatum jokingly told him there were no hard feelings for Hawk having gotten him shot. Pete tried to talk him into asking Monroe for a permanent job on the Triple-P. "You know dang well he'd hire you, even if he had to let one of us go."

"Is that so?" Hawk joked. "Well, I wouldn't want one of you boys to lose your job. Besides, I've got a job that's been waitin' for me to get my behind back down to Fort Ellis. I don't know how much longer the army can operate without me to tell 'em what to do."

He went to bed that night with confidence that all his gear was in good shape and ready to pack up in the morning. He opted to start out a little later than he normally would have in order to take advantage of another good breakfast under his belt. By the time he finally climbed up into the saddle, he was beginning to regret that decision. For there was a long round of good-byes and Pete must have talked to Monroe the night before because Monroe offered him a job on the ranch. He declined, of course, even though he was tempted to accept in spite of his dislike for working cattle, because this was the closest he had ever come to being a member of a family. *Hell,* he told himself, aware that he was revisiting thoughts he had thrashed through the night before, *that warm fuzzy feeling would wear off in another week.* Then he'd remember that he liked it best alone, without too many folks to crowd him. So he said his good-byes to the ladies, even a brief farewell to Miss Emily, who had Lily wheel her out to the porch. She took his hand again, thanked him for helping keep her family safe, then cautioned him to be extra careful on his ride back to Helena. "There are men who would harm you," she warned. He assured her that he surely would be careful, thinking that there always were men like that in this part of the territory. Then he remembered to tell the women how good their cooking was—so they would welcome him back, although he doubted he'd ever see them again. By the time he had finished with a manly handshake with Tommy, the sun was well up when he finally headed Rascal up the path to the river trail toward Missoula.

It was midmorning when he passed Skinner's store and thoughts of the Triple-P were already fading away, replaced by his usual anticipation of what might lie on the trail ahead. Financially, he was well fixed for the coming winter with money to buy extra ammunition as well as any cooking supplies he might need in the event he was not hired by the army before next spring.

As he headed on to Missoula, he thought of Roy Nestor. A truly bad man, but was he worth taking the remaining days of summer to track down? Nestor had not only murdered Jamie Pratt, but he had also tried to kill Hawk. His attempt had failed, his two paid assassins killed, and Nestor sent running for his life. If that was enough to change

Monroe's determination to track him down, then it should also be enough to satisfy Hawk's personal need for vengeance. At least, that's what he decided on this sunny day in late summer as he rode up the Bitterroot Valley. He had no scores to settle. Eager to get back to the life he knew best, he pushed his horses a little harder, planning to make camp at Fort Missoula that night.

There was little difference in the scene that he rode in upon when he reached the army post that evening. Like before, the fort was in the early stages of construction with no progress that he could see. There were quite a few more men there than there had been when he had camped with Monroe and Rachel before. But they were far short of the two full companies that had originally started construction before the Nez Perce came over Lolo Pass into the Bitterroot Valley. After making his camp in the same spot as before, he was visited by a soldier on sentry duty who was delighted to share a cup of coffee with him since his post was not easily seen by the sergeant of the guard. "Don't look like much work has been done on the fort since I passed through here a while back," Hawk said. "But it looks like you've got a lot more men."

"Hell," the soldier replied. "These men ain't here to build the fort. They were all wounded fightin' the Nez Perce at Big Hole Basin.

They were brought back here to recover."

"Well, I'll be . . ." Hawk started. "I thought the Nez Perce passed on through real peaceful and weren't lookin' for a fight."

"I reckon they weren't, but our boys caught up with 'em at the Big Hole and there was a big battle."

"They whip the Indians?" Hawk asked.

"Hell, no, they got away, gave our boys a helluva fight, then slipped out on 'em and headed toward Yellowstone country. And that's why there ain't no soldiers here to build this fort." Hawk was surprised they had heard nothing about the battle, not even in Stevensville. "Where you headed?" the soldier asked.

"Fort Ellis," Hawk said. "I'll head out for Helena in the mornin'."

"Best keep a sharp eye when you head down that way," the soldier said, "especially if you're thinkin' 'bout takin' the Mullan Road. With most of the troops gone after the Nez Perce, there's been a little more trouble with Sioux raidin' parties along that road—mostly between here and Helena. They know there ain't no patrols sent out from here right now."

"Oh?" Hawk replied. "What about Lieutenant Conner's camp down near Fagan's tradin' post, is it still there?"

"For a fact, I don't know," the soldier replied. "We ain't had no contact with 'em is all I can tell you." This was not good news to Hawk. It meant he was going to have to be extra careful. A picture of Miss Emily popped into his mind and he recalled the solemn warning she had given him about people who would do him harm. *I guess you were right,* he thought. Anyone could caution you to be careful, but that old lady acted as if she was getting her information from some mysterious source.

He considered leaving the road and riding down the opposite side of the river. But the ride would be so much easier on Rascal and his packhorse that he decided to stick with his intention of taking the Mullan Road down to Helena. With that in mind, he planned to start out early in the morning, figuring on reaching Fagan's that night after a full day's ride. "Well, I'd best get back on my post," the soldier decided. "The sergeant of the guard's likely to come sneakin' around, tryin' to catch me asleep. Thank you for the coffee." He picked up his rifle and started back toward the unfinished buildings. "Watch your back on that road tomorrow," he called over his shoulder.

Intent upon crawling into his blankets early, Hawk pulled his horses in close and hobbled his packhorse, There was no need to hobble Rascal, the big buckskin would not wander far from his master's side. Before the sun revealed itself the following morning, he was in the saddle and on his way.

CHAPTER 15

"I think we are wasting our time coming back to this trail again today," Running Bird complained. "There have been no more wagons since the Nez Perce rode over the Lolo Pass and the soldiers went after them."

"Running Bird is right," Crooked Leg said. "It is too late in the summer for the white settlers to be traveling farther west. It is almost the moon of colored leaves. Soon the snow will fall and there will be no one on this trail. Maybe we should go back to the others." The rest of the fourteen-man war party had decided to move on to the northwest after finding no wagons on the Mullan Road.

"You talk of snow and yet the sun is still hot," Spotted Pony replied. "The white man is too crazy to know how fast the seasons will change."

"Maybe Crooked Leg is right and we should have gone with the others to hunt on the other side of these mountains," Running Bird suggested. "Our food is almost gone."

"If you had not gone with me before, you would not have that rifle you carry," Spotted Pony reminded him, "or the bullets to shoot it. There is plenty of time to hunt for the coming winter."

331

"I know why you keep coming back to this place," Crooked Leg, who knew his friend the best, said. "You still look for that devil who killed your brother. He is gone. He just passed through this way and now he is gone and you must cast him from your mind."

"I come to this place because it is the best place to attack the wagons that bring guns and bullets," Spotted Pony insisted. "We will need them to fight the Blackfeet." This was a subject very much on all their minds, for they were raiding far out of their own territory. He started to say more but was interrupted by Running Bird.

"Hush! Someone comes."

The three Lakota warriors crawled closer to the brow of the ridge. Below on the road the soldiers had built, they saw a rider approaching, leading a packhorse. He was still a good seventy-five yards away, but it was obvious that he was alone. "See," Spotted Pony said, "two horses, guns, and a loaded packhorse. This will be a good . . ." His voice trailed off as he suddenly stared as if stunned.

"What is it?" Crooked Leg asked. A moment later, he gasped, "Feather In His Hat!" All three stared dumbstruck then as if seeing a vision.

"He has come back!" Spotted Pony whispered, having recovered from the initial shock of seeing the man he had vowed to kill. He would have charged down the slope to attack had not

Crooked Leg grabbed his arm and held him. "I knew he would come back."

"Wait!" Crooked Leg commanded. "He has killed your brother. Would you have him kill you as well? If you go running down this hill, he will see you and kill you before you can get close to him. He is no ordinary white man. His medicine is strong."

"He must die by my hand," Spotted Pony declared, still trembling with anticipation. "It is my right. I have sworn to kill him and Man Above has brought him here to this place for my vengeance."

"It is your right and we will respect it, but why let him know that you have seen him? It is better to surprise him. We will help you ambush him," Running Bird said. "This is not a good place. He would see us before we could get close enough. Better down there where the road makes a turn through the trees closer to the river." He pointed to a bend in the road and Spotted Pony quickly agreed, anxious to start. So they backed carefully away from the top of the ridge, down the other side where they had left their horses.

Hawk had not taken the soldier's warning about raids on the Mullan Road lightly. He went by way of the road to cut the time it would take to ride from Missoula to Helena, but he knew the risk was greater by doing so. Consequently, he was alert to the sounds of the forest, the river, and the horses. It was a state of alertness that he was in the habit of maintaining any time he was alone in a hostile land. On this day, however, he seemed even more alert than usual and he had to admit that it was because of Miss Emily's solemn warning that he should be cautious. *Hell, I'm always cautious,* he thought, then laughed at himself and said, "Except when I ain't." *What a scary old lady,* he thought.

His eyes automatically scanned the high ridge on his left for any hint of movement. As he continued on, he looked ahead about a quarter of a mile to a curve in the road as it entered a stand of firs close to the river. He couldn't help thinking what a good place it would be for an ambush, but it was just one of a handful of such places he had spotted since leaving Fort Missoula. Just as he had done in those sightings, he continued on until suddenly Rascal's ears flickered back and he snorted. With no more warning than that, Hawk immediately hauled the reins sharply to his right and gave the buckskin his heels, heading for the bank of the river some ten or twelve feet below him. The shot that rang out at that moment passed high over his head as Rascal dropped down over the bluffs.

Sioux, he thought automatically as he lay low on the buckskin's neck, his immediate goal a search for cover. Several more shots split the morning

334

air and he was almost jerked from the saddle when his packhorse went down, but he released the lead rope in time to recover. Below the bluffs now, he raced toward a deep gully formed by a stream emptying into the river. It was not the best he could hope for, but it was the closest and its sides were deep enough to protect his horse from rifle fire from above the bluffs. *What a waste,* he thought, thinking of his packhorse. It had to be a wild shot because he was sure they had intended to gain two horses with their attack. He looked around him for a quick assessment of the spot he had landed in. It would do, he supposed, as long as they didn't cross over to the other side of the river. If they did, his backside would be unprotected. It occurred to him that he always seemed to find himself in this situation, backed up against a river. The question now was, how many? As near as he could figure, the shots had come from a dense stand of fir trees at a point where the river took a sharp turn back to the south and the road followed it. He couldn't be too certain, however, because he hadn't had the opportunity to do much looking while he was trying to keep from ending up like his packhorse. As far as the number of his attackers, he decided they were no more than two or three, based on the volley of shots he heard. With that assumption, he was not inclined to sit there and hold them off until they decided to cross the river where they could shoot into the open mouth of the stream. He didn't plan to be there when that happened, so it was time to go on the offensive. He was confident that Rascal wouldn't be in any danger as long as he was protected there in the gully. Even if the Indians came across the river, they would be able to see there was no one but Rascal in the gully. And Rascal was too fine a horse to kill. He would be better off out of the way of gunfire, so he tied his reins to a bush growing out of the side of the gully.

Before slipping out of the gully, he first needed to better pinpoint his assailants, so he crawled up to the edge of it and fired three shots at the stand of trees as rapidly as he could squeeze the trigger and crank in another cartridge. His volley was answered immediately, kicking up dirt on the edge of the gully. In the short time before ducking below the rim, he saw only one muzzle flash, but he counted three shots, fired too rapidly to have come from one rifle. With some idea of the size of the party he was fighting, he slipped out the mouth of the stream and ran downstream. Hunched over as he ran, he was able to remain hidden beneath the river bluffs. When he had run far enough to put him beyond the point where the river turned onto the first part of an S curve, he dropped to his knee behind a clump of bushes. Panting heavily from his sprint, he labored to slow his breathing down in order to hear any small sounds that might give him a clue to his assailants' whereabouts.

"Ay-ee!" Spotted Pony cried out in anger when Hawk had suddenly veered off the road and down the bank of the river. "How did he know?" He had shot at him in frustration, causing Crooked Leg and Running Bird to fire, too, and he knew right away that it had been a mistake. For now the hated white man not only knew about the planned ambush, but due to their haste, one of them had killed a good horse.

"I think this white devil's medicine is strong," Running Bird said. "We must be very careful."

"Look," Crooked Leg said. He was still staring at the gully from which the shots were fired and he could just see the ears of the buckskin horse Feather In His Hat was riding. "He is still in the gully. I think he means to stand us off there."

Spotted Pony stared at the bluffs and the river behind them. "I think he plans to trick us," he said. "He thinks that we will come for him from the road and from each side. I think he is not as smart as he thinks. This is what we will do." He sent Crooked Leg to circle around the trees to his right, then he sent Running Bird to do the same to his left. "You will keep him from escaping to either side while I cross over the river. He has nothing to protect him from behind." They all agreed that this was the obvious plan of attack and while his two companions hurried to take their positions, Spotted Pony jumped on his horse and sped off upriver to find a place to cross without being spotted.

Feeling confident that he could not be seen over the bluffs, Hawk hurried out the mouth of the gully into the river, holding his rifle above the water as he made his way across. The water was a little over waist deep on him, so he waded with his cartridge belt around his neck. There was a good possibility that he might be seen when he reached the other bank and climbed up out of the river. So he headed toward a clump of willow trees whose branches hung out over the water. *So far, so good,* he thought as he climbed up through the willows without a shot being fired in his direction. *Now, if I can find a good place to watch that gully—and that looks like the spot,* he thought, looking at a shallow cut halfway down a hummock that sloped down to the river. *This ain't the first time I've used this trick,* he couldn't help recalling, *and I can't think of a better plan for the fix I'm in right now.* There was nothing left but to wait to see how it all worked out.

He didn't have to wait long before he spotted a warrior working his way cautiously along the opposite river bluffs to the left of the gully he had abandoned. He raised his rifle and sighted it on the warrior, but did not pull the trigger. He was sure the warrior couldn't see over the side of the gully, so he waited, confident that there would be another advancing on the right side of the gully. A moment later, he sighted him, closing in. *Now, if I figured this right,* he thought, *the third one will be showing up in the bluffs below me on this side.* He waited patiently in spite of the two open targets he could see across the river. The third man should have shown up by then. Maybe he was wrong. Maybe there were only two, but if that was the case, what were they waiting for? His answer came immediately in the form of a shadow cast upon the ground below him. He had been outfoxed! The Lakota warrior Spotted Pony stood at the top of the hummock above him, his rifle aimed at him.

"How strong your medicine now, Feather In His Hat?" Spotted Pony sneered. "How fast you turn to shoot?" he asked in his broken English, challenging him to try.

Hawk knew he had no chance, no matter how fast he might be. There was no way he could turn and shoot up over his head before the Indian pulled the trigger. The dominant emotion he felt was disgust at having been outfoxed. Fear was an emotion he had no experience with and he had always expected his luck would run out one day, just as every man's did. *Best I can do is maybe put a bullet in him, too,* he thought, and prepared to make his final move. For even if he managed to kill the warrior standing above him, his chances of defending himself from the other two were slim.

"Know that it is Spotted Pony of the Lakota that kills you," he said. "You kill my brother. You die now."

Even before he spun around, Hawk heard the rifle shot. Shocked and confused, he just managed to avoid the falling body of the warrior as it crashed heavily into the trench beside him. With no time to figure out what had just happened, his reactions took over in time to permit him to turn back to get off a kill shot on one of the warriors across the river. At almost the same time, a shot from above him knocked the remaining warrior down. He couldn't believe he was still alive. It could only be an army patrol tracking the hostiles. Anxious to find out who had saved him right in the nick of time, he started to climb out of the trench, but was stopped stone-still by what could only be a hallucination. "Roy Nestor!" he exclaimed.

"Hello, Hawk," Nestor sneered, while holding his rifle on him. "It's kind of a queer turn of things, ain't it? I mean, it looks like I just saved your bacon, don't it? Who'da thought I'd be the one to come along to save your ass? Only, it ain't gonna work out that way, 'cause I just didn't want no damn Injun takin' the pleasure of killin' you. Them Injuns almost spoiled my party, but I just let 'em set you up for me. When I saw what they had in mind, I just stayed right behind 'em. They didn't even know I was followin' 'em. They was so fired up on the chance to kill you, and I always was a better tracker than you. And I know all your tricks. This here is the same one you pulled on me that night on the Missouri when you damned near killed me. Yes, sir, if there's one thing I know, it's that you're just full of tricks. I know what you're thinkin' right now, so why don't you just drop that Winchester before I cut you down?"

Hawk could see that he had little choice. If he had any chance at all, it would be to keep Nestor talking. Knowing him as well as he did, he was sure he wanted to gloat over his upper hand before killing him. He also knew that, slim as it was, there was a chance to put a bullet in him, if he could act fast enough. So he put his rifle down, as ordered, propping it against the side of the trench so as to make grabbing it easier.

Nestor was quick to respond. "Uh-uh, that ain't gonna work. Pick it up by the barrel and toss it outta that trench." He chuckled, obviously enjoying his advantage. "I told you, I know all your tricks. Too bad Lieutenant Conner ain't here to save you now, ain't it?"

Reluctant to do so, but knowing he'd be shot right away if he didn't, Hawk tossed his rifle down the hummock. When he did, his eye settled on Spotted Pony's rifle, lying at his feet near the body. Was it ready to fire? From the angle he viewed it, he couldn't see if the hammer was cocked. That could be critical in the event he made a play for it, and that rifle was the only chance he had. It might mean the difference between living and dying. He was betting on a cartridge in the chamber ready to fire. The Indian was just ready to pull the trigger when he was struck by Nestor's bullet. He had to have cocked his rifle.

"You thought I was runnin' from you, didn't you?" Nestor asked.

"That's what I figured you were good at," Hawk replied, goading him to continue running his mouth.

"Smart-ass right to the end, ain't you? Well, you can see now that I weren't runnin'. For the past week I've been lookin' for you—wanted to pay you what I owe you. I've always been a better man than you—better scout, better tracker—and that's why I'm standin' up here holdin' the rifle and you're standing in a damn ditch that's gonna be your grave." He paused to see if Hawk had any comeback for that, but Hawk didn't respond, so Nestor continued. "I think maybe I'll hack off your topknot and send it to Lieutenant Meade. You was always his favorite. Maybe I'll send a piece of you to your good friend Lieutenant Conner." He brought the rifle up to his shoulder.

"Yessir, I've been lookin' forward to this. Maybe I'll start by shootin' you in the foot," he said, thinking about the missing toes on his right foot, the result of Hawk's humiliating him in the street at Bozeman.

Hawk finally decided he was not improving his chances for survival by letting Nestor run on about his hatred for him and he was just wasting time, so he figured to take his shot. "You know, Nestor, you always were full of shit. I don't know if you can even hit me from that far away."

"Why, you son of a bitch," Nestor blurted, and pulled the trigger. Anticipating his reaction, Hawk dived at the same time, picking up Spotted Pony's rifle as he rolled over the Indian's body. Nestor's bullet caught him in the side, but not before he put a shot in the middle of Nestor's forehead. His body dropped like a lead weight, facedown on the slope of the hummock, then slid slowly down to settle on top of Spotted Pony. Hawk sat staring at him for a long moment to make sure he was dead, barely able to believe the events of the past few minutes. Nestor was dead, all right. A neat bullet hole almost dead center his forehead verified that. Hawk was well aware that luck had a huge part in it, for he had tried to hit him in the chest, but his shot had been high. He could blame it on Spotted Pony's rifle if he needed an excuse. But being completely honest about it, he felt he was lucky to have hit him at all, considering the desperate move he had been forced to make. Whatever, he decided, if it was fate that stepped in, fate was a hell of a marksman, with a shot right between the eyes.

For a long moment, he continued to sit there and stare at the twisted features of the corpse. He never would have figured Roy Nestor had the guts to come after him. The two men had a strong dislike for each other almost since the first day they met. There had been a competition between them since the first, but Hawk had never realized the extent of it until now. He had always attributed Nestor's attitude to a contempt for everyone and not just him.

A pain in his side brought his attention back to the present situation. He was alive, but he hadn't escaped unharmed. He looked down at his buckskin shirt to discover a large blood-soaked circle. "I swear," he muttered, "I'm just bound and determined to mess up my one good shirt." He pulled the shirt up to look at the hole in his side, which was still pumping blood freely. "Damn," he swore. "That don't look good." *I'm still wearing a bandage on my shoulder, now this*. Holding his hand tightly over the wound, he climbed out of the trench. His clean shirt was in his saddlebag, he would stuff it inside his shirt to stop the bleeding. Although in some pain and leaking blood, he didn't feel incapacitated, so he walked down to the water's edge so that Rascal could see him. He whistled, but the big buckskin failed to respond. He remembered then that he had decided to tie him. "Damn," he swore again, this time at the horse. "Can't you even untie a simple knot? I reckon you need fingers for that," he allowed on second thought. "What the hell . . ." he mumbled, and waded into the river.

Definitely hampered, but determined to reap the benefits of his double encounter, he took some time to find Nestor's horse and packhorse to replace his packhorse shot by the Sioux. He gathered all the weapons and ammunition he could find, then went through Nestor's packs, taking anything of use to him and discarding the rest. The last thing he did was to ride through the thick stand of trees at the curve of the river where he found the three Indian ponies tied. Thinking them worth the effort, he fashioned lead ropes for what was now a string of five horses to trail along behind Rascal. By then, it was getting along in the afternoon, but he figured he could make it to Conner's encampment if he was still there. If Conner was gone, he could still make Fagan's trading post before dark, even though he was feeling a great deal of discomfort in his side. On the other hand, he felt that he had an obligation to return to the Triple-P to tell Monroe and the others that Roy Nestor was dead. He knew Monroe was carrying a heavy load of guilt on his shoulders for not tracking his brother's killer down. Maybe the news would free him of the burden. After all, Hawk figured, a man's mind ought to be free of guilt so he can enjoy his honeymoon. He thought about it for a few minutes. He was closer to Fagan's than he was to the Triple-P and he was already feeling the effects of his wound more and more. He decided to keep going toward Fagan's and bypass Lieutenant Conner's camp. Conner had no surgeon with his company, so the next best thing to a doctor would be Minnie Red Shirt, Rubin Fagan's wife. His wouldn't be the first gunshot wound she had worked on. Judging by the blood he had already lost, he was afraid he might not make it to the Triple-P.

It took him longer to get started than he had counted on. By the time he transferred all the packs from his dead horse to Nestor's packhorse, he was moving slower and slower. And by the time he got all the horses ready to travel, he was operating on little more than willpower. But he was determined not to be brought down by Roy Nestor's hand. *If I go under, I'll be damned if I'll let it be because of that son of a bitch.* When he figured he was at last ready to start out again, he realized he didn't have his hat, so he went back to the trench where Nestor's body lay sprawled across Spotted Pony's corpse. He found his hat sitting upside down beside them. He picked it up and brushed the dirt off, pleased to see that his feather was still firmly in place. Up in the saddle again, he adjusted the cotton shirt he was using as a bandage to stop the blood that by then had soaked the whole side of his buckskin shirt. With a good twenty miles to go, he started for Fagan's.

Second Lieutenant Peter Wallace halted his patrol when his scout signaled him to come forward. Wallace rode up to see what had caused his scout to stop. "Yonder," Ben Mullins said, and pointed toward the bank of the river. "I pulled up here and sat for a while to see if there was anybody else besides them horses. That feller on the ground ain't moved and the horses ain't, neither."

Wallace didn't see the man he referred to at first, but he saw the buckskin horse with a lead rope tied to the saddle with five horses behind it. They were simply standing there, heads down, patiently waiting. Then he saw the body lying facedown. He turned and signaled the men to come forward. "Be careful we don't ride into an ambush," he said, and started down through the bluffs to the river. "It could be what it looks like and it could be a little surprise waiting for us." It wouldn't be the first time the Sioux had set bait for an ambush.

With every man in the patrol alert for Indian mischief, the detail rode down to the riverbank to find the situation exactly as it appeared from above. A dead man, apparently having reached the end of his string. Mullins dismounted and walked over to the body. He reached down and rolled him over on his back, then drew his hand back, startled. "That's John Hawk!" he exclaimed.

"Damn," Wallace responded. "He must have run up on that party of Sioux we're looking for. Lieutenant Conner's gonna be disappointed to hear about this. He and Hawk rode on a lot of patrols together." He shook his head slowly while he decided what to do about it. "Couple of you men give Ben a hand. Pick him up and lay him across his saddle. We'll take him on back to camp. We don't have anything with us to dig a grave and a man like Hawk deserves a decent burial." He shook his head again and declared, "That's just a damn shame."

"Too bad, ain't it, Lieutenant?" one of the troopers commented. "He almost made it to camp—ain't but a half a mile away."

Ben Mullins remained standing by the body, staring intently at it. Finally, he surmised, "Ought not bury him anywhere."

"Why?" Wallace asked.

" 'Cause he ain't dead," Mullins replied.

Minnie Red Shirt walked into the back room where a bed had been set up for her patient. Standing at the foot of the bed, her hands on her hips, she prepared to scold him for sitting upright. "You start that bleeding again, I cut your throat and be done with you, I think." He had already lost a lot of blood before the soldiers brought him to her. Now it seemed he was determined to start it again in spite of her efforts to make him give it enough time to heal.

"I declare, Minnie," Hawk replied. "I never realized what a fine-lookin' woman you are when you get mad. You oughta get mad more often."

"Ha!" Minnie responded. "You never see me when I really mad. You keep starting that wound up, then maybe you see." She walked around to the side of the bed and placed her hand on his brow. "Fever gone," she said, nodding to herself. "When the soldiers bring you here, you look like dead man. I say, why you bring him here? Dig hole, put him in it."

"I ain't ready to go yet," Hawk said. "There's a lot of places I ain't been, a lot of trails I ain't scouted." He didn't tell her that he had survived out of sheer refusal to die by Roy Nestor's hand. "I think it was that coffee of yours that saved my life. You make mighty good coffee. I hope you came in to tell me you were fixin' to bring me a cup."

"Ha! I come to see if you dead or alive. Two soldiers in store, talking to Fagan." Ever since Hawk had known her, she had called her husband Fagan. He figured it was because everybody else called him Fagan and not Rubin. "They want to know can they see you," she continued. "I tell them I see if you dead. Maybe I tell them go away, you not awake." She spun on her heel to leave.

"You wouldn't do that," he called after her. "Tell 'em to bring some coffee with 'em." She didn't reply, just hurried on her way to the store. He smiled, knowing her bark was so much stronger than her bite. And he knew he would always be grateful for her care. It was a safe bet that the two soldiers who came to see him were Lieutenant Conner and Corporal Johnson and after a few minutes, they came in the door.

"Well, you don't look dead, does he, Johnson?" Lieutenant Conner walked over and extended his hand. "It didn't look too good for you when Wallace brought you into camp."

"I thought you were dead," Johnson said. "If it hadn'ta been for Ben Mullins, ol' Lieutenant Wallace mighta buried you."

"Everybody keeps tellin' me I looked dead," Hawk complained. "Hell, I'm about ready to ride outta here."

"He talks big," Minnie said as she walked in holding a coffeepot and three cups. "He can't get outta bed yet." She held her hand out to permit them to take a cup from her fingers. Then she filled the cups and left the room to let the men talk.

"We're pulling out of here day after tomorrow," Conner said. "I was hoping you'd be ready to go with us." When Hawk asked where they were going, Conner told him they had been called back to Fort Ellis. "Company from the Seventh Infantry is gonna take over the road between Helena and Missoula. And damn it, I want you back."

"I told Lieutenant Meade I'd be back as soon as I took care of that little business with Monroe Pratt," Hawk said. "But I ain't hardly fit to ride just yet, and when I am, I've got to ride up to the Bitterroot Valley to let Monroe know he don't have to worry about Roy Nestor no more. Once I get all that done, I'm yours. Although I might have to make a short stop in Helena. There's a little lady there who asked me to stop by to see her." He called a picture of Sophie Hicks to mind and the last time he ate breakfast in Sophie's Diner, next to the hotel. *You never can tell,* he thought.

"All right," Conner said. "But I'm expecting you back. I want your word as a gentleman."

Hawk said, "My word as a gentleman ain't worth much. You'd best take my word as a scoundrel. That'll be worth a whole lot more."

Books are produced in the United States using U.S.-based materials

Books are printed using a revolutionary new process called THINKtech™ that lowers energy usage by 70% and increases overall quality

Books are durable and flexible because of smythe-sewing

Paper is sourced using environmentally responsible foresting methods and the paper is acid-free

Center Point Large Print
600 Brooks Road / PO Box 1
Thorndike, ME 04986-0001 USA

(207) 568-3717

US & Canada:
1 800 929-9108
www.centerpointlargeprint.com